SILVER FOX

SILVER BROTHERS SECURITIES

LACEY SILKS

"You don't choose your family. They are God's gift to you, as you are to them." ~ Desmond Tutu

She twitched, breathing heavy. I looked up to meet her dreamy gaze and her shoulder jerked. "Can't blame a girl for enjoying a man's touch."
I grinned. "Glad to be of service."
"What else can you do with your hands?" She bit her lower lip.
"Patience, my love. Patience."
~ Silver Hunter ~

James Silver, a billionaire CEO and seasoned private
investigator, never expected Laura Young, a striking rookie
cop, to turn his world upside down. Their undeniable
chemistry sparked during a memorable night, but Laura's
strong-will led her to disappear without a word, leaving James
to wonder what might have been.
Two years on, their paths cross again—Laura, now arresting
James, reignites a flame that he thought had extinguished.
Determined not to let her escape again, James seizes this
second chance.
Laura's brief but unforgettable encounter with James Silver
had seemed like a fleeting fantasy. But after discovering his
complicated personal life, she realized she made a mistake
leaving, and now harbors a secret she must reveal.
As fate brings Laura and James back together, she grapples
with revealing her life-altering truth, and accepting his.
Confronting their past and the undeniable bond they share,
they fight for a future, together.

Silver Fox is the sixth novel in the *Silver Brothers Securities Family
Saga* and should be read after *Silver Santa*. Intended for mature
audiences.

$\mathcal{I}$ searched through the colorful rack of costumes for the perfect Halloween dinosaur outfit. Not for me. For my son. Three years ago, motherhood hadn't been near my radar, but neither was James Silver, the man who knocked me up. Three years later, with a badge on my chest and a best friend for a partner, I was rocking single parenting like Mary Poppins.

"I found it." Allie removed a furry brown onesie with a white-tipped tail. "It's perfect for Foxy."

"No more foxes. He's got a fox toothbrush, PJ, slippers, and bed sheets. It's enough. Foxy needs to get into normal things, like dinosaurs."

"Because dinosaurs are missing from his life."

That tone.

Allie's judgment carried far, but we'd gone through this before. Foxy's father could never be in his life. I dropped my arms to the sides and swiveled on my foot, facing my best friend. The stink-eye she gave me fueled an urge to rescind her godmother title.

"Your mother called—checking to see if you're alive. She hasn't heard from you in six months."

Maybe it wasn't about Foxy's father after all.

"Did you tell her I'm alive?"

"No, I told her she can find you at Evergreen Memorial. Of course I told her you're alive, and I told her Foxy's doing great too."

She wouldn't.

My throat seized. "You didn't."

"No, I didn't, but it's about time you told her she's a grandmother. Your father would be happy as well."

"Not happening. I'm not giving my son a grandmother who sends a hundred bucks for his birthday instead of hugging him. No thanks."

"Laura…" She touched my shoulder. "They say a grandmother's love is unlike any other. And since you're a mother now, you have more in common."

"You think that because your mother is great. She gives you love, and you give her…safety and tequila. All I ever gave my parents were gray hairs."

"My mother's a mess just like yours. Maybe a different kind of a mess, but still a mess. Point is, she should know. Maybe she'd surprise you."

I sighed. "I'll think about it, but that's all I can promise. Now, help me find a costume. Our morning break is almost over."

Allie scanned the remaining rack of Halloween costumes. Who was I kidding? I could never rescind her godmother title. She was the best, and she was correct. As screwed up as our family dynamics were, they were still my family, and I missed them. Except, my parents had expectations I couldn't meet. Their disappointment carried all the way from Manhattan and their home in the Hamptons. Avoiding the doctor duo was a challenge, but easier accomplished from further away.

So, I'd kept my pregnancy to myself and now thrived as a single mother. Changing things up wasn't on the calendar, and

Allie confirmed I was alive whenever she answered my mother's calls.

She picked a dinosaur costume, dangling the monstrosity in the air. "A T-Rex with plastic claws. You could poke a kid's eye out."

"Clearly, the fox one wins. It's safe, perfect, and cute." I checked my watch. "And our break is over."

I paid for the costume and threw the bag inside the cruiser. I secured my seatbelt and took a sip of my cooling latte when the dispatch call came through.

"Two armed suspects seen entering the Cameo building near Fifth and Park. All units respond."

I spat out my coffee and fumbled with the cup holder, "Allie, that's us."

My streak of welfare checks and no arrests had earned me the longest time without a bust at the precinct. The snickers behind my back were getting annoying, but today, I would prove them all wrong.

My partner reached for the receiver. "Ten-four. Unit twelve-oh-one in the vicinity responding."

We shot out of the cruiser like two rookies and ran a quarter block to the Cameo building, where we stopped at the corner and assessed the area. A businessman lit a cigarette outside the door. A couple passed a homeless man sleeping on a bench, then entered the building. We watched for clues, but there were none.

"No visible chaos," I said.

"No sign of commotion."

"Seems quiet for an armed entry."

"Maybe they're professionals."

"I'd love to cuff a pro more than I'd like to scratch that two-year-and-nine-month itch."

This was my day. I could feel it in my bones.

"You've had no sex in two years?"

"Two years and nine months. Foxy's conception was my last. This bust is better than an orange in your Christmas stocking."

She looked at me like I was crazy. "Fuck, Laura. That's bad. I bet you forgot how to orgasm."

"Nonsense. I flicked one off under the shower this morning."

"Argh, Laura. I didn't need to know that."

"Shouldn't have asked then. Let's be cautious in there."

I fixed my shoulders back, and we walked to the revolving door. Inside, business carried on as usual. A handful of office workers were waiting for the elevator, and a security guard was sitting at the information desk.

"You think it was a prank call?" I asked her.

"Or whoever ran in here is already upstairs. Let's take the stairs."

"No, wait. Look at the stiff guard."

We approached the desk, and I lowered my voice. "Sir, did you call in an armed entry?"

"Yes—third floor. He's on the third floor. Black hoodie and a patch of silver hair."

My best friend's forehead creased.

"How many exits?"

"He took the south stairwell. North is closed off for renovations."

I scanned the area. Two suits were standing by the elevator, along with a stressed woman who seemed in dire need of a vacation. More entered the front, followed by the homeless man in a black hoodie.

"Clear the area and stand at the front. Don't let anyone else inside until they're all out. Back up will be here soon," I said, and followed Allie's lead up the stairs.

We took the stairs two at a time all the way to the third floor. My chest compressed, my heart hammering and ears drumming with the sound of ticking time. Sweat dripped down my back. The nerves were new; they'd started when I returned to work after my short maternity leave, forcing me to leave my baby with Mrs. Brewers across the street. With motherhood came the additional need to survive for my son. While I was lucky to have a wonderful nanny, she was getting more kids, and Foxy was getting sick more often.

Allie grabbed my arm before I opened the stairwell door. "Laura, please be careful. My godson needs his mom home tonight."

"Fifty percent more police officers died in the line of duty this year than last." The worry coasting over her eyes turned into fearlessness, but I continued anyway. "And since we're not ready to be a statistic, you be careful as well."

She punched me playfully on my arm, and I swallowed past the lump in my throat. "This could be your first bust."

"Not if we keep standing here."

Using her body, she pushed me aside and opened the stairwell door. I followed her down the hallway. After the second turn, a man entered an office. The door shut behind him, and Allie ran forward while I stood in the middle of the hall.

The black hoodie he was wearing was the same one as the homeless man's.

"That's his partner," I said under my breath, but Allie had already burst through the office door. By the time I arrived, she had someone on the ground.

I turned on my heel and ran back to the stairwell. Downstairs, the foyer filled as security ushered everyone outside. I scanned the area, my eyes stopping on the homeless man leaning against a tree. He was watching the exits. I left through the side door and ran around the corner so I could come up behind him. The stretched hoodie over his wide shoulders was the same one as the attacker's upstairs. I removed my gun and aimed at the man's back.

"Hands up!"

His shoulders jerked as he startled.

"NYPD. Step away from the tree and put your hands up."

He lifted his hands in slow motion, palms flat to the front and stance wide.

"Hurry up."

"You've got the wrong man, officer." His deep voice stirred fuzzy memories, but I pushed past the tingling at the back of my mind. I was going to cuff this co-conspirator, no matter what.

"Don't fucking move." I stepped closer. As his arms rose, his hoodie lifted above his belt, exposing a weapon. "Is that gun behind your back registered?"

I removed the gun from behind his belt, noting his tight ass.

"You're under arrest for breaking and entering. Anything you say can and will be used against you in a court of law."

"Breaking and entering? At least make up something believable. I didn't break in."

The cuffs clicked, the final piece of my memory slotting into place.

Oh, my God. That voice.

The dread that someone wanted to complicate my life ran through my veins.

"Fox." His name slipped from my tongue.

"Laura? Laura, is that you?"

His head turned with a snap of the neck, and my body went limp. The one man I'd been avoiding for two years was now standing less than a breath away from me. And the best plan my brain could come up with was to take him to the station. If they locked him away for possession, I could kill two birds with one stone: score my bust and disappear. The plan flew through my mind like a stray bullet, until the smell of him invaded my lungs, and the bullet settled near my heart.

"Fox?" His name curled along my tongue. I hadn't spoken

his real name ever, but I certainly held it close to my heart. "I mean, James? Is that you? What the fuck?"

He stood still, as if he shared my shock.

"You're reading my mind. Uncuff me." He twisted sideways.

"I can't. I already read you your rights."

"You mean, you mumbled my rights."

"Shut up. You're under arrest. What are you doing here?" I asked him.

"If I'm under arrest, I believe I get a phone call before I answer your questions, officer."

He was right. And I already knew what he was doing here. My two-way radio confirmed that backup had arrived for Allie. She was getting a ride with a colleague.

"Looks like we're ready to go."

"Laura, take off the cuffs. I'm not the guy you're looking for."

"I beg to differ." He caught onto my hushed breath, and I realized my mistake. The spark in his eyes lit my blood on fire, and I swallowed to clear the rushing heat. It didn't work. I doubted anything would work when his smoldering eyes did their magic. Although the crazy morning we'd spent in Colorado seemed long ago, every minute had stayed fresh in my mind.

"If you run the number on the gun, it's registered to Fox Silver. Take the damn cuffs off, Laura."

His tone drew me out of my daze.

"Ninety-eight percent of criminals try to persuade an officer to remove their cuffs. That's criminal. You're under arrest, and you're coming with me to the station."

"You're making a mistake. I'll be out of the station before you fill out the paperwork."

Backup arrived for Allie, and I directed them inside before I turned back to James.

"Wonderful. Then you won't mind coming along, after all."

"I don't have time for this, Laura. I'm a busy father with obligations who's trying to catch a criminal."

His fatherhood was why I'd left without saying goodbye—and the woman who'd interrupted our stay with her pregnant belly. I wasn't about to compete with the mother of his child, and I wouldn't let my son be second, either. My only other choice was disappearing.

"Laura? Are you even listening to me? There's somewhere I need to be, and if I don't leave right now, I'll miss the appointment."

"All right. We can leave right now. In my cruiser."

"Oh, great. I would really appreciate a ride—"

"I meant *you* in the back of my cruiser."

"You're really gonna do this?" He closed his eyes and took in a calming breath.

A pinch of regret loomed in my chest. "I'm just doing my job."

"Your job?' Anger flamed in his bright eyes. "For fuck's sake, Laura. You were a nutcracker three years ago."

Fury steamed out of my ears.

"Well, then, I guess this nutcracker just got her bust."

I opened the back door and pushed against his heavy body, but he resisted, turning my way. The corner of his mouth lifted, and a dimple sank into his cheek.

Damn.

"Will you not embarrass me and let me ride shotgun?"

My heart hammered in my chest, constricting my lungs. A tingling sensation scattered over my skin, reacting to his dangerously sexy tone.

"Rules are rules, Mr. Silver. Suspects ride from the back. I mean, in the back."

Fuck, neither one sounded innocent.

He smirked.

"Get in." I gripped his bulging arm and nudged his mass of

muscles inside. Jesus, was he ever strong. I gathered my wits and pulled away from the curb.

"So, what happened to you in Colorado?" he asked.

A better question was, why was the sky blue and his girlfriend pregnant? Why did he seduce me when he had a family, and why did I let him?

Play dumb.

"What do you mean, what happened in Colorado?"

I pushed on the gas, throwing him against the back seat. He groaned, and I checked the rearview mirror as he sat closer to the partition between us.

"I mean, why did you leave?" The deep tone rumbled through his chest, and a memory of his beautiful torso flashed through my mind. I cranked the window open for some air.

"There was an avalanche. The mountains got dangerous, and..." I stopped along with the car, waiting for the pedestrians to pass. "And I went to see my sick friend."

I started rolling again.

"And you didn't call?"

I pushed on the brake, and his face pressed against the wired divider. At this pace, we'd never get to the station, but I wasn't about to explain how I despised love triangles and players.

"Look, I had a good time in Colorado, but as you can see, I'm more than a nutcracker now."

"Right—you're a cop who's busting a guy for nothing. Significant improvement."

Was that sarcasm in his voice? I checked the rearview mirror as he rolled his eyes.

"You know nothing about me, Silver. I'm great at my job."

Eighty percent of relationships started with lies; except we had no relationship. I had been good at my job until Mrs. Brewers took another child to babysit. Foxy caught one bug after another, forcing me to cut back on my hours.

"You're definitely great at running," he mumbled and sat back in his seat. I was not about to get into this with him while on the job. Any woman in my shoes would have done the same. I said nothing else until we arrived at the precinct and I put him in a room for booking. I had just signed off on the paperwork when Sargent Dwight called me over to his desk.

"The gun is registered. Mr. Silver's lawyer says you should have checked before booking him for possession."

"He got a lawyer?"

"The Silvers always lawyer up. You would have known that if you followed protocol, which you didn't. I don't want to demote you, Young, but—"

"Demote me? Sir, I know I've been off my game the past couple of months, but I can do my job."

He loosened the tie around his neck.

"You're a good cop, Laura, and I need you here, but you will need to apologize to Mr. Silver."

"So he's walking?"

"Your bust is a no-bust. What do you want me to hold him on?"

Good genes, bright blue eyes, and a body to die for? I shrugged instead.

"I haven't seen you slip like this before. Is something going on at home?"

Did three stacks of laundry, a sink full of dishes, and a sick two-year-old count?

"Foxy's puking again. He's getting all kinds of germs when Mrs. Brewers brings on new kids, so I'm looking for a new sitter, and I'm… I'm sorry about the gun. I won't slip again, sir."

"All right. Go pay your dues and make sure the lawyers are off our back."

"Yes, sir."

I turned and saw him standing by the main desk. He was leaning forward, resting his elbow on the counter, charming the secretary. The overgrown beard was new, but it matched his long lashes. If it weren't for the darker circles underneath his eyes, I'd argue he looked hotter than the night we met. His gaze lifted and caught my stare.

I fixed my shoulders back, lifted my head, mustered my confidence, and straightened my spine, taking calculated steps to the front.

"Hey," I said. "I'm sorry about the power trip. I shouldn't have arrested you."

"Don't worry. I won't press charges if you have dinner with me."

"What?"

"I thought we could catch up."

"Dinner?"

"That's what I said."

"I don't think my boyfriend would appreciate that."

"So you're not single? You're seeing someone?"

"Yes."

Sometimes my lies came out so beautifully. How could I deny the talent? Besides, didn't he have a family to worry about?

The disappointment in his eyes stopped my next breath. I didn't expect the sudden clench around my heart, either. The precinct door opened, and I thanked the lord for some air.

We turned to the entry at the same time. A blonde bombshell was pacing down the hall like it was a catwalk.

It was her. The woman from Colorado.

Her long, flowing dress clung to her delicate curves, and her hair fluttered in the draft. Her earrings matched the diamond tips in her long nails, and her purse matched her shoes. I rarely noticed such details, but it was hard not to notice hers.

"There you are, Fox. I can't believe they impounded your Bentley. We're running late, and I have the car running. I'm going to sue whoever is responsible for this."

That would be me. Normally, I didn't stoop to begging, but I would if it meant I'd keep this job.

She hooked her arm underneath his, but he peeled her clingy fingers off one by one. What was her name again?

"Thanks for coming, Tiffany."

Right. Tiffany.

"Ms. Tiffany, I'm sorry for keeping Mr. Silver so long—"

"You're the one who did this?" She eyed my badge. "Officer Young?"

"Yes," I turned to James. I'd rather swallow my pride here than have Tiffany sue me. "I should have never arrested you. I'm sorry."

His chin lifted, and he winked. "My offer stands, Officer Young. We have a lot to talk about. Have dinner with me."

Tiffany took hold of his hand and pulled him toward the door. "Come on, Fox. We don't want to be late."

He stopped, retreated a few steps, and pointed with his finger like he was giving a lecture. "The gun is not the only thing you were wrong about, Laura."

Sergeant Dwight came up from behind me. "I left my wife's homemade cough drops on your desk. I hope your little boy feels better soon, Laura."

My lashes flipped fully open while James's eyes tightened at the corners.

"Ahem, thank you. I've got to go."

I darted to the back room and waited until James Silver, aka Fox Silver, aka my son's secret father, had left with his baby mama.

Chapter 2

James

$\mathcal{I}$ gripped the steering wheel, carefully turning at the corner as Tiffany applied her lipstick in the mirror. The past ten days of doctor visits had me on edge, and I was sick of letting life run me down. This morning, I expected answers.

"Thanks for picking us up." She flipped the visor back into its position.

The girls sat in the back seat. Laila held her favorite teddy bear underneath her arm, and her sister stared blankly out the window. Kensi's pale-yellow skin worsened daily, and I prayed Dr. Hippo would have the answers and solutions that I didn't.

"You're welcome. What happened to your car again?"

"The mechanic happened. Some new guy poured in the wrong transmission oil and nearly broke the thing."

"Take my SUV while you wait for your car."

"Thanks, Fox. You're a gem. But they've already offered me an Aston Martin."

"Well, we can't miss this appointment, so you're stuck with my Bentley for now."

She lowered her hand to mine. I switched the gear, slowing in the park neighborhood.

"I enjoy being stuck with you and the girls. It's just like old times."

Except it wasn't like old times. Back then, we were in love when we adopted Kensi. The newborn girl created a bond I never expected. Life was perfect—until it wasn't, and co-parenting became our only option.

"I'm sure the doctor will tell us she's lacking vitamins; that's all. We didn't think we could figure out Laila's autoimmune disease, and look at her now. She's thriving."

Kensi's tummy aches had turned into sleepless nights because she couldn't stop throwing up. Her skin color was off, and the doctor suspected liver failure. We were getting the diagnosis today. I glanced in the rearview mirror as she closed her eyes and drifted off. She was more tired this month than last, and I prayed Dr. Hippo had our answers. He was working at the emergency clinic today and had squeezed us in for a chat. The pediatric hepatologist looked nothing like Kensi's favorite zoo animal and everything like the men Tiffany was into.

I stopped at a red light as my phone dinged with an incoming message that Laura had the day off. I turned southeast to the local park, where she took her kid for walks. I'd seen them there twice in the past week.

"I have to make a brief stop. Do you mind?"

"We can't be late. I cleared my schedule for the day."

"You don't have a house to stage or an office to furnish?"

"I have my priorities intact. How is my lipstick?" She turned in her seat and pouted. "Did you know this shade of pink is Dr. Hippo's favorite?"

"Priorities." I snickered.

"Fox Silver, are you jealous?"

Her hold over my hand shifted to my knee and then up my thigh to my groin. My ex had a knack for pushing boundaries, but her later manipulations had torn us apart. When my condom broke during breakup sex, she told me she'd take a morning-after pill. She lied, and nine months later, we had Laila, complicating an already complicated relationship. I removed her hand from my dick.

"Stop it, Tiff. We're here."

I circled the park, and spotted Laura near the swings. I pulled in by the park's entrance and pressed my foot harder on the brake. She was standing with her back to me, pushing on the swing. The skin-tight leggings outlined her toned legs right up to the short, fuzzy sweater which exposed her flat stomach. The army boots paired well with the camouflage colors. She looked hotter than the nutcracker and the cop outfit combined.

"Where's here?" Tiffany's voice jerked me awake, and the fantasy of peeling leggings off Laura's ass faded.

"I have an errand to run. It shouldn't take long. Wait here with the girls. I'm leaving the car running if you want the heater."

"Where are you going?"

I unbuckled and hopped out of my seat, then lowered to the window.

"Stay in the car." I lifted my finger. "I mean it, Tiff. I don't care what sale you see in the window display or if you have a craving for a mocha-cookie-crumble frappuccino. Stay with the girls."

"Is she someone special?"

She was someone special three years ago, and just as special the day she arrested me. It turned out her roommate and best friend was working a case with me at Silver Securities. We were bound to run into one another eventually, and I preferred the moment to happen on my turf. For the past ten days, I had shamelessly stalked Laura's house, but there seemed to be no logic to her schedule, and I missed her most of the time.

I checked my watch and hurried across the lawn. The sunny day held a hint of fall in its breeze. I kicked through scattered leaves, and Laura turned at my approach. Her eyes widened and her backbone clicked into a rod as she stepped in front of the swing, stopping me mid-step. She stood, open-mouthed and blinked rapidly.

"Motherhood suits you." I removed my hands from my pockets.

"What are you doing here? Are you following me?" Her attention scattered across the park before returning to me.

"Sort of. I wanted to talk to you. I feel bad about leaving things the way we did."

"I apologized."

"Laura, this isn't about your stupid arrest."

The few feet between us were too many. The longer I stood in her presence, the stronger I felt the urge to make things right. She stared at me, chewing on the inside of her cheek.

"Since when does Fox Silver do personal visits with the women he fucks?" She snorted.

"Since when do you call me Fox?"

"Heard it at the station." A shrug rolled over her shoulder, like seeing Tiffany throw her arms around my neck hadn't affected her. Like I didn't affect her. My nerves stripped bare in front of her. I didn't know where to begin. My life was nothing short of complicated, but she... She brought back the little bit of hope I'd lost. Her lungs swelled with a breath, lifting her breasts.

"You don't live far from Oyster Cove Bay." I leaned against the swing's post, and she caught me staring at her full chest.

"Wipe that smirk off your face."

"Sorry, can't help it. They've grown."

"It's called breastfeeding, although I'm weaning him off. You searched me out here to tell me I have big boobs?"

"How's your little boy feeling? The captain's cold remedy worked?"

"Ah, I get it..." Her brows narrowed and her eyes grew

distant, and I decided it was time to go in for the kill before she pushed me away. We could play this little guessing game for a while, but I didn't feel like losing precious moments. I had questions, and she had the answers. Life was too short as it was. I didn't want Laura missing from mine any longer.

"Is he mine?" I blurted.

She lowered her hand to the swing and stopped the momentum.

"What?"

"Your baby. I mean, we…you and I…in Colorado."

"What?" she repeated.

I glanced behind her to the toddler in a swing, kicking his legs back and forth. The fox-face costume with a mesh cutout for eyes and mouth couldn't have been comfortable. Poor guy. If he were my son, I'd never let Laura dress him in that. It wasn't even Halloween.

"How old is he?"

Her nose crinkled. "He turns two on December first."

"And what zodiac sign is that?"

"Since when are you into astrology?"

"So a Scorpio? Is he as feisty as his mother?"

"Sagittarius. Don't you think I would have said something sooner if he were yours?"

Would she? Why wouldn't she?

"Right. I'm sorry."

"Don't you have your wife and kids to worry about?" She looked around, swinging her head back and forth. "And didn't I ask you about your wife and daughter the night we met?"

"Those were hypothetical questions."

"Okay. Let's not make them hypothetical. Is your wife going to jump out from behind the bushes anytime soon?"

I glanced back over my shoulder, because I wasn't sure Tiffany wouldn't. Except she wasn't my wife. Thankfully, the grass was still dewy, and she wouldn't risk ruining her heels.

"I didn't have a wife back then, and I don't have one now."

She squinted. I had been waiting for three years to see her stunned face. She'd made a mistake leaving Colorado, and she knew it.

"But you have a—"

"I have two daughters. Kensi's seven, and Laila turned two last March."

A gulp jerked her chin. "Congratulations."

"I'm co-parenting, and I've been single since before Colorado, I guarantee. So, who's the lucky guy?" I nodded to the little boy.

"Not you."

"Okay, I get it. We started off on the wrong foot. I'm sorry."

"You mean, when your pregnant girlfriend showed up moments after we… Well, you know what we did."

Our morning locked away in a maintenance room returned every night in my dreams. That was almost a thousand nights with her and without her, and the constant morning wood didn't help. I missed her, but as a new father with responsibilities, finding time for someone who didn't want to be found proved difficult.

"Is that why you left? Because you saw Tiffany pregnant? She said someone helped her out from the spa—"

"No?"

"Was that a question?"

"No?"

I shook my head. "I thought I had you figured out, Laura Young. You weren't someone who jumped to baseless conclusions."

"The pregnant belly wasn't a baseless conclusion."

"Tiffany surprised me in Colorado. We weren't together, and I wish you hadn't left, so I could explain, but I guess I'm too late." I pointed behind her. Her little one was swinging his or her legs back and forth, looking to Laura for help.

"Are you together now?" she asked, throwing me off as I remembered Tiffany in the car.

"No, I'm a single, co-parenting father."

"Ossy, Ossy," the boy cheered from the swing.

"What's Ossy?" I asked.

"Ahem." Her eyes flew from the toddler to me. "It's his name. He's saying his name. Ozzy."

"That's cute. My mother used to call me Foxy, and I couldn't pronounce my name, so I used to say Ossy."

"Huh, that's cute."

The morning clouds passed, and the sun warmed the playground. The sound of laughing children carried through the park. After we had Kensi, I wanted a boy, but then Laila was born, my world turned upside down, and I fell in love with my second daughter.

"Is it after Ozzy Osbourne?" I asked her.

"No, after the guy from *Survivor.*"

She pushed the swing back and forth again, watching me watching her and the kid. She looked good as a mom; tired, but I bet the bags under my eyes outshone hers.

"You grew a beard?" Her mouth cranked up in the corner. "When did that happen?"

"When my time got cut short by diapers, mixing formulas, and emergency doctor visits. You know how it is. Can I ask you a stupid question?"

"Why not? I'm pretty sure I can't stop you."

"Why a fox costume?"

She stared at her son for what felt like forever and when her gaze returned to mine, regret flashed in her eyes. She blinked twice, and it was gone.

"The dinosaur costume had plastic claws hazardous to a child." Her focus lifted from her son to me. "And he likes foxes. I guess he takes after his Mama."

Was that an olive branch?

"Are you married?"

She recoiled back. Maybe it was the wrong olive branch?

"How did you come to that conclusion?"

"Well, you have a kid, and you certainly don't look interested in me, so I'm assuming you're happily married to Ozzy's father."

"Eighty percent of single mothers are happier single than married. So no, I'm not married."

I laughed. A car horn sounded in the distance.

"So you're single?"

"Technically, yes. I am. But I'm not dating. The breastfeeding and bra pads scare men off."

"So the boyfriend doesn't exist?"

She rolled her eyes. "No, he doesn't."

"I'm not asking to get into your bra. We'll leave that for the second date."

"Since when do you leave bras and panties for second dates? And how is a second date possible when I haven't agreed to the first one?"

"You haven't kicked me to the curb yet."

"That's hard to do when we're already outside."

"Next time I'm next to you, I'll make sure we're inside and alone."

I stepped forward, but she stretched out her hand, stopping me

She stopped the swing's momentum. "Flirting with me is dangerous, James."

"Colorado was dangerous."

A spark flashed in her eyes.

"It was also special and I'll never forget it."

She shuddered. "I don't have time for players in my life."

"Why do you think I'm a player?"

"Oh, Fox? Fox!"

Fuck.

Tiffany.

"That's why."

My ex hurried across the lawn in her high heels, holding Laila in her arms.

"I gotta go."

"Of course you do." She waved me off.

"It is just that… We have something." I ran backward, waving. *Doctor's appointment* would have sounded a dash more intelligent, but who was I kidding? I turned into a complete mess, forgetting all responsibility in her presence.

I caught up to Tiffany. Where the fuck was Kensi?

"You left Kensi in the car? Alone? What the fuck, Tiff."

"Watch your mouth. I'm not the one who's chatting with a woman in the park. Don't we have a doctor's appointment? We're going to be late, Fox."

I secured Laila in the car seat, took the wheel, and pulled into the traffic.

"We won't be late. I'm never late."

And if Laura was still single, maybe I wasn't late for her, either.

TIFFANY SCROLLED through her phone in the waiting room, Kensi played Tetris on my phone, and Laila slept in her stroller. I paced up and down the hall. By the time Dr. Hippo called us into his office, I'd turned into a complete mess.

"Kensi is suffering from acute liver failure. Her liver function is deteriorating, and I've already placed her on a transplant list."

Tiffany sat openmouthed, gasping air like a guppy. She wasn't the perfect partner, but she was a pretty good mother. She'd do better when Kensi felt better and they could return to their manicure days at Grace's spa.

"Daddy, am I going to die?" Her large brown eyes held onto mine. God, how I wanted to take her pain away.

I picked her up in my arms. "No, you're not, baby. She's not, Dr. Hippo, right?"

He removed a lollipop from his shirt pocket and gave it to Kensi. "Young kids are very resilient. They're our best patients, so we're going to do everything possible to make you feel better soon."

I didn't think lollipops worked, but Kensi's smile said otherwise.

"Here, you can give the other one to your sister when she wakes up." He stuffed an extra one in her pocket.

"Is this our only option?" Tiffany asked.

"I'm afraid it is. Children don't wait as long as adults, but in Kensi's case, the sooner we find a matching donor, the better."

"Can you take mine?" I asked.

"And mine." Tiffany squeezed my hand. "We'll both donate."

"I'm glad you brought it up, because that's definitely an option. We will have you both tested for compatibility, but I must warn you, not all parents are automatic donors, and given Kensi's adopted, the chances are lower. This is a great start, though."

"Thank you, Dr. Hippo."

I had my bloodwork done first, took Laila into my arms, and left Tiffany with Kensi and the nurse. My ex suffered from Vaso-vagal and took longer with bloodwork. Kensi volunteered to stay by her mother's side to keep her spirits up while I paced down the long hospital hall with Laila sleeping in my arms. I pushed the stroller with one hand and I stopped in my tracks on the second pass by the pediatric unit where Laura sat curled on a seat. Ozzy slept in a stroller next to her. The area was undergoing renovations and was nearly empty. I walked up and touched her shoulder.

"Laura?"

She startled. "James?"

"What are you doing here?"

She sat up, straightened her legs, and swept her hand over her eyes. "We slid down the slide at the park and landed wrong. Ozzy's arm… I'm waiting for Ozzy's x-ray results, but he's calmer now, so I think it's likely a sprain. I hope it's just a sprain."

She looked like the mess I felt on the inside. Finding out your kid was hurt ached deep in a parent's chest. And she was doing it all alone.

"Can I wait with you? This is Laila, my younger one."

Her grateful eyes met mine. "Yeah, that would be nice."

I texted Tiffany to meet me in the car and took a seat across from Laura. Laila stirred in my arms, relaxing into my hold. Her tummy had settled since this morning.

"You didn't call Ozzy's dad to the hospital?"

"He's not present in our lives."

"Didn't work out?"

"One-night stands rarely work out."

I winced at the jab.

"I'm sorry, I didn't mean—"

"No need to apologize. When I met you, I honestly thought you'd be more than a one-night stand."

Her large eyes grew wider.

"So you're single."

She sucked in her cheeks. "I like my life. It's not easy, but you know how it is with kids. One moment, you think your life is on track, and the next, your kid has a sprained wrist. I hope it's just sprained. It could have damaged the growth plate. Every four seconds, a child is treated for an emergency." She glanced down at the stroller.

I barely knew this woman, yet I'd felt she belonged with me from the moment we met in Colorado. I should have never let her go.

"What are you here for?" she asked.

"More bloodwork."

"Are you okay?"

"I'm fine. It's Kensi. My seven-year-old. She's been sick for a while."

"I'm sorry. I didn't know."

"There's a lot you don't know about me." I cleared my throat. "I just found out Kensi needs a liver transplant."

"Oh. I'm so sorry. That's way worse than a sprained wrist. Sorry."

"Only proves you right. One moment you're tucking your little one into bed, and an hour later you wake up because they're screaming in pain. It's the worst when they hurt and you can't do anything."

"It is."

Her eyes softened. She pulled her tongue along her cracked lips, and while I knew she was likely thirsty, it was the sexiest thing ever. Three years later, I still had it bad for her.

"You thirsty?" I secured Laila on my hip and crossed the hall to the vending machine. I punched in the codes as she called from behind.

"Can you get the orange-flavored dark chocolate as well? I stupidly skipped breakfast, and it's already—"

"After dinner. Sure. Orange-flavored dark chocolate, coming right up."

I punched in the code for a water bottle, and picked a couple of bars for the girls and Ozzy, in case he woke up. I emptied most of the coins from my pocket and handed the snacks to Laura.

"Thank you. Orange-flavored chocolate is my favorite."

"I didn't know that about you."

"There are a lot of things you don't know about me." She winked.

"So, have I earned enough pity to have you agree to dinner with me?" I sat down beside her.

"I'm not sure, James, but this is a good start."

I closed my eyes. "It's been so long since I heard you speak my name. Feels nice."

"You're delusional." She snickered, breaking my moment. Laura leaned forward and lowered her hand to mine.

"Likely as delusional as the day I met you," I whispered.

"Let me think about the dinner. I appreciate you staying here with me, James."

A text came in from Tiffany that she'd finished, and Laura received Ozzy's sprained wrist result at the same time.

"How did you get to the hospital?" I asked her.

"Uber."

"I'll drive you two home."

She moved her hand off mine. "We can take a cab."

"Don't be afraid, Laura. I don't bite in front of kids." I removed my phone from my pocket. "What's your number?"

I typed her in as a new contact and sent a quick emoji message. Her phone dinged, she opened the screen and laughed. "What's that?"

"A flower bouquet, dinner plate, and dancing."

"Hmm, how romantic. You do everything while holding a sleeping toddler in your arms?"

"Definitely not everything. You should know; and if you don't, I'm willing to remind you."

Chapter 3

Laura

James made a quick introduction by his Luxury Escalade SUV and helped me secure Foxy in the back seat. Thank God for costumes, face masks, and men with extra car seats. Tiffany sat in the front and their two daughters in the back.

"Do I know you from somewhere?" she asked.

I caught James's gaze darting to the rearview mirror. He took an early exit off the interstate and headed to the coast, opposite from where I lived.

"I arrested James last week. You saw me at the station when you picked him up."

"Ahh, that's right." She turned to James. He pressed harder on the gas, pushing me back in my seat. "She calls you James, like your friends do, and you rarely make a habit of helping cops who arrest you, so—"

"That's because I've never been arrested before," he grunted.

"Glad to have popped your cherry, James."

Not sure where that came from. Tiffany turned in her seat, vying for attention.

"But she wouldn't call you James if she didn't know you—"

"We're old friends. Everything else is none of your business."

"Oh, there you go, getting all defensive with me when all I'm seeking is the truth—"

"You and truth?" He snorted and pulled into a gated community.

"Why do you always interrupt me?"

I played with Foxy's costume tail and listened to the two of them bicker. It was cute. They kept a low tone to avoid upsetting the kids, but Tiffany manipulated the conversation like a professional, and James saw through her cleverly constructed sentences.

She was in love with the man, and she was working on a new design project at the Silver Securities headquarters. She was either good at her job or James had a soft heart. Maybe it was both. The man I'd thought was a player seemed committed to his daughters and kept the mother of his children in his life.

James parked the car in front of a beautiful, modern house. He unbuckled and walked around to the passenger's side and opened Tiffany's door. She took his offered hand, stepped out, and held him in an uncomfortably long embrace. He walked her to the door, made sure she was safely inside, and returned to the car.

"Sorry about that. I'm going to drop the girls off at my mother's, and your place is next."

"They're not staying with Tiffany?"

"She has an early meeting with her design team. She's in the middle of a project, and the girls stay with me permanently. I enjoy having them at home. My parents are helping me out tonight."

Our eyes linked in the rearview mirror. It must have been nice to have parents you could rely on. Mine didn't even know they were grandparents, and I preferred keeping the news to myself.

"You're a good father."

He smiled, and his attention returned to the road. "Are your parents nearby?"

"Yes, and no. They're busy doctors."

"Doctors? I didn't know your parents were doctors."

"Well, it's not like we spent a long time together…you know, to learn everything."

I regretted the words as soon as I spoke them because, truth be told, I didn't need twenty-four hours to know James Silver stood for loyalty and devotion. But then Tiffany happened, and my emotions took over.

"The time we spent together was long enough to learn what I needed, but not long enough to get what I wanted." He smiled again, and shivers nipped at my spine. My heart beat off its regular pattern, and I checked on Foxy's mask. So far, he'd behaved better than usual, likely because of the pain medication kicking in. Thank goodness, he had no need for a cast.

James drove the rest of the way to Oyster Cove Bay in silence. He pulled up in front of a gate, keyed in a code, and dropped the girls off with his parents. Twenty minutes later, he parked in front of the rental home I shared with my best friend, Allie. I unbuckled Foxy from the car seat and scrambled out from the car, holding him sleeping in my arms. I turned around and bumped into James. He scooped Foxy into his arms and carried him up the steps to the front door.

I watched James hold his son in shock, but the realization Foxy was with both of his parents for the first time stirred warmth around my heart. The initial fear coursing through my veins quickly turned into something new. Something I hadn't felt before. I didn't want Foxy to feel the loss of a father, but James would never forgive me for keeping my son to myself.

He reached the top step and turned around. "You have keys, right?"

I rummaged through my purse and found the keys. I pushed

the door open and turned back around, reaching for Foxy. "Here."

James set him back in my arms.

"I'll be right back. I need to put him in bed."

"All right."

I grabbed Foxy's bottle from the fridge, along with the magnet baby picture stuck to the front, and took him upstairs. I placed the bottle in a warmer, changed him into his fox pajamas, and sat by his big boy bed. Allie had helped me pick out the wooden bed for his forest-themed room last week. I pushed his dark hair away from his forehead. His blue eyes shone brightly as he devoured the bottle, dozing off. He looked so much like his father. After Foxy fell asleep, I removed his bottle and tiptoed downstairs, where James was relaxing on the couch.

"You're still here." I walked around the kitchen corner, leaving the empty bottle in the sink.

"I got your stroller from the trunk, and since you mentioned coming back, I made tea and ordered food." He pointed to the family room table, and I sat down on the adjacent couch. The spicy aroma of Thai food stirred my hunger alive.

"Not sure if that's too spicy, since you're nursing, but from what I recall, you love spice."

"Good memory. It's perfect. Thanks. I'm weaning Ozzy off my boobs." I opened the carton and plated shrimp pad Thai.

"That's good to know."

The day's toll weighed heavily on my aching body. "I'm sorry it took so long. I wanted to feed him, and I like to know he's sleeping before I leave."

"It's all right. Completely understand. The girls love me tucking them in."

"Shouldn't you be doing that now?" He reached to the table and passed me the cup of tea. The gentle touch of his fingers over mine sent an electric current through my veins.

I sipped on the honey-lemon brew. "Did you add a touch of ginger?"

"Found some in the fridge. Kensi and Laila love it when their grandfather reads them bedtime stories. Laila pulls on his gray beard and giggles because he makes funny noises."

"That's nice."

"He installed a playground in his backyard and bought special fishing gear for the girls. My parents love having them over, and I can't deny, I appreciate the help. They're amazing."

The sudden feeling of an enormous loss stirred in my chest. Foxy didn't know any of his grandparents. I took another bite of my shrimp. The spice cleared my nasal passages and watered my eyes.

"You live close to them?" I coughed into my arm and wiped the burning tears.

"Next door. It's a quiet neighborhood."

"And Tiffany?"

"She lives nearby, but we haven't been together for years. I think Kensi's illness tore us apart, and… Other things. She's a good mother. Your parents must be thrilled to have a grandson," he said out of nowhere.

"Well, they're not, because they're not really in my life."

"Why not?"

"Too busy."

"You or them?"

"Both. I concentrate on bringing justice and peace, while they stay cooped-up at the hospital."

"You mentioned they're doctors so, you're both similar."

"How so?"

"You both save lives."

He wasn't supposed to take their side, yet it didn't feel like he had. Fact was, my parents were excellent surgeons. They just weren't great parents.

"Sure. They save lives, but I know how to raise a child."

"I take it childhood sucked, so you didn't follow their footsteps into medicine."

"Childhood was fine, but being a teenager kind of sucked. Police work brought back my focus. I moved out at eighteen and haven't looked back since."

"So, I take it you've always been independent."

"Mostly."

"And where does Ozzy's dad come into the picture?"

"I already told you—he doesn't."

At least, he hadn't until now.

"Come here." He grabbed my hand, pulled me off my seat, and brought me down on the couch beside him. "Lie down."

He gently pushed on my shoulder, and I lowered to the cushioned seat. He drew his hands over my thighs, down my shins and to my foot. The delicate touch over my toes sent shivers up my spine. My breaths quickened as his thumbs pressed into my sore soles, numbing my body and mind.

I lifted my head. "What are you doing?"

"Trying to relax you, but I'm not sure that's possible. Lie back."

"I can relax." I shot up, and he chuckled, guiding me back to the couch. He lifted my foot into his hands and kneaded the sole. My muscles went limp as his expert fingers pushed underneath, working through the tightness.

"I'll miss work if you keep this up."

"How so?"

"You're putting me to sleep."

"Words every man wants to hear. Allow me to correct my mistake." He drew his hands higher to my calves and pushed through the muscle. He slowly dragged his fingers along my flesh, over the knee to my thigh.

I bit my inner cheek and my eyes flew open. "What have you been doing? How's Silver Securities?"

He lowered his hands back to the safer spot below the knee. "You're aware your friend is working for us?"

"All I know is that Allie's on a secret assignment. We don't share intel details."

"Do you miss working with her?"

"Like a pair of well-worn shoes. She had my back, and I had hers. They haven't assigned me a new partner yet, and I'm doing paperwork. God knows how long they'll keep me. I've had one too many strikes against me at work."

"You can only move up from there."

"I doubt it. It was easier with Allie. Like I said, she had my back." I closed my eyes for a longer pause. "I missed my noon shift today. Fo—ozzy…" I swallowed the mistake. "Ozzy had his accident at the park, and I had to call in."

James looked momentarily confused. "They should understand because accidents happen."

I opened my eyes. "Not five times in a month. I'm a great cop, but my son's a priority, you know?"

"I know, but you must be tired because you're calling your son Fozzy."

He was right. I had nearly slipped, and I couldn't let it happen again.

"I'm sorry things didn't work out with Tiffany."

"Thanks. Building trust is hard. Fixing broken trust is even harder."

I swallowed past the squeeze in my throat. "She broke your trust?"

"Tiffany poked holes in my condoms."

My brows lifted.

"She surprised me in Colorado."

"But you tried working things out?"

I knew they had. I'd seen so firsthand when I came back to

tell him I was pregnant. They were a family, and I didn't belong.

"We did, but you know what they say: once a liar—"

"Always a liar." It seemed like my road to forgiveness lay filled with razors and stones.

"Tiffany told me she'd take the morning-after pill. It was supposed to be break-up sex, but the stupid one-night stand made me a father."

If he only knew.

"What Tiff did was unforgivable."

He pressed harder into my foot, and I winced.

"Was that too hard? I'm sorry."

"No, I'm sorry."

His forehead creased, and I closed my eyes. I truly was sorry, but I couldn't tell him so when he was pouring out his heart and turning my body into butter.

James wouldn't forgive me unless I earned his trust. Life would be easier if James knew the truth and Foxy had a father in his life. A lump of regret formed in my throat. I'd been single parenting for so long, it was getting to me, especially since things could have been different. I needed a break, and I couldn't afford one. My heart pitter-pattered against my ribcage. His undivided attention to my foot was sending all the right signals, fogging my brain.

"Are you falling asleep on me?" he asked.

I yawned. "No. I'm sorry. I'm just exhausted."

He reached behind him, pulled a blanket from a corner basket, and covered me. Finding the right moment would be difficult. Right now, it would be suicidal.

I stretched my arms above my head, and his mouth curved sideways in an irresistible grin.

"I try to stay away from you for three years, and now you find me?" I whispered. Why had it taken him so long?

"So you *have* been avoiding me?"

Him; my parents. "I'm too busy to avoid."

"Come on, Laura, let me take you to dinner. On your own time and schedule. I'm all open."

So was I, but I couldn't. "James, I'm trying to tell you, I can't date you right now. My life is—"

"Complicated?"

"Like taxes."

"Taxes?'

"They're complicated."

"Right. So you're dumping me for the second time?"

"I'm not dumping you. We're not together. And I'm complicated."

He drew his hands up to my calf and massaged his fingers over the muscle again. I was melting into the couch, and my resistance waned.

"Pursuing you will be a lot of fun," he growled. The deep, rich, and resonant rumble carried a note of Barry White and lust.

"As nice as the idea of dating sounds, I'm just not ready," I whispered.

"Just relax, okay? Close your eyes."

He kneaded my aching muscles as I listened to his calming voice. My eyelids dropped as he took me back to Colorado and our time in the mountains. Having someone at home, to talk to and hear your troubles, was nice. Tiffany was a lucky woman, and James obviously valued her as a mother, despite her flaws; but could he ever forgive me?

I woke up on the couch to a screaming toddler and jumped to my feet, trying to get my bearings. I ran up the stairs two at a time. Foxy's tears stopped the moment he saw me. He sat up in his big boy bed, grinning through tears.

"Good morning, sunshine. Mamma's here." I picked him up and realized the sun shone high through the window.

"Crap."

"Crap," he repeated.

"What?"

"Crap," he said again. "Ossy crap."

"You can't say *Foxy*, but you can say *crap*? If your daddy only knew."

Where was his daddy, and what happened last night? I had tea, lay down on the couch, and James massaged my feet until I fell asleep. I hurried downstairs and into the kitchen where my empty teacup sat in the sink.

Fucking chamomile tea: a girl's best friend and now my nightmare. James and his relaxing massage, along with the tea, had lulled me to sleep.

I was late for work, and tardiness was unacceptable by the force. Calling in late this late was bad enough as it was. I carried Foxy to the changing table and dialed the station. I left a message I was taking the day off and quickly changed Foxy's diaper. Sargent Dwight returned my call by the time I'd brushed his teeth and set him down in the playpen.

"Good morning, sir."

"It's almost afternoon."

Shit. "I'm sorry, sir. I should have called in sooner."

"Laura, I know it takes time to get used to a new partner, but you've been missing work. It's time to think about a leave of absence."

Fuck.

"Sir, it's not about my new partner. It's flu season, and the little one's been getting sick—"

"Take a couple of weeks off, Laura. Get your life in order and come back focused. That's an order."

An order? I swallowed past the squeeze of my throat.

"We'll pay the leave. You're a good cop, but I need you at your best, so we have no more unwarranted arrests."

"Yes, sir."

"I'll see you soon, and let me know if you need any help."

"Thank you, sir."

We hung up, and I turned to Foxy. "At least, I'm not fired, kid. I guess it's just you and me today, babe. And for the next two weeks."

Truth was, the time off couldn't have come any sooner. I made breakfast, had a cup of coffee, and checked in with Allie, who was shacking up with Tristan Silver. My best friend was finally getting what she'd wanted: revenge and safety.

After breakfast, I canceled the babysitter for the next two weeks and drove with Foxy to the hospital. Dr. Hippo was on call that day in the pediatrics unit. He checked Foxy's sprained arm and gave him a strawberry lollipop.

"He's doing great. The swelling has gone down. A few more days in the wrist guard and he'll be back to sliding in the park in no time."

"I think we'll keep our distance from the slides for a while. Thank you, Dr. Hippo."

"You're welcome."

"Dr. Hippo, I actually have a technical question."

"What is it?"

"Can you tell me a little about liver donations?"

"Sure. Who needs a liver?" His keen eyes sparkled.

"I don't even know if I'd be a match, but if I were, I'd prefer to keep the donation anonymous. Is that possible? And what would I need to do?"

"We'd start with a simple blood test first. After that, we'd do some tissue sampling. Anonymity is definitely possible. I'm assuming you have a specific person in mind for the donation?"

"Yes. Kensi Silver."

"She's my patient, actually. And her case is urgent."

"Yes, I know. Her father is a friend of mine, and the reason I'd like to keep this anonymous."

His forehead creased, and his brows drew closer together. The distant look in his eyes as he stared right through me gave me the chills.

"I understand." He typed a few keystrokes into the computer and printed a requisition. "The lab is down the hall. They'll draw your blood, and we'll be in touch."

He glanced at the paperwork. "Laura Young? As in, Alice and Tom's daughter?"

"You know my parents?" My voice cracked.

"Everyone knows your parents. I worked with them at Manhattan General."

"Yes, that's their home base."

"I didn't know they had a grandson."

I scrunched my shoulders against my neck, cleared my throat, and lowered my head. "That's because they don't know they have one."

My hushed voice lingered in the air, like a pause button, until Dr. Hippo broke the silence. "Given your parents' profession and yours, you're aware that life is not easy. But it is short, and I wouldn't waste time trying to fix what can't be fixed, but what can. Life, health, and relationships fall into the second category. Also, I'm not one to judge when I shall be judged as well. I only want to help, Laura, and everything said between us remains confidential."

"Thank you, Dr. Hippo. I truly appreciate your help."

"Laura, your file here from eight years ago says you were pregnant, and that the baby—"

"Yes, sir. I'd like that part of my life to stay confidential as well."

"All right. For what it's worth, you have as much drive and independence as your parents do. And it seems like your heart is in the right place, too. Reach out if you need anything, and I'll call you with the blood results."

"Thank you."

We shook hands, and I went to the lab with the requisition for the bloodwork shaking in my hand.

Chapter 4

James

$\mathcal{I}$ sat in a mini chair with my knees up to my chin, sipping tea from a plastic pink cup, opposite my daughters. Laila was wearing her Sunday dress and a sparkly tiara, while Kensi had opted for a homemade warrior outfit, which came with a ladle as a sword.

"Daddy cookie." Laila pushed another oatmeal treat between my lips.

"Thank you. It's delicious." I said with a mouthful and turned to my mother. "Was this Tiffany's idea?"

"No. The girls did everything. Kensi set the table and the cups."

"What about the cheese grater?" I pointed to Kensi's chest, and the girl grinned from ear to ear.

"That's my breastplate." She took the ski goggles off her head and lowered them to the table. "But I don't need my visor when I eat."

I loved my daughter's wild imagination. She'd stopped playing with her friends a few weeks back because she wasn't strong enough to last through a soccer game. But her little sister and grandparents occupied her better than any school.

"And who are you supposed to be?"

She looked at me like I'd lost my mind. The jaundiced shade of her skin was becoming more prominent daily. A nurse checked Kensi in the mornings, mid-day, and before bed, but I worried those days were running out too quickly.

"I'm Kensi, Daddy. A strong woman who accepts no rejection."

I tilted my head sideways. "Who told you that, Kens?"

"Mommy."

"And the tiara and dress?" I pointed to Laila.

My mother set a plate of baby cupcakes on the table. "That was my idea. Doesn't she look cute?"

"They'll get a sugar rush, Mom."

"It's a good thing those are sugar-free." She winked.

I'd once heard somewhere that sons choose women who remind them of their mothers; I'd be lucky to have a partner with my mother's compassion, wit, and selflessness.

"Thanks, Mom."

"You're welcome. Now, maybe one day Laila will want hiking gear, but now, she wants a tiara. Or maybe you'll have a boy and you'll get to dress him in fireman outfits. My point is, if Laila wants sparkles, she gets sparkles. She's a toddler, James."

"Okay, okay. I get it, and I'm sorry."

She ruffled the top of my head, and I reached up to fix it.

"Mo-ohm," I whined, raking my fingers through the perfectly combed strands.

"Daddy, cookie." Laila fed me another biscuit.

"Hey, Mom," I called out through the falling crumbles. "Remember the two security guards we hired for Colorado? Hunter had them dressed as nutcrackers..."

"I know exactly who you're talking about because the girls came highly recommended. One of them got sick on the trip and the other one left after the avalanche."

Laura.

"Who recommended them?"

"Your father's surgeon, Dr. Young. One of them was his daughter. He works at Manhattan General. His wife leads cancer research there as well."

"Tom Young was dad's surgeon."

"He wouldn't have made the recommendation if she wasn't a good fit. What was her name?" My mother shut her eyes and opened them again just as quickly. "Laura. Laura Young. Wasn't she a good fit?"

"Yes, she was perfect."

My mother's brows lifted..

"What do you know about Dr. Young?" I asked.

"Which one? The surgeon? Great, as you know. His wife works in cancer research, and he saved your father's life. He bragged about her prestigious awards at every appointment. He bragged about his daughter graduating from the police academy as well. They're both extremely talented doctors and very committed to their work. I imagine their daughter is just as great at her job."

"She's good, but it's not easy for a single mother."

"How do you know she's a single mother?"

I rose from the mini chair that barely fit my ass and stretched. My bones ached. My cousin's planned operation couldn't come fast enough, so I could rest. The girls retreated to a corner fort built from cushions, pillows, and blankets.

"I bumped into Laura at the hospital and drove her and her son home."

"Dr. Young is a grandfather? Your father saw him a few months ago for a routine checkup. I'm surprised he didn't mention anything."

"Apparently, the Youngs don't know it either, because she hasn't told them."

"Oh, my goodness. Well, I rarely butt in, but—"

I laughed out loud. "You stick your nose where it doesn't belong like a backseat driver."

"If I didn't stick my nose in some things, you'd have a third one on the way."

"I was drunk, Mom." I remembered the evening Tiffany had attended our family event when Laila was one. Well, most of it, at least. Tiff poured me one whiskey after another and we ended up in the bathroom, her against the wall and me fucking her from behind. I shuddered.

"I guess I should thank you. How is Dad doing?"

"No complications. Your father's down to semi-annual checkups, thank goodness."

"That's good. That's really great." I looked out into the distance.

"James, why are you interested in the Youngs? Is their daughter in trouble?"

I wasn't sure how to answer that, because I didn't know myself. Family was everything to me, and I had a difficult time understanding why Laura hadn't told her parents she'd had a baby.

"I hope not. Do you have the surgeon's contact information?"

"I do. I'll text it to you." She picked up her phone and sent me the details.

"Dr. Hippo specializes at Memorial General as well. It's where I'm getting my bone marrow biopsy next week."

"Why are you getting a biopsy?"

"My bloodwork came back with low platelets and a possible neutropenia which could be from an infection. I may not be a viable donor for Kensi."

"Maybe you should re-schedule for sooner. Like for today."

"You're worried?" I asked.

"No, I'm not. You're young and fit. Whatever you face, we face together. But the sooner you know, the better. Your father made a donation to that hospital after his surgery. I'm sure we can get you in sooner."

"You think it's that important?"

She touched my shoulder. "It would make me feel better."

"All right. I'll call Dr. Hippo today." I covered her hand with mine. "No worries, Mom. I'm sure everything's gonna be fine."

Kensi smoothed her hand over her tummy and I rushed to her side, lifting her into my arms.

"Does it hurt, baby?"

"A little."

I turned to my mother. "Does she look more yellow to you today?"

"It's my camouflage, Daddy."

I set her down on the couch.

"She had a good night's sleep, which is far more than I can say for you. You've been working insane hours. Please tell me you're not skipping sleep."

"Not trying to. The woman I dropped off at home last night was Dr. Young's daughter."

"The nutcracker?"

I nodded. "Yeah, her."

"And?"

"And that's it." I checked my watch. "I got to go. I'm signing off on the furniture for the new department and meeting Tiff for lunch."

"Can't someone else do it?" she asked.

"You'd think." I turned to the girls. "Will you be good for Grandma?"

They both sent me air kisses, which I caught and placed over my heart.

"I should be back by early afternoon. Thanks, Mom." I kissed them both, squeezed my little girls tightly, and left.

"Tiff? What are you doing here?"

My ex was sitting cross-legged on top of my mahogany office desk. The slit in her skirt ran up her thigh, and she was wearing a revealing top I'd once favored.

Oh, shit.

I left the office door ajar. "I thought we were meeting in the new area?"

"I wanted to see you first."

"Is everything on schedule?"

"It is, but I'd love to hear more about the team you're preparing this for. The space seems special. Tristan is asking for many perks he didn't have before."

"You should ask him about the perks, but if you want my opinion… What Tristan wants, Tristan gets."

"What is it *you* want, James?" She hopped off the desk and sauntered my way.

Tiffany was persistent, and she hadn't given up on me or on our perfect little family, as she called us. The girls bound us for life, and their mother would always remain in mine.

"I want to sign off on the delivery and whatever else you need." I checked my watch. "Are you ready to go? I have an appointment with Tristan, and a biopsy at the hospital later."

Her shoulders dropped as I pulled the door open and gestured her to the hall. She stopped in the doorway and turned around, bumping into my chest. I should have seen that one coming.

"I'm sorry. I just, well, who's coming with you?"

"Nobody."

"But who's gonna drive you back?"

"George, the company's driver."

"But—"

"Tiff, it's fine. It's just a biopsy. Cross your fingers that it's nothing, so Kensi can have my liver. Concentrate on finishing the office space, and I'll call you as soon as I'm done. And George is driving me back."

"All right." She smoothed her palm over my chest. "I want you to know you can count on me, James."

"Tiff—"

"I know I've said it before, but it's true."

"Thank you. I appreciate it. Are the girls staying at your house this weekend?"

"Yes, but I can't pick them up until the evening."

Of course, she couldn't.

"You know what? Why don't you come by Sunday morning? No point dragging them out before bedtime."

Hopefully, my parents could watch the girls. They lived closer than Tiffany, anyway, and I had one last job before easing my workload.

"Sounds good."

"What are your plans on Sunday?"

"I booked a spa day at Grace's."

"Sounds like the perfect girl's day."

I could see Tiffany smiling out of the corner of my eye.

We toured the area Tristan had planned out for the new department. Tiffany's talent had earned her company prestige for a reason. They'd designed the space with thought and care: gray and white elements with a touch of silver added modern sleekness. The pillow-filled couches, cushioned seats, and an area with giant white beanbags near the windows added coziness.

"So?"

"Where do I sign?"

She held out a tablet, and I swept my finger across the screen. She loosened her hold on the device, and I caught the screen in my hands, which brought my face down to hers. She went in for my mouth, but I turned my head sideways, and her lips smacked over my cheek.

I stood tall and stepped back. "Tiffany, I hope I didn't give you the wrong idea."

"What wrong idea is that? That you're a wonderful father, a great businessman, and an exquisite lover? That I want you, James? I thought my intention was clear."

Her hands drifted underneath my suit and around my torso. I stepped back again, putting some space between us.

"You'd better update your intention if you want to work with me again."

"If we were a family again, would it be so bad? Don't you miss waking up next to me?"

Truth was, I did miss a woman's warm body in my bed, but it wasn't Tiffany's, and I wasn't revisiting a conversation we'd had in the past. There was no return to that road.

"I prefer our current co-parenting arrangement. I have a meeting before the hospital, Tiff."

"It's that woman we drove, isn't it? Laura? I saw how you looked at her."

I ignored her comment, as it was none of her business.

"I'll see you this weekend. The girls will have their backpacks ready." I lowered my hands to her shoulders and steered her to the exit. "You know the way out."

"Good luck at the hospital today, James," she said as I walked away.

"Thanks, Tiff."

I continued down the hall to Tristan's office and found him fidgeting with a pair of fluffy cuffs. He had it bad for the new hire at Silver Securities.

"Who are those for?"

"Don't fucking ask. Allie sent these as a gift, and I'm not sure whether they're for her or me. You're early."

"I signed off on the furniture, and I'm curious whether you'll finally let me know what you're doing with the space."

"Human trafficking division. Unfortunately, the demand is out there. Are you ready for the auction?"

"I'm always ready. Are you?"

"No. We'll meet with Allie this weekend. I told her I'm bringing someone single."

"What for?"

"So she can bring a date for you. The woman has a kid and she sounds like a good match for you. I got it right, didn't I?"

Technically, I was single, but I also wasn't looking for a date. Unless it was Laura. But if Allie was bringing a friend, chances were great it would be her.

"Sure, why not? It should be fun. You said she has a kid?"

"A boy."

"And the father?"

"Not in the picture at the moment."

Perfect.

"Allie said they're figuring things out."

I chuckled. *Figuring things out.*

"Looking forward to it, my cousin, but I'm sure that's not why you asked me to join you here."

I plopped down on the couch in his office and stretched my legs out in front. My head felt heavy, and a sudden wave of exhaustion passed through my body. I cranked my neck sideways and forced myself to sit straight up.

"You're right. Thanks for coming. I know you have your appointment today."

"In exactly an hour. What can I do for you?"

"I have my hands full with Kendra's case, and I need your help to find an investigator for the new department. Someone with experience, but trainable, who would make a suitable partner for Allie."

"So it's official? You're going to hire her?"

"She's perfect for the job. I'll surprise her as soon as we get Kendra. So? You up for it?"

"You're making me responsible for hiring a new investigator?"

"That's right."

"Nothing good in recruiting?"

"Personal acquaintances always work best. I can't ask my brother because his hands are full with Kendra. Gabe is in Austria. Hunter's not old enough, and our fathers barely retired."

"All right. I'll do it. Anything else?"

"How are my nieces? And how is it possible none of us are a match for Kensi?"

My brothers and extended family had rushed to get their bloodwork done as soon as they'd found out about Kensi.

"I don't know, but at least, I am. I just need a few more tests. Speaking of which, I'd better get going."

We gave each other a brotherly hug, and George, the company's chauffeur, gave me a ride to the hospital.

The bone marrow biopsy wasn't painful, but definitely uncomfortable—and definitely worth it. I dressed, and Dr. Hippo came into the room, smiling.

"I have good news for you, Mr. Silver."

"You can't have my results that quickly, can you?"

"No, we'll have yours in a few weeks; but if we're lucky, we won't have to wait too long for Kensi's surgery. We've done a few preliminary tests, but we may have found a matching donor."

"You're serious?"

"We should have the final results after the weekend, but it looks promising, so far."

"That's great news. Who's the donor?"

"It's an anonymous donation."

"Wow. This feels like a dream."

I'd tossed and turned every night since Kensi's diagnosis, and barely ever slept through to morning.

"Please let them know my gratitude. Given compatible results, when could we do the surgery?"

"Given the donor's ability, within days."

I felt like I'd gotten a new lease on life. My daughter would get her liver, and she'd live.

"Thank you, Dr. Hippo. Please let me know if you hear anything else."

"I will. Good to see you, Mr. Silver."

I took the staircase downstairs and went to grab a coffee at the hospital's snack shop, when I noticed a familiar brown head of hair in the line ahead of me. I tapped the guy in front of the shoulder.

"Hey, you mind if I scoot ahead of you? I know that girl."

He looked me up and down, and I handed a crisp twenty into his palm. "Your coffee's on me. Keep the change."

"Sure, bro."

I did the same with the next three guys, and sixty bucks later, I was standing behind Laura. The last guy let me butt in for free.

"Hello, Officer Young."

She whipped her body around. Her eyes popped open, and she puffed out a long breath as she searched for her words. She had let her hair down from its usual bun when she was in uniform. It was longer than when we'd met, and sexy. She made the MILF vibe difficult to miss.

"What are you doing here?" she asked.

"Bone marrow biopsy."

"For Kensi's transplant?"

"Yes, and no. Just crossing all the t's and dotting all the i's. What about you?"

She cleared her throat. "My parents work here."

"I thought you weren't on speaking terms."

"We're trying to reconcile." Her gaze skidded from one end of the room to the other. "Isn't that odd? We don't see each other for three years, and then I run into you twice in the past couple of weeks."

"Three times," I corrected. "This is our third. We could have had a fourth, or even a fifth, if you'd returned my calls."

"Sorry. I've been busy. Reconciling."

"So, now that you're not busy, you'll agree to a date with me? How about Friday night?"

"I don't think I can get a babysitter by then, and I already told you, I'm not dating."

I called bullshit on that, but if Laura showed at the Marina this Friday, I wouldn't have to call it out.

"Can't blame a guy for trying. How's work?"

"Work is one of the reasons I'm here. I'm on mandatory leave. Two weeks."

"What happened?"

"Motherhood and not enough sick days. The boss wants me to think about my life and priorities. My son is a priority."

"Next?" the barista asked, and Laura turned to place her order.

She waited for me as they prepared my coffee, and we walked shoulder to shoulder to the parking lot.

"How did it go with your parents?"

"I wasn't able to see them. One's in surgery and the other one has a full day of patients."

"So, you're free for the afternoon?"

"If by 'free,' you mean pick up my son from Allie's care at the park, make dinner, throw in a load of laundry, and think about my life as homework, then yes, I'm free."

"Funny. Well, if you're not free, then I guess I'm going to throw my sales pitch now."

"Sales pitch? What are you selling?"

"Tristan is setting up a new department at Silver Securities. Allie will be the lead, and she'll need a new partner."

"Wait a minute." She stopped. "Are you saying what I think

you're saying? Are you offering me a job? And if so, is this a pity offer? Because I don't do pity, and you don't even know what I can do—"

"I'm well aware of your abilities, Laura. You showed me some of your best moves in that maintenance room."

"Why do you do that?"

"Do what?"

"Make serious offers, and then joke about them."

We started walking again. She clicked a car key button and a Wrangler's lights flickered about ten parking spots down.

"I'm not joking about the offer."

"Yes, but when you refer to my abilities, and then us having sex, in the same conversation as offering me a job, it sounds like you want a prostitute and not an investigator."

"You'd get to work with your old partner," I coerced.

"I can't deny that sounds appealing."

"But?"

"No but. I need to think about it."

"What's there to think about? A pay increase, benefits, and flexible work hours."

Why was she so hesitant?

"You're offering me a job after I arrested you?"

"We're not all perfect, are we?" I winked.

She fought a half-cocked smile. "You want the answer now?"

"No."

"Then I'll think about it."

"As you do, mention nothing to Allie. It's supposed to be a surprise."

"Great. More secrets I have to keep from my best friend."

"What other secrets are you keeping?"

"There's a reason they're called secrets." She winked. "I should get going. I have to pick up Ozzy."

I stood in the parking lot by her Wrangler. That car looked like it had seen better days.

"So you'll call me?" I called out after her.

"I'll think about it. Why don't you send over the details?"

"All right. Sounds good. Have a good weekend doing laundry."

"Thanks. You too."

She jumped in her car and took off, tires screeching. I stared after the car, timing my next step.

Chapter 5

Laura

$\mathcal{I}$ stood frozen in front of James Silver as he lifted my hand to his lips and placed a scattering of pecks on my skin. Goosebumps spread from each spot he kissed. My breaths shortened and my knees barely held up. They had set our table on the outdoor deck at the Marina, and this blind date Allie had insisted I attend was my biggest nightmare. I never told my best friend that James was Foxy's father. I should have. She'd put two and two together when she saw my face, and his face, as James walked into the Marina, but it was already too late.

Keeping the truth from my best friend had been a mistake. Had I been honest with her, I wouldn't be looking into James' smug face as he towered over me, trapping me in his presence and silently challenging me on my assertion I wasn't ready to date. My heart was beating in some weird pattern that cut my breath short, and I was afraid to meet his gaze because, only a few days ago, I'd been adamant. I told him I wasn't ready to date. Yet here we were. On a date. I anchored myself to the deck and braved looking into his bright blue eyes.

His brow wiggled, and I cracked a smile. He was making

this too easy for me. James pulled out my chair, and I slid into my seat, throwing Allie a dirty look.

Thankfully, most conversation at the table focused around next week's operation to rescue a kidnapped woman. I focused on the menu and ordered way too much food for one person because it was easier than watching James scratch his freshly trimmed beard as he concentrated.

The waiter brought out our food: three plates for me and one for everyone else.

"You've got an appetite," James said from the side.

"Not true," I said. "I'm nervous, and I do stupid things when I'm nervous—like order too much food."

"I always thought you had nerves of steel."

"My nerves don't work around you."

He chuckled and dug into his lobster. I stuck a fork in one of my scallops and held it in front of his mouth. "Try. They're delicious."

"Are you doing that because you won't be able to finish?"

"Can't waste food."

The amused look on his face was cute. I stuck another scallop on the fork and fed him. His appetite had no limit. James helped me with my three plates. Allie and Tristan had finished earlier and gone for a walk around the deck to feed the seagulls, leaving us alone. I sat back in my seat and sipped on iced tea.

"So, no time for dating?" he asked.

There it was. I sighed. "I couldn't say no. Allie vetoed me."

"Do I want to know what that means?"

"It's a thing we have. You're not allowed to argue a veto, and we each get one every year."

"And who makes up these rules?"

"We do. Best friends know what's best for the other."

His confident smile crept higher and higher. He leaned

forward, forcing my gaze to his. "So, you're saying your best friend thinks I'm good for you?"

"No. I'm saying my best friend has one coming her way."

"Don't be upset. Maybe one day you'll thank her."

His eyes crinkled with a smile. He was enjoying this too much.

"When are you getting your biopsy results?" I asked.

"The doctor said next week."

"That's good. And how is Kensi feeling?"

"She's stable, but we're still waiting for something solid."

I was waiting for an answer from Dr. Hippo as well. He could call with the results from my liver tissue match any day now, and the sooner he called, the better. I had two weeks off, and Mrs. Brewers was on standby for babysitting. Thank God for babysitters who lived across the street, and ones who took kids on short notice. When Mrs. Brewers had told me she was sick today, I was ready to cancel, but Allie dropped Foxy off with Tristan's sister. If James had a clue his little cousin was watching his son, he'd flip. My window to tell James about Foxy was closing. I had to turn this date around.

"Allie and Tristan work well together."

"They're a good fit, but I'm glad they gave us a moment. It's personal."

My heart dropped into my stomach and my throat sealed as I prepared for the bomb to drop. Oh, God, did he know?

"Okay?"

"How would you feel about working so close to me?"

I cleared my throat. "I believe it's a great opportunity. Silver Securities has an excellent reputation."

"You're avoiding my question."

His eyebrow lifted. The subtle shift of confidence on his face sent my heart out of synch again.

"Why don't you answer the same question? How would you feel about working with me?"

He angled his body closer to mine. "I let you get away from me last time, and I'm not doing it again."

My body heated before going numb. Why wouldn't I give this a try when his intention was so clear? But how could I start a relationship with a lie? A big lie? The decision would be easier if James knew the truth.

"I don't know, James. I have to think about it." Sweat dripped down my hands and I rubbed them down my pants to dry them.

"What's there to think about? Flexible schedule, full benefits, and an increase in salary. We're a family-oriented company, so you'd have all the time you need for Ozzy. In fact, we're also setting up childcare at work, so your son would be a couple of floors away from you."

"I can't deny your offer sounds tempting, James."

"Yet not tempting enough. What can I do to sway your decision?"

"It's not you." Of course, it was. "I have a lot going on right now, and wouldn't want to take on anything I couldn't handle. And I'm handling a lot. I'm afraid I wouldn't be a good hire. We both know the work requires full attention, which has been difficult."

He shifted closer. "I don't need an answer right now. The offer's on the table. Think about it. No pressure."

Air whizzed out of my lungs.

No pressure.

Working with Allie again would be amazing, but James would be my boss. My son's father would be my boss, without knowing he had a son. If I agreed, though, it would put some pressure on my stupid ass to tell him the truth before my start date. My stomach swirled with the chocolate mousse I'd finished earlier, and I took a sip of water.

"When would I start? I have a few things to take care of in the next two weeks."

Buying time seemed like a viable option.

"It's up to you. We're completely flexible. The department's set to begin operations as soon as we have Kendra."

"The kidnapped girl you're rescuing next week?"

He nodded. "The new department is a necessity. Human trafficking will concentrate on saving sex-trafficked women. There are girls as young as seventeen, pregnant and alone, without medical care, losing babies, trafficked and passed on from one man to another."

I froze. My stomach squeezed and pushed up, jerking my shoulders forward.

"Laura? Laura, what's the matter?"

I grabbed the closest thing within my reach, which was James's jacket, and threw up inside the pocket. My vomit spilled out onto the floor.

James passed me a napkin while holding back my hair.

"I'm so sorry." I heaved in air while wiping my mouth.

"Are you all right? We should go to the hospital—"

I wiggled my finger left and right. "No, no. I'm fine."

"You don't look fine, and my jacket tells a different story."

He stood up, removed the jacket from his chair, and walked over to the trash near the kitchen door. He picked up a fresh glass of water on his way back and set it in front of me.

"Drink. You need to hydrate. I'm going to the kitchen to check in with Olivier."

"Don't. It's not the food."

"Then what is it? Do you feel ill?"

A worker came to the table and I stood up, weak in the knees. James held me by the elbow and we moved over to the railing as the maintenance guy swept the mess off the floor. I felt awful and embarrassed for him.

"I'm fine now. I think I'm just nervous about spending this time with you, and I'm so sorry about your jacket, James. Seventy four percent of blind dates fail."

"Let's not get ahead of ourselves. You haven't burned down the building–"

"Yet."

He chuckled. "You sure you're alright?"

"Yeah, I'm sure. I'm sorry."

Fortunately, Allie and Tristan appeared from around the corner and walked back to our table, hand in hand.

"They're coming back," I said.

"Whether you agree to the job or not, please don't say anything to Allie. It's supposed to be a surprise. But I really hope you agree."

He wound his arm around me. The warm hold sent comfort through my veins and trepidation to my heart. What was happening here?

"What are you doing tonight?" he asked, and I looked up into his persuasive eyes

The answer was nothing. I'd planned to pick up Foxy from Emma's and go home, but she'd offered to watch him until the morning, so I was free. He smoothed his hand over mine as Allie and Tristan came up to the table. Tristan wrapped his arms around her and brought her closer to his body.

"I've settled the bill, but we have one more pit-stop tonight. We'll take Allie's car, and James can take mine."

"Where are we going?" I asked.

"To play dress up." Allie hooked me under my arm. "Wow, you don't look so good. What's that smell?"

"I need to use the bathroom." I pulled Allie along with me.

"We'll meet you in the parking lot," Tristan called out behind us.

Thankfully, the Marina had a fancy bathroom with mouthwash.

"Why did you throw up?" She tucked my stray hair behind my ear.

"I don't know how long I can keep lying to him."

"Maybe it's time to tell him the truth."

"If I tell him right now, he'll never forgive me."

"Then remind him what he's missing first, and then drop the bomb."

"That's like going nuclear."

"Well, then you gotta nuke him good."

I gave her a hard eye roll. "What if he hates me?"

"Did you see the way he looks at you? The man is still in love with you."

"Still in love? He was never in love with me. Allie, we spent one night together." One amazing night I would never forget.

"And you share a child. There's obviously a connection there."

She was right—except, James didn't know about the greatest connection we had. I cranked my neck to the side and gathered my wits.

"I have to pick up Foxy."

"Emma said he can stay until morning. I already told her he will. " She wiggled her brows. "This is the chance you've been waiting for. Don't mess it up."

"Did you know eighty-eight percent of people lie to their partners?"

"You don't have to be a statistic, babe. I know you can do it."

"I'm gonna try, babe. I truly will."

She hugged me hard, and we returned to the parking lot. Moments later, we were driving toward Manhattan. James cranked up the radio, and I used the time to gather my thoughts. I went over all the possible conversations about Foxy in my head, and all of them ended with James hating me.

Half an hour later, James pulled up to a boutique. Its owner, Mary Wagner, welcomed us at the door. Dark curls spilled over her shoulders as she embodied Elvira Addams in Madonna's style. I helped Allie change into a suitable outfit for the auction where they'd pawn her.

"You know what you're doing, right?" I asked her in the change room. "Because Foxy needs his godmother."

"I got it. I promise," Allie assured me.

"Hey, James."

Our heads flew to the voice behind the curtain, and I popped my head out of the change room.

"What's up, Gracie?" He waved to a beautiful woman walking down the staircase.

"I'm still looking for that date for the masquerade. You interested?"

"I don't do tuxedos," James grunted.

"You're a Silver. You can do whatever and whomever you want." The woman busted out a laugh.

I stepped out of the dressing room and watched as Gracie walked down the glass stairs.

"If that were true, my baby brother would do you, Gracie."

"Don't speak the demon's name."

"Hunter's been asking about you."

Grace let out an exasperated "Argh..." and stomped down the last three steps.

Their bickering was cute. Tristan's cousin, from his mother's side, had spunk.

"It doesn't change the fact I'd like to skin him Silence of the Lambs style. Tell him I'll be ready to accept his apology when he matures, which is...ahem...never."

James stood up and wrapped his enormous arms around her in a bear hug. "I missed you. Sorry about my brother."

She handed him a small gift bag and whispered something in his ear.

"Are you coming, Laura?"

Allie nudged my back, propelling me forward. James took my hand without asking again, kissed Grace on her cheek, and waved at Allie and Tristan. "I'll see you two in the morning. Don't stay up too late."

I followed his lead back to the car and took the passenger's seat. James buckled his seatbelt and turned my way.

"I couldn't wait to get you alone again. Are you in a hurry to get home?"

"Didn't you say you needed to pick up Laila?"

"No, I just wanted to get out of there so I could have more time with you. Do you have time?"

"I pick up Ozzy in the morning, so yeah, I have some time."

A sly smile lifted the corner of his mouth. "Great. I want to show you something. It's not far."

His dimple pushed deeper into his cheek, and I melted into my seat. He had that sexy, mysterious look patented. Ten minutes later, James pulled into his private parking spot at Silver Securities. We took the elevator to the fifteenth floor. Motion censored lights flickered on.

"I know I said I'd give you time to decide, but I wanted to ensure you saw the full picture of the operation you'd be leading with Allie."

I smiled. "All right. Show me what you've got."

He pressed his finger to a pad, and the glass door slid open. The grand tour of the office floor where Allie's future team would operate had my mind spinning. The resources to help here were absolutely incredible. The secret I'd have to keep from my best friend was big, but it wasn't my first, nor my second. After the tour, we took the elevator to the corporate floor, where he insisted on showing me the view from his office. I walked around the spacious room. The gray and white decor with a touch of silver boasted elegance, strength, and power. I slid my finger over the polished mahogany desk.

"I must say, the technology at Silver Securities is impressive, and the design team did a great job with the space downstairs. It's cozy."

"I'm glad you like it. You'd lead a team of twelve, in charge of everything from planning a rescue operation to dealing with the aftermath. The rescued woman passing through your office would receive physiological and emotional support. I know it'd be a change from working the streets, but it would be more fulfilling. Last week, my brother brought a pregnant seventeen-year-old in to a safe house. She would have lost her baby if she'd stayed with her abuser."

Shivers nipped at my spine. I knew I could do the job. Bringing down human trafficking hit a sweet spot deep in my chest. The number of times we'd found an infant's body dumped because the child had resulted from rape was one too many.

I pressed my palm against the window. Such a beautiful skyline masked the crime below.

"I'm sorry about your jacket."

"It's replaceable." His voice was low, and I was afraid to turn around.

"What did Grace give you?"

"A gift for you. Whatever it is, I hope I get to see you wear it."

My skin prickled with goosebumps as his intention overtook my senses. I swallowed with a click. "The view isn't so bad either."

The lights dimmed behind me in the window's reflection, and my pulse quickened.

"I agree." James's warm breath dusted the back of my neck, and I turned to face him. He stood tall, his thick thighs against mine. The potent scent of his cologne hit me. The peppery, cedar aroma with a hint of rose spun my head until I looked up and met his blue eyes. His gaze anchored me.

"Laura, there's another consideration I'd like you to make besides the work."

I swallowed a knot of apprehension as he held his breath. "What is it?"

"Give me a chance." His throaty voice vibrated through the

air and landed on my skin. The waves oscillated down my throat and chest, and settled below my belt.

"A chance for what?" My whisper broke into staccato.

The bottomless depth of his gaze pulled me into a hold I didn't want to escape. He lifted his hands to my arms, squeezing gently. Every part of his muscled body touched mine as his hands slid up and down my arms. The emotions criss-crossing his face tempered my fear. I should have tried harder.

"A chance to make Colorado right."

His mouth drifted closer in slow motion. I closed my eyes, and his hot lips touched down in a sensual kiss. My lips parted for his tongue, and the world ceased to exist. A torturous stampede of regret and gratitude rushed through my insides. Fate had a funny sense of humor if she thought I'd tell him right now because this stolen moment was just for us.

The ground sank beneath me as my knees gave out, but James held me so tightly in his arms, I couldn't fall. He wouldn't let me fall. The kiss deepened, and the protective shell around my heart cracked. I'd secretly yearned for him since the moment I'd left; more so, when my pregnancy test showed a plus sign. The soul-piercing kiss whisked me back to Colorado, where I'd given him everything he wanted and stolen what should have been ours.

Why did I walk away so fast?

I walked backward, following his lead, until my ass hit his mahogany desk.

His hands searched over my clothes for access. I rubbed my thigh over his confined erection. Arousal surged through my veins. He was hot back then and hotter right now. I pulled away, took a hold of his v-neck shirt, and dragged it over his head. My hands grazed down the ladder of his beautiful abs to his erection. I kissed him between smiles, and he grinned against my lips, gently biting on the flesh. I fumbled with his buckle and unfastened his pants. My fingers brushed the dark sprinkle of hair near the top where the pink crown of his cock poked through.

He sucked in a sharp breath and pulled away, pressing his forehead against mine, heaving air. "Laura."

"James."

Was this not my moment? What if it wasn't?

"I… I'm not sure about this. My life is complicated."

"Like taxes," he said.

I chuckled.

"My life is complicated, as well, so we're one for one so far." His hands curved over the nook between my shoulders and neck, and I gripped his wrists.

I closed my eyes. "This feels right, James."

Yet, it was so wrong. How could I keep this secret inside myself? Then again, how could I tell him the truth? Every ticking second was too much time wasted already.

"I want to make it feel better."

Promises and lies never blended well. His promises and my lies—but stopping now was impossible. Allie was right. Nuclear was my only option.

I kissed along his jawline until I found his mouth again. He hooked his fingers into my stretchy jeans and pulled them off my ass, never breaking the kiss. My panties got caught in his hold, and a cool drift breezed over my heated flesh as he lifted me to the desk. My hot ass squished against the polished surface, sliding back until I nearly knocked off the fancy digital clock. He pulled away and removed my shirt over my head. His eyes grew wide at the sight of my breasts.

"I just stopped nursing, so I'd stay away from this area." I pointed to my cleavage.

"Any area I should particularly focus on?" His crooked smile sank his dimple into its irresistible spot. His mouth, hard on mine, forced me down to the desk. He let go and trailed kisses down my body. I turned my head sideways. Manhattan's night skyline blurred in the distance. His mouth reached my throbbing heat, and my lower back arched. I tightened around his two fingers as he slid them inside of me, licking down my slit. He closed his mouth over me, flicking his tongue in an unforgiving rhythm while finger-fucking me. I pulled his head off my pussy and used his shoulders to pull myself up to sit.

He lowered his boxers, and his cock sprang free. The sound of a drawer opening rolled through the room. He reached within and removed a condom.

"You sure those aren't poked?"

"The drawer only opens with my thumbprint, so they're pretty secure."

He ripped the packet open and rolled the latex down his length. The main vein running up his cock pulsed in the faint light. I was throbbing everywhere, and my knees parted of their own accord. James lined himself up at my opening and thrust hard inside. My body flew up on the table as I gripped tightly around him. He held me in his arms and took my mouth as his hips rolled back and forth, heightening the friction between him and my clit. We clung to each other, skin-to-skin.

God, he was the hottest man I'd ever been with. Delight pulsed between my legs as I wrapped them around his hips. He thrust harder, his hands supporting my ass on the sleek desk. I breathed in his grunts, and he swallowed my moans until my limbs lost all will and the connection between us reached its height. I pulled my mouth away from his and came hard around him. His hips jerked twice more and then he stilled, gasping in my shaky hold. He withdrew, removed his condom and trashed it. Then, he stepped out of his pants, lifted me off the desk, and carried me to a couch. He removed my shirt and covered us with a blanket, and I settled in his hold.

A thousand questions stormed in my head.

"Next time I have you, it will be in my bed," he whispered, and I couldn't help my grin.

"Why are you smiling?" His heavy breath blended with mine. "I know that was amazing, but I can do much better."

I had no doubt he could. "I just fucked my boss-to-be on his desk," I said.

"Does that mean you're taking the job?"

"I'm not sure yet. So far, the benefits seem to outweigh the drawbacks."

"What drawbacks? There should be none."

What about exposing my heart, family, career, and future? What about exposing me as a liar and a fraud?

"I misspoke. I can't see the drawbacks anymore. But I should go home."

"I can drive you in the morning."

"I can take an Uber."

"Veto," he murmured in my ear.

"You can't veto me."

"I believe I just did. You stay here with me until morning. I'll sneak you out through a private elevator, take you to breakfast, and then you can pick up Ozzy."

"I'll have to brush my teeth before breakfast."

"I keep a spare toothbrush here. Now stop making excuses and let me enjoy holding you. I've missed three years already. I'm not missing any more."

Exhausted, confused, and satisfied, I snuggled into his body. My cheek lay flat against his naked chest, and I listened to his calming heartbeat. The rhythmic beat eased the anxiety tied around my heart. His light snore rumbled underneath me when a text pinged on my phone. I snuck out from his hold, wrapped another blanket around myself, and tiptoed to my jacket over his chair.

I found my phone and pulled my finger across the screen. The text nearly stopped my heart.

Teresa Silver: I'd like to meet for lunch this weekend. Please bring my grandson.

Chapter 6

James

"Good morning, Mom." I strolled through the front door of my parents' house.

"Daddy!" Kensi and Laila ran to my side and gave me a hug.

"Morning, girls. What are you baking?"

"Pancakes and muffins. Grandma's making croissants for later."

I inhaled the fresh pastry aroma. Comfort and security hung permanently in the air at my parents' house. I wished Laura hadn't left my office five days ago. I'd woken up that morning, intending to share breakfast, but she was already gone. She'd left a note on my desk that we'd catch up during the week, and I'd heard nothing since. The past five days without her, as I waited for my biopsy results, felt torturous. The girls stayed home with their grandparents next door, while I lost myself in casework.

"Breakfast smells delicious."

The girls ran back to my mother and glued themselves to her side by the kitchen pantry. She kissed them both on the tops of their heads and started listing all the baking she'd planned for the day.

We'd pulled Kensi from school three months ago when her health took a turn for the worse. Sick seven-year-olds shouldn't have to worry about school. I'd hired a nurse to stay at my parents' house, monitoring my girl when I worked. My mother, meanwhile, watched Laila, because she was a superhero.

I stole a hug from the girls and took my mother into my arms.

"You call me as soon as you know." She squeezed me tight. "You don't know how much you have to live for."

I glanced over her shoulder at the girls. "Oh, I do."

"No, you don't. Trust me, you don't; so you need to be well, you hear me?"

My mother looked different this morning than yesterday. She looked truly worried, which kicked up an instinct in my chest. Perhaps she was right.

"Everything's going to be fine, Mom. I'll call you as soon as I can. Love you." I kissed the top of her head the same way she'd kissed my girls and left for Manhattan General.

As Dr. Hippo's first appointment this morning, I walked through his office door on time. I gave him a firm handshake, as if that would change the biopsy result, and sat in the chair across from his desk. My knee bounced.

"Good morning, Mr. Silver."

"Please tell me you have good news for me this morning, Doc."

"I have good news and bad news. Which one would you prefer to hear first?"

Fuck.

I pulled a breath in through my nostrils. "Let's start with the bad again."

"While you're a match for Kensi, you're not a candidate for her because of a chronic disease called hairy cell leukemia, or HCL."

"Did you just say leukemia?"

"I know it sounds scary and overwhelming, but let me assure you, ninety percent of HCL patients live to their normal life expectancy. In fact, most die from something completely different. Your biopsy revealed point-zero-two percent of hairy cells. That's what we call early detection."

"What kind of treatment am I looking at? Chemo?"

"The low ratio of hairy cells requires no treatment. Your bloodwork will be monitored every two months."

God, could he suck any more air out of the room?

"Hairy cell leukemia grows at an extremely low rate, but your immune system works overtime, causing chronic fatigue."

Apparently, he could.

"The diagnosis also explains your enlarged spleen, which could present itself as pain underneath your left ribs."

I sat open-mouthed and replayed his words in my head.

"Well, how long until treatment?"

"That varies by patient. Six weeks, months, or even years from now is possible. I'll refer you to a homeopath. Keeping fit, healthy, and not stressed is one key to beating this disease."

"Not stressed? You're aware of what I do for a living, Dr. Hippo. My two-year-old has an autoimmune disease, and my seven-year-old needs a liver transplant. I think I'm ready for the good news."

I gripped the chair arms and my knuckles whitened. He waited until my fury settled, and I was grateful for his understanding.

"The good news is the potential donor I mentioned last week matches with all of Kensi's markers."

"All eight?"

"Yes. The donor is ready for surgery on Monday."

I shot up from my seat. "That's a perfect match. Are you serious?"

"Yes. I don't joke about patient care, so yes, I'm serious."

"This is a miracle, isn't it?"

"I often think of anonymous donors as angels because of their altruistic nature."

"Whoever it is, you tell him or her they have my full gratitude. Thank you, Doctor Hippo."

"You're welcome. The secretary will email you all the details."

I left his office with the word *leukemia* ringing in my ears, yet I couldn't resist an upbeat step. Kensi was getting her liver.

I sat down at a corner table as the two doctors I'd asked to meet passed through the side door.

Perfect timing.

I waved at them both and stood up from my seat to greet them.

"Mrs. Young, Mr. Young. Thank you for meeting with me. I value your time and your work—"

"It's nice to see you, Mr. Silver. How is your father doing?" Mr. Young shook my hand and took his seat.

"Great—you saved his life. My mother tells me if you hadn't operated on him, his ticker would have given out. She sends her regards and thanks you."

"I'm glad to hear he's well. You said on the phone Laura's in trouble. What kind of trouble? How can we help?" Mrs. Young leaned forward in her seat.

"I may have misspoken. She's not in trouble, but her work at the force is pushing her limits. I'm considering hiring Laura for a position at Silver Securities, and I'd like to ask you a few questions."

"You've made a generous donation to my wife's research. The next hour is yours, Mr. Silver."

"I'm not sure if she mentioned it, but I'm seeing Laura."

Mr. Young cleared his throat. "Our daughter hasn't exactly picked up our calls over the past few years."

"But she's a very smart and courageous woman," her mother added.

Although Laura wasn't courageous enough to tell them they were grandparents.

"Should I worry about her working in human trafficking?"

"Laura will be saving people from slavery?"

"Sex trafficking, to be exact. Young girls who've seen what no one should see. Fearful pregnant girls who have no one."

The Youngs exchanged a knowing look, and I wondered what had passed between them. Her mother leaned in closer, securing my full attention.

"Laura has lived through more than most her age. She's worked hard to get where she is. We've always known she'd succeed at any path she chose, and we're thrilled she's thrived at the police force, but we haven't spoken in months."

Her eyes fell sad, and I shifted in my seat. "I'm sorry for your pain. I know we've just met, but I also know she loves her family."

"Thank you."

I pulled my hands along my pants, wiping off the sweat.

"Mr. and Mrs. Young, I know we just met, but I must ask why Laura would object to having a baby. Not that we're thinking about babies," I hastened to add. "It came up in the conversation and surprised me."

He glanced over at his wife and lowered his hands beneath the table, taking hers. That glance, though, and the uncertainty in their eyes, had me pinned in my seat. The air between us thickened with a thousand emotions. Her mother wiped a tear from the corner of her eye, while her father braced his elbows on the table and lowered his head into his hands.

"Laura's traumatized. She'd be afraid to lose another baby."

Lose another baby?

I angled my head in a questioning matter, and the Youngs exchanged another look. *What the fuck was going on here?*

"Mr. and Mrs. Young, as you know, Laura's line of work will not always be safe. Anything you can tell me could make a difference between life and death. I protect all of my employees, and I want to protect Laura as well. More so, I care deeply for her."

Her father looked up. "Do you love her?"

"Yes."

The reply came out so fast, I had no chance to stop it. All on its own. And I couldn't take it back. I didn't want it back. *How did this happen? When did this happen?*

Her mother's face softened. She chewed on her upper lip the way Laura did, and filled her lungs with a courageous breath. "Lara has a rainbow baby. The girl was stillborn."

My lungs collapsed and my mouth dropped open.

"Laura was seventeen and planning to go to medical school, but after being raped and finding out she was pregnant, she changed. We... We thought we were doing the right thing, and we wanted to guide her, but she wasn't the same after the attack. She dropped out of school and spent nights and days working out, and working and saving money while her belly grew."

She was raped?

I shook my head. "What do you mean, you thought you were doing the right thing?"

Mrs. Young sat straight up and took her husband's hand again.

"We tried to explain that science was in her blood, but Laura pulled out of school and away from her family. She cursed medicine because no doctor could save her baby, and she went into police work. We've barely been in touch ever since."

Oh, fuck. No wonder she'd kept her distance.

"I'm so sorry for your loss," I said.

Her father cleared his throat. "We're not bad parents. We

just haven't figured out how to get our daughter back."

I checked the time. "I understand. Sometimes trauma forces us to take paths we don't expect. I'm sure Laura simply needs time. I'll make sure she checks in with you more often. Thank you for your time and confidence."

Mrs. Young took my hand. "Please—you can't mention this conversation to Laura, but I hope you can bring our daughter back to her family."

"I won't say anything, and I will do my best to ensure Laura thrives."

I left them at the table and headed for the elevator. This weekend, Silver Securities would lead an operation to rescue a family friend. Today was all about clearing the mind.

The elevator door dinged open, and my morning instantly brightened. I walked inside and stood beside Laura.

"James?"

"Laura? What are you doing here?"

"We have to stop meeting at the hospital." I laughed out loud when we said the same thing.

"This hospital is my home away from home. I had an appointment. You?" The garage button had been lit, and I leaned back against the wall.

"I...ahem...just saw my parents. We're reconciling, and I'm hoping they'll finally have the time for me and Ozzy."

I lifted a brow. "Really?"

"Yeah. Why are you so surprised? Fifty-eight percent of estranged families reconcile."

And how many lie about actually reconciling?

I tipped my head sideways and pressed the emergency button on the control panel. The elevator halted, and she steadied her stance. The lines of her neck moved as she swallowed, and I stepped closer, forcing her back against the wall. Bob, the security guard in the downstairs lobby, came on the intercom.

"This is Fox Silver. Look away from the camera, Bob. I'll let you know when we're done."

"Ma'am, I wouldn't be doing my job if I didn't ask you whether you're all right."

She trembled in my hold, but a slow smile slid up the corner of her mouth. "I'm fine, Bob."

"You hear that, Bob? She's fine." I lowered my lips to her ear and whispered. "Very fine. Why did you leave my office so fast in the morning?"

Her throat lurched with a hard swallow.

"Bye, Bob," I said.

"See you at the Christmas party, James."

I closed in. "How did it go with your parents?"

"You don't look like you believe me."

"Did you tell them about Ozzy?"

"Okay, there, Mr. FBI. What's with so many questions? I had to leave early to pick up my son. I'm cleaning up my life, but there is a process to that."

Her gaze slowly lifted to mine. Her large eyes were outlined with long lashes. Her confession sounded amazing, but I fucking couldn't wait to shut her up. Right after she explained why she'd lied.

"I just had coffee with your parents," I said. "We had a lovely conversation."

Her backbone straightened and the fierce woman who'd arrested me snapped back to life, whipping out her protective shield.

"You did what?"

"I had to interview them. For your job at Silver Securities."

Her brow lifted. "You were snooping."

"The more important point here is, you lied to me. Why did you lie?"

"You told them I'll be working for you?" She ignored my question.

"For me, with me, underneath me. Yeah, I covered all that. Did you know my parents know yours? Doctor Young, your father, operated on my father."

"Of course, I knew. How do you think I got the nutcracker job in Colorado?" She chuckled, but her eyes held a semi-distant look. "My father saved your father's life. I guess your parents felt they owed them a favor."

"So my father's bad heart is the reason I met you?"

Amusement rippled across her face. Finally. I wasn't sure how long I could keep this elevator stuck between the third and fourth floor before someone called the fire department.

"It's like we were meant to be." Laura shrugged. "Sixty-eight percent of people meet their partner through an acquaintance."

"Partner?" I stepped closer and gripped her hips. "Is that what I am to you? A partner?"

Her shoulder lifted in a quick shrug. "I'm not sure what you are, yet, Fox Silver, but you're definitely something."

My mouth closed in on hers.

"I prefer it when you call me James," I whispered against her lips.

"But Fox sounds sexy, especially when Tiffany says it…"

I yanked my head back. "Are you jealous, Ms. Young?"

Her lips rolled inward, and she made a pinch with her forefinger and thumb. "Possibly? A little?"

"Does that mean the answer to my job offer is yes? I must warn you, you'll be on-call day and night." A rush of adrenaline flew through my veins.

"I believe I could get a better offer."

"Tell me what you want and I'll make it happen," I said.

"Stay alive this coming weekend, and we'll talk after then."

She pulled away. I groaned and pressed the emergency button again. The elevator brakes let go, and we descended to the garage.

"I don't understand why we have to be stuck in an elevator

to have a decent conversation. Did I fuck the wrong way? Because I don't make a habit of sleeping with women I'm not interested in."

She quivered in my hold, as if remembering our night at the office. After fucking her over my desk, we'd made love on the couch. The lustful night was just a prelude, though, because I needed her again. I needed her in my bed.

"No, James. You fucked just right." She sighed. "Like I said, stay alive this weekend. And how could I complain about being stuck in an elevator with James Bond?"

"Interesting. Did you know Bond's women fucked him at his command?"

"You mean like dogs? Is that what you want?"

"No. I want much more than a bitch. I want a fierce, powerful mother who listens to her instinct, and that's you. I want *you*, Laura."

She shifted away. "What were you doing with my parents?"

"Interviewing them for your job. Honestly, I thought you'd be more interesting," I lied. She was so fucking interesting, I had no spare tires for the ones she'd blown in my mind. "What were you doing at the hospital, if not to reconnect with your parents?"

She waved her hand in dismissal. "Woman stuff. Fibroids from too many tampons. Ninety-five percent of women develop one or more uterine fibroids during their reproductive lifespan."

"That's a lot, and you're right. I didn't want to know."

"Truth is, I've been having stomach pains and had to check them out."

She swayed on the balls of her feet until the elevator opened, and she stepped out. I followed her down the parking aisle. "Well?"

"Well, what?"

"What did they find?"

She gulped. "Gas."

"Gas?"

She nodded and winced in pain, grabbing her right side.

"You all right?"

"Yeah. Let's hope it's not an appendix." Her face twisted in pain and she let out a grunt. "Maybe it's more gas."

"What did you eat?" I asked.

"Nothing different."

She tried to stand straight, but winced in pain.

"Well, what are you doing now?" I asked.

"Going home. I have a million and a half responsibilities awaiting." She grabbed her side again.

"Okay, I'm driving you home. When does this fibroid pain go away?"

"I'm praying the answer is soon. Are you sure you want to spend time in a closed vehicle with a gassy woman?"

"I have two brothers."I reached out for her car keys and took her hand in mine. "I'll have someone drive your Wrangler home before the end of the day."

"Thank you."

We walked to my car, and my phone rang the moment I pulled out of the garage.

"Hi, Daddy," Kensi chimed through the Bluetooth speaker.

"Hi, baby."

"Grandpa wants to take us fishing."

"That sounds like fun."

"When are you coming home? I made a new sword and armor with grandpa."

"I'll be there in the afternoon, princess. How's your baby sister?"

"Laila's tummy is good."

"And yours?"

"Huwts a little."

"We'll make sure you're all better soon, okay, baby?"

"Okay, Daddy. I love you."

"I love you more."

We hung up, and I merged onto the freeway.

"You're a wonderful dad." Laura sighed, and I glanced sideways. She held a dreamy look in her eyes.

"You're a good mom, too."

She laughed. "You don't even know me."

"I know you take care of your son with no one's help. That's pretty big."

"Why would Laila's tummy hurt again?"

"She has an autoimmune disease, but it's manageable right now."

"Right. You mentioned that before. It's the worst when you want to help them, and you don't know how. They cry and cry because they can't verbalize what's wrong."

"Before Laila's diagnosis, we thought we were doing something wrong, but it wasn't us. Thank God for Dr. Hippo."

"He's great, isn't he?" she said.

"You've met?"

"He treated Ozzy's sprained wrist in the emergency department."

"How is he doing?"

"Much better. Thank you."

"And you? When can I see you again?"

"How about when I come into work?"

"You'll do it?"

She nodded, and I punched through the air with delight.

"Were you really at the hospital snooping?"

"That, and I found my kryptonite."

"I thought I was your kryptonite."

I grinned and took the exit off the interstate.

"You are. I can't donate my liver to Kensi because I have hairy cell leukemia."

"Leukemia?"

"Apparently it's the good kind."

"I don't think *leukemia* and *good kind* belong in the same sentence. Are you starting treatment?"

"There's no need to kill my immune system because there's not enough leukemia inside me to kill. But I thought I would give my girl a liver. And I can't."

"At least Dr. Hippo found a donor for Kensi."

I yawned and turned onto her street. "How did you know Dr. Hippo found a donor?"

A gulp jerked her chin, and she forced a smile.

"I ran into Tiffany earlier. She told me the good news."

Her eyes shifted sideways, and I assumed Dr. Hippo had already called Kensi's mother. I parked in front of Laura's apartment, turned off the car, and hurried around to the passenger's side. Laura took my offered hand, and I helped her out. We walked up the steps to her door.

"Thank you. I'd invite you in—"

"Don't, because I'd have to decline. I have late work tonight, and I have an early morning with Kensi."

She lowered her head, and I touched her chin to lift her eyes back to mine. "But I can't wait to see you again. What happened in my office wasn't a one-time thing."

She bit her lip.

"We're both busy, but I will make the time for us. I want to make time for us."

She rolled her lips inward to contain a smile, and I lowered my mouth to hers, sealing my promise. She tasted like orange and chocolate.

"I'll see you soon," I said against her lips with reluctance.

"See you soon."

I waited until she locked the door behind her and left, feeling like I was leaving my future behind.

Chapter 1

Laura

$\mathcal{I}$ dressed Foxy in his Sunday best and straightened his bowtie.

"Guess where we're going today?"

He rolled his plastic car along the kitchen counter, oblivious to the fact that he was about to meet his grandmother. I looked him over once more, combing my fingers through his hair.

"You're going to see your new grandmother, and hopefully she won't kill Mommy."

The text from Teresa Silver last Friday had hit me like a train, and I'd snuck out of James's office before he woke. I wasn't sure how she knew about Foxy, but I had my suspicions. James' mother had invited us to her house, and if I were lucky, I'd leave in one piece. I could only pray she'd give me enough time to explain and tell James on my own.

I buckled Foxy into his car seat and drove to Oyster Cove Bay. Twenty minutes later, the driveway curved three times before I came to a stop in front of a mansion. James lived next door. I'd been in his driveway before, but never inside. I took a deep breath, removed Foxy from the car, set him on the ground, and took his hand.

"Come on, baby. Let's make a good impression."

He gripped his fox toy in his free hand, and we walked up the porch steps. The front door swung open before we reached it, and Teresa greeted us with open arms and an enormous smile.

"Finally. I've been counting the minutes."

She lifted Foxy into her arms and gave me a hug while holding him. "It's nice to see you again, Laura."

He clung to her like a monkey, gripping her curled hair. I followed them inside the spacious home.

"It's nice to meet you as well. I'm sorry—"

"Now, now. Let's not start our day with apologies. Settle in. We have lots to talk about. Coffee or tea? I made a milkshake for Foxy. Do you know if he likes strawberries?"

I returned her kind smile. "They're his favorite right after raspberries."

We continued through the foyer, where exposed beams ran the width of the room. The two-story front entrance reached the roof. A decorative net hung on the side wall. Below, water dripped into a koi fish pond. Above us, a giant antler chandelier hung from the supporting joist. I stopped and turned in a circle, taking in the homey space.

"Now, I heard you're not supposed to give berries to children under two because they're likely to develop allergies. How old is Foxy?"

"He turned two in August."

She walked back toward me, looking up. "My husband made that." She pointed to the chandelier. "The boys helped collect the pieces."

"They killed the deer?"

"No, honey. Those antlers were shed."

"It's beautiful."

"Thank you. My boys are very handy." She turned back to Foxy. "And Grandma has to make up for your second birthday.

Does he like cupcakes? He liked the ones Emma made last weekend."

She confirmed my suspicion she must have found Foxy when she visited her sister-in-law's, where my son had a new babysitter.

I followed her to the kitchen. She handed a cupcake to Foxy, set him down on the floor, and spun around.

"Now, if I do the math right, he was conceived in Colorado, correct? Coffee or tea?"

"That's correct, but I didn't poke holes in his condom. Coffee, please. I have a feeling I'm going to need lots of coffee."

"Aha, I see he's told you about Tiffany." She poured me a cup of fresh brew and set the cup in front of me. "Hazelnut-vanilla is all right?"

"Yes, thank you. Mrs. Silver—"

"Please call me Teresa. Foxy already calls me Nana. Why are you so stiff?"

I glanced over at my son on the family room floor. He'd made himself comfortable in a pile of toys I assumed Teresa had bought during the week.

I set down the coffee cup and looked back at his grinning grandmother. "Teresa, why are you being so kind to me?"

"I figure if I'm kind, I get to spend time with my grandson. When you get to my age, you've lived through a few ups and downs, so I try not to judge. The situation may feel like everything you've dreaded, but to me, I have a grandson, and I couldn't be more grateful you brought him."

Would telling James the truth be as easy as this? Was I over-reacting and over-thinking?

"Thank you. I truly mean that."

"I know. Jesus, just look at him. He looks just like James when he was two. Has he seen his son?"

"Foxy was dressed in a fox costume, so technically, he hasn't seen him."

"Clever. I love the name you chose."

"I'm more lucky than clever, and James thinks his name is Ozzy."

Her head tipped sideways. "After the guy from *Survivor*?"

I allowed a crinkle of a smile.

"So, are you waiting to tell him until Foxy can pronounce his name?"

I chuckled. "I'm afraid he'll realize how I've lied to him the moment he lays his eyes on his son. You're right. The resemblance is uncanny. I'm… I'm trying to find the right time."

My son's darker complexion definitely came from James. He would be as handsome as his father one day.

"Did you see the lighter strand of hair on his left?" I asked, between sips of my coffee. How did she make me feel so comfortable so fast?

"Just like James."

"I've always wanted Foxy to have a father, but you can't make honey without bees. But then James walked back into my life, and everything changed. Suddenly, the dream of a full hive was within my reach." I said.

"A hive? Sweetheart, I've never heard anyone compare our family to a hive, but you're part of our hive and you'll be part of it, forever." Her gentle voice brought Foxy's attention to his grandmother. He stood up and carried a ball her way. She bounced it on the floor. He laughed and returned to his new toys.

"Thank you for the toys. I can see how much you already care about him. He's very lucky."

"It's my pleasure. I love my grandbabies and their mothers. All right. You need to start at the beginning."

I sucked in a stuttering breath. "I came back, Teresa. I was afraid at the beginning of my pregnancy because we barely knew each other, but a month away from giving birth, I came to tell him. I drove to his house, parked the car, and then I saw them in the window: a perfectly happy family. Kensi was coloring on the dining room table, Laila was bouncing in a swing, and James and Tiffany were dancing in the middle of the room. And then he kissed her. That's how I knew I'd lost my chance, and I didn't want to break them up."

"They're not together any longer," she said. "They tried, but it didn't work."

"I know that… Now. Nothing can make up for the fact I kept James from his son. I'm a cop, and there's not much I fear, but I've never been so scared in my life. I could lose so much."

"But think about what you could gain. My son is a forgiving man."

"Who else knows about him?" I nodded toward Foxy.

"Emma, her mother Wilma, and my husband Jake. We were at my sister-in-law's for an evening tea when your friend dropped Foxy off with Emma."

"It's nice you have so much family around."

She reached across the counter and took my hand in hers. "So do you, Laura. Believe it or not, we're your family now, and the sooner you speak with James, the better. Accept his job offer. Reconnect."

"How do you know he offered me a job?"

"James confided in me. He also told me about the arrest and about your blind date. He's already talked to your parents once."

"He said it was part of my job interview."

"Need I remind you that James is an investigator, and he's earned his nickname for a reason?"

"You're right. I think my time is limited." I lowered my head into my hands.

"Why haven't you told your parents about Foxy?"

My head flew up, and she scrunched her shoulders against her neck. "When James asked me for your father's contact information, I got in touch with your mother. Don't worry. I said nothing."

"Teresa, there's more to this than I can explain."

She covered my hand with hers. "Try me, honey."

"I'm not proud of the choice I made. My parents would have been disappointed the same way they were when I got pregnant at seventeen. It wasn't even my damn fault, but I lost my baby girl."

"What?"

"I was attacked in a parking lot. I've told no one, and you can't either."

"Oh, honey, I'm so sorry about your loss."

"I'm protective of Foxy because I can't lose him, and honestly, I don't see that changing any time soon. But I also know how much he would benefit from having his father in his life."

"So would you. Start with your parents. Think of them as your practice run before you tell James. This is something you want to tell him yourself, Laura. James is an excellent investigator."

"I know. I'll tell him right after Kensi's surgery."

"Why not before? It's the perfect time to bring some happiness to his life."

"Because I'll be busy."

"What's more important than telling him?"

"Kensi's surgery."

Her brows drew together.

"I'll be unavailable during her surgery and a bit after." I filled my lungs with a breath of courage. "Because I'm her match."

"What?"

"They're taking a piece of my liver out for Kensi next week, and I've told no one except you."

Out of nowhere, she got up from her seat and threw her

arms around my neck. A tiny sob escaped from her chest, and I smoothed my hand over her back. "I would love for you to spend some time with Foxy during my surgery and recovery. I mean, my babysitter's available but I thought you'd like to get to know him? I'll tell James the truth as soon as I get better. He'll be too busy with Kensi over the next few weeks, so I should have enough time to recover."

"What is your cover for the surgery?" she asked.

"I don't have one yet."

"Let me worry about that because, knowing my son, you'll need one."

"You're going to help me?"

"We're family, and family helps one another. We'll employ Emma to keep her eyes and ears open, and we'll figure out what to do about Tiffany."

"What do you mean, Tiffany?"

"She's been trying to get back with James for years. She still loves him, and she won't give up easily. Tiffany will dig for dirt, and she knows how to dig."

"So you're not a fan?"

She burst out a laugh. "No, I'm not. Thank God you showed up when you did. Now, let's go have some brunch. Do you prefer a strawberry or melon daiquiri?"

I hugged her so hard that afternoon, I felt the squeeze in my muscles by the evening. Teresa's warm soul changed the trajectory of my day. When I'd arrived in the early morning, I'd expected murder, yet she'd shown me kindness and offered support, along with encouragement. She was everything I'd always wanted in a mother, and her immeasurable love overlooked my flaws. Teresa would not only keep my secret, she would also help me reveal the truth after my surgery.

⁂

I opened my eyes to bright light, straining my blurred vision. My head throbbed. The smell of sanitized air swirled around my nose, and my mouth tasted like the desert.

"Water," I mumbled, and someone passed a straw to my lips.

I sucked until the cup emptied and shifted in the bed. A throbbing pain assaulted my side.

"Don't move." I heard a whisper and turned my head sideways to meet Teresa's grateful eyes. "The surgery finished a few hours ago, and everything went well."

I swallowed past the rough spot in my throat. "Kensi?"

"She's doing well. I can't stay long, but I've brought backup. Emma's nearby because Allie's still in the hospital."

"How is she doing?"

"She took a bullet, but they saved Kendra."

"And James?"

"He's busy with Kensi and Laila. I think you have a few quiet days ahead."

My phone dinged on the side table.

"It's James. He says Kensi's recovering well. He's thanking me for the daisies I sent to Kensi, along with a fox stuffy. He says that was cute, and he can't wait to see me."

"You see? Everything will work out."

I typed a quick reply about how happy I was about Kensi and how I couldn't wait to see him.

I turned my head Teresa's way. "Thank you for sending the flowers and the toy."

"Oh, that's not on me. That's on Emma."

"Hi, I'm Emma." The spunky teenager waved from the corner chair, and I realized I was in a private room. Vases of flowers lined the windowsill and dresser.

"I know who you are, Ems. You babysit my son."

"I thought I'd introduce myself again, in case you had a concussion."

"I had a liver transplant, not a concussion. Thank you for sending the gifts."

"You're welcome. You're lucky your best friend survived her gunshot. No one's even asking about you."

Wonderful.

"Don't worry. I'm a great secret-keeper."

"No one's asking? Really?"

"James is with Kensi, and Allie's sleeping. You don't have many people, do you?"

"You sound like a rehab nurse from hell."

"Thanks. It's okay if you don't have people. We're family, so I can be your people. I changed your chart to show appendicitis, just in case someone checks."

"What if the nurse checks?"

"You can leave the nurses to me. They love me here, and the chocolates and donuts I leave at their station. I've got to go to school now, but text me if you need anything."

I felt like I'd landed in a hospital from heaven. I'd never had this much support in my life. My head flew up just before Emma left.

"Wait—if you're both here, where is Foxy?"

"He's with Grandpa Jake, who's showing him the donkeys right about now. They're expanding the chicken coop this afternoon, but I can bring him by after his nap. See ya." Emma waved and left.

I settled back in the bed. "You have donkeys and chickens?"

"Just chickens. Foxy loves farm animals."

I smiled. "He does. Thank you, Teresa. Thank you for everything."

"You're welcome. You can trust James as much as you trust Emma and me."

I pulled my hand across my eyes, clearing the crust and fog. "I know. As soon as I heal and I'm back at work, I'll tell him."

She drew her head back quickly. "How soon are you planning to go?"

"It depends on how long it takes to heal from appendicitis. I can't tell James about this surgery."

"Why not?"

"It's not the way I want to get him back. Besides, I didn't do this for him. I did it for Kensi."

She covered my hand where the butterfly needle connected to an IV and leaned in. "There's nothing wrong with saying you did it for them both. You're a hero. You saved my granddaughter's life and gave me a grandson."

I returned her kind smile. "You have a gift of lifting people up, Teresa."

"Glad to hear it's working."

A light knock sounded on the door, and my mom's head popped inside. My father pushed in from behind her.

"Mom, Dad. What are you doing here?"

Teresa stood up from her seat. "Alice, Tom. It's nice to see you again."

"Teresa?"

"I was checking in on my granddaughter and saw Laura through the door when I passed by her room."

"Is your granddaughter all right?"

"Yes, she's recovering well from her surgery. I should get going. Take care, Laura."

"Thank you, Teresa." I waved goodbye, and she left.

My mother took the seat beside my bed. "You donated a piece of your liver?"

"The chart says I had an appendectomy."

"I know what the chart says...and what the hospital records say. Which is another enigma I can't understand."

"Damn it! It's because I want the donation to be anonymous. That's all. I can't believe you checked the hospital records. That's a crime."

"Doesn't apply when you're trying to reach stubborn family members and they don't answer your calls." My father groaned. "What's going on, Laura? Why are you ostracizing us?"

"I wasn't trying to," I whispered.

I wasn't about to tell my parents they were grandparents from a hospital bed, but the time for the truth was drawing near.

"We should have dinner together when I get better. I'll bring dessert."

My mother smiled. "That would be nice. I'm taking a leave of absence in a week, so I'll have more time, I promise. Who's helping you recover?"

"Don't worry. I've got this. They'll release me in a couple of days."

"Is it James?"

I tilted my head.

"He told us you're dating."

He did?

"Yes, it is. His little girl is the liver recipient and the reason I'm keeping this donation anonymous. I don't want him to know."

My parents exchanged a look, and something I wasn't privy to passed between them.

"What's wrong?" I asked.

"Nothing, dear. We're going to hire a nurse for you."

"I'm fine, and I can do this on my own."

"Stubborn and independent." My father swung his head in disappointment. "We'll see you soon, Laura. Get some rest."

I puffed out a frustrated breath and settled back in my bed. I closed my eyes, and a snapshot of Kensi swinging on a tree swing floated through my mind. James stood nearby with Foxy in his arms and Laila on her first toddler bike. The sun beamed, birds chirped, and our big, happy family laughed. I fell asleep with the image in my head and slept through the day and night.

Chapter 8

James

I knocked on Laura's front door and bent down to pick up the giant bouquet of daisies. They were tied with a red bow, which held a get-well note from Laila. Kensi remained at the hospital, undergoing tests, but so far, it appeared the transplant was successful.

"Who is it?" she called from the other side.

"Delivery for Ms. Young." I lowered my tone.

"Leave it at the door," she growled.

"Can't leave it. It's a live delivery, Ms. Young." I tried again, holding my laughter in and the flowers in front of the door's peephole. The lock clicked open, followed by the door and her gasp.

"What is this?"

She peered through the gap in the door created by the chain lock.

I shimmied sideways so she could see my face. "Heard you had an appendectomy, and apparently, daisies cure everything. Can I come in?"

She closed the door to unlock the chain, then reopened the door, and I stepped inside.

"Where did you hear about my surgery?" She pointed to the

right. "The kitchen table is empty." I set the vase down, removed the bag of hot food from my arm, and set that on the table as well.

"My mother ran into yours at the hospital. Why didn't you tell me you were having surgery?"

Her nose crinkled.

"It happened too quickly. Ms. Young?

"Since when do you call me that?" Her lip curled inward to contain a smile as she shrugged a shoulder. "That's cute."

"You could have called." I lifted a brow.

"You were busy with Kensi, and the appendix burst, so they had to operate immediately. They sliced me open, took out the organ, cleaned out my guts, and I still got a postoperative infection."

"All the more reason you should have called. I was a few floors away, and you sent Kensi a gift, while I sent you nothing."

"What do you mean, nothing? You just brought flowers and food, which is awesome because I'm starving."

"Still wish you had called."

"It was nothing."

I grabbed the containers and followed her to the family room. She held onto her right side as she limped to the couch. I sat beside her, and she winced in pain. Jesus, she looked so tired.

"They released you too fast."

"I'm sure the doctors knew what they were doing, but I'm glad you're here." She smiled. "Did you come bearing my new employment papers?"

"No, I came with chicken soup, creamy donuts, and a foot massage. Also, I'm here if you need laundry done or dishes washed." I set the opened soup container in front of her.

"Wow, full service. I appreciate the offer, but I'm not having you touch my laundry. We're not there yet."

She stirred, picked up the soup container, and scooped a spoonful into her mouth. Her deep sigh of delight resonated in my bones. I'd never met a woman whose food consumption delighted me.

"Baby, believe me. I've seen many skid marks and period stains."

She nearly spat her soup out and covered her mouth. "That makes it even worse."

"Eat more. I take it, it's good?"

"Delicious. Thank you. How did you know a way to a girl's heart is through her stomach?"

"I prefer getting to your heart by other means."

Her cheeks flushed an enticing shade of pink. She ate three-quarters of the soup, set the container aside, and relaxed back into the couch.

"That was delicious. Thank you."

"You're welcome."

"Now, I believe you mentioned other means to my heart?" she snickered, and amusement rumbled through my chest. Her lower lip curled inward, and she chewed on the flesh before rising to her elbows.

"Be careful, Laura. I'm about to lose control."

"I thought that was the idea." She grinned. "But I really need a bath, and it's difficult with the bandages."

"All right, let's get you upstairs."

I helped her up as she winced in pain. We stood in front of the bathtub like it was a maze. Her bandaged side and fresh stitches had to remain dry.

"It would have been easier in my shower. How do you normally do this?" I asked.

"I sit in the tub and use the showerhead."

Her gaze met mine. Fire glittered in her eyes as she curled in her lower lip.

"All right. Let's get these clothes off you."

I slowly helped with her shirt, then removed her cotton bottoms. She stood in front of me in her panties and bandages, her arms over her chest, covering her breasts. A green shade colored her skin near the surgery area.

"What's this?" I pointed to the oval scar near her rib on the opposite side.

"I took a bullet once. Went right through the back."

"What? For who? How?"

"On a school trip to DC. The sniper was aiming for the VP, and I saw a reflection in a window. Got me a letter of recommendation to the academy. They also sent me a lifetime White House pass during visiting hours. I thought it was pretty cool."

"That's ballsy of you."

"I can't take the credit. It was instinct."

"Exactly why you should take credit. That's incredible. Just when I thought I knew everything about you." I shook my head in disbelief.

"You have no idea," she mumbled.

"What else are you hiding?"

"How much this fucking thing hurts." She grabbed her side.

"Are you ready to get naked?"

"No."

.I lowered her panties and my dick twitched. She dropped her arms to the sides, letting her breasts spill out. This was not a time for a hard-on, but how could I help it? She was gorgeous.She grasped my arm and stepped into the bathtub. I clipped her hair up into a bun and turned on the water.

"It's easier if I stand," she said, reaching for the showerhead.

"I got it." I turned on the tap and waited for the warm flow.

She stood still in the bathtub as I aimed the water, avoiding the bandages. She turned around. The view of her pear-shaped backside was a painful reminder of how much I missed her.

"This feels nice. Thank you," she whispered.

"You're welcome. Hold onto the showerhead. I'll lather you up."

I poured the lilac body wash onto a sponge and began the meticulous and torturous process of washing her. The longer I circled the suds over her skin, the more confined I felt in my jeans. I drew the soap over her shoulders and down to her breasts, careful not to soak the dressing. I cleared the soap with a soaked cloth and continued down the exposed ribcage, down her belly and to between her legs.

She twitched, breathing heavily. I looked up to meet her dreamy gaze and her shoulder jerked. "Can't blame a girl for enjoying a man's touch."

I grinned. "Glad to be of service."

"What else can you do with your hands, Mr. Silver?" She bit her lower lip.

"Patience, my love. Patience."

She stopped, and I refocused on her inner thighs and pussy, pretending I didn't just call her *my love.* I pulled my fingers along her legs up to her apex, washing her thoroughly. Her muscles tensed, and I looked up as she bit her lip.

"Rinse."

She aimed the water at the front and I spun her around by the hips. I added more body wash near the shoulders and circled the sponge down her back to her beautiful ass. Her cheeks tightened. I pulled the suds over her behind and between the cheeks, dropped the sponge, rinsed her back, and tapped on her inner thigh. Her legs parted.

I slid my hand between her soft thighs to her pussy. She quivered in my palm. I pulled my fingers up her swollen folds, circling over her clit. She braced her hands against the wall and pressed her cheek over the tile.

"James."

Hearing my name on her lips stirred my need. Her silky skin, tough like a seal's but soft, bent to my hand's pressure. I adored kissing her backside and touching her like she was mine.

She breathed heavily. I pulled my hand away and turned her around to face me. Her eyelids drooped, and her lips were raw from biting. I wrapped her in a towel and carefully lifted her into my arms. She wound her arms around my neck.

"Where are we going?"

"To finish what I started," I said against her mouth, kissing her.

I carried her to the bedroom, set her in the middle of her bed, and removed the towel. She lay naked in the moonlight's glow. Silver light shimmered over her skin.

"You're so beautiful."

I lowered to her legs and kissed my way from the knee to over her thigh. She sank into the sheets, and I grazed my lips over her pussy, looking up. Her throat lurched with a hard swallow, and her ribs sank in. I held her steady by the hips and pulled my tongue along her slit. She tasted like lilac and honey. I closed my mouth around her clit, and her lower back caved. Her flesh swelled between my lips as I kissed the tender spot and slid two fingers inside her. She whimpered.

"James."

Her tiny spurts of breath echoed between my slurps, and it was the most beautiful sound I'd ever heard. She grabbed my head, raking her fingers through my hair, pressing me harder onto herself. I flicked my tongue quicker and pushed my fingers deeper. The first spasm shook through her body.

"James..."

She pressed her hands to my head, lifted herself to my mouth, and I devoured her until she screamed my name.

"James! Oh God, James."

Her body spasmed and her pussy pulsed between my lips. I kept pressing with my tongue, sucking every last second of her orgasm, until she pushed my head away and settled in the sheets. I crawled up her body to spoon her, my hand snaking around to her front and cupping her breast. I listened to her slowing breath.

"You obliterated me."

"That was the idea."

"Hmm…" she cooed in my hold, her ass writhing against my hard dick. "This feels nice."

"What feels nice?"

"You holding me like this." She wiggled her ass over my erection. "What will we do about that?"

"That will have to wait until you've healed. You could barely hold yourself up in the shower."

"Again, that's because you obliterated me. I'm sure we could—"

"No, we couldn't, babe. Not the way I want to take you."

She reached behind herself and rubbed over my dick. The skilled snap of my button and zipper gave me no way out. Not that I wanted one. She shimmied lower, and I removed my jeans. Her icy hand slid over my cock, burning against my hot skin. My thoughts fogged, and I forgot what I was going to say as she wickedly wrapped her fingers around me and stroked up and down.

"You don't have to fuck me to get off, baby. I bet you won't last three minutes."

Her dirty mouth turned me on and my head gave into the pillow as I gave into her hand's wicked technique.

"You don't understand, babe." My ass tightened with each stroke, and she gripped me tighter. "I'll want to fuck you. After that, I'll want to fuck you again."

"That can't happen until the stitches come off, but let me see what I can do in the meantime."

She cupped my balls in her other hand and brought them higher, pressing her finger underneath. I sucked air into my lungs and all the blood rushed to where she held power over me.

"Laura…" I breathed, and she sat up, carefully repositioning herself. The instant thought of my cock in her mouth gave me a rush, and I pushed into her hand just as she lowered her lips to my crown.

Her head bobbed, and I started the countdown to where she brought me undone. She worked me in a delicious rhythm before she let me go deeper and quicker.

I grasped her ass with one hand and dug my fingers into her skin. Her mouth dripped with saliva as I reached for her head, quickening the motion. A zap snapped in my spine and flew to my balls. I tensed and pushed once more, spilling in her mouth.

"Ahhh…" I groaned.

She kept my cock in her mouth until I finished and then licked up my shaft with her full tongue, firing up my arousal all over again.

"Two minutes and twenty-seven seconds." Her smile swung free.

"You timed me?"

She pointed to the clock shining a red twelve-thirty on the ceiling above her bed.

"It's a gift from Allie. I needed a second alarm clock because, sometimes, Ozzy keeps me up at night, and mornings can be tough. You know how it is."

She reached for a tissue and wiped her mouth, then settled on the bed beside me.

"I do."

"I'm happy Kensi's doing well. Seventy-five percent of children have no surgical complications, so the numbers are on her side. Are you staying home now?"

"I'll be taking care of Kensi when she's discharged in a couple of days. Come to think of it, she's a mini version of you:

stubborn and focused. She insists she's ready to leave the hospital now."

Laura chuckled. "Maybe the girl knows what's right for her."

"I know what's right for her, just like I know what's right for you." I pulled the covers over her body and rose onto my elbow.

"That's patriarchal," she murmured, and closed her eyes.

"If I don't take care of my girls, then who will?"

A cautious smile crept up the corner of her face. "Can I tell you a secret?"

"Sure."

"I'm not used to people taking care of me."

"Why not? You care for people all the time."

"That's different. It's my job to keep people safe."

"What if I kept you safe? Both you and Ozzy."

She stilled in my hold. I watched in the moonlight as she blinked rapidly.

"Me and Ozzy?" she whispered.

"Yeah. Both of you. Where is Ozzy?"

"He's with the sitter." She yawned through a giggle. "I swear you sucked the life out of me."

"Relax, Laura. I'm thinking we should delay your first day of work."

"Don't. It's fine. I'll be fine. I'll likely have paperwork and human resources training the first week. That's desk work, so I won't strain anything. And Allie's coming back."

She pouted, and I relaxed behind her.

"All right, but I'm not letting you out of my sight."

Thunder rolled far in the distance. She snuggled into my side and murmured, "I'm hoping you won't."

It was supposed to be this easy, wasn't it? Having a woman in my arms who synched with me to the second. Laura was a breath of fresh air and the partner I'd missed in Tiffany: someone I could trust and count on.

She drifted off to sleep in my arms within minutes. I covered her with the comforter, dressed, and walked past what appeared to be Ozzy's room. The wood-themed room filled with fox toys, a fox wallpaper border, stuffed foxes, fox sheets, and a fox nightlight took me aback. I remembered him in a fox costume at the park. Laura had a thing for foxes.

But were foxes Ozzy's obsession or Laura's? Was she into foxes because of me? Was I reading too much into this?

On my way downstairs, I bumped my head into a picture frame on the sidewall. I clicked the flashlight on my phone and straightened the frame. In the picture, Ozzy was sitting dressed as Robin Hood in a forest- and animal-themed setting. The cute boy couldn't have been much over one. I stepped down the stairs to see the age progression in the next frame. He was a pumpkin on a farm in that one. The ones lower were a fireman, a doctor, and a police officer. But the last picture of him dressed in a checkered shirt and a bow tie completely held me in my tracks, and I couldn't stop staring. His dark hair was brushed to the side, and his bright blue eyes shone like two little gems. He was a beautiful child, and definitely took after his beautiful mother.

Chapter 9

Laura

Three weeks had passed since the liver transplant, and today marked my third official day at work. Teresa picked Foxy up in the mornings before James arrived in his Bentley like a knight in shining armor. We drove to Silver Securities in Manhattan every day, listening to eighties and nineties stations. The surprise for Allie last week went without a hitch, and our human-trafficking department was off to a great start. I helped a girl off the street and secured her a job at a café. After her, the calls started coming in, one after another.

As I'd predicted, James stacked enough work on my desk to keep me at the office and off the street for months. We'd reorganized the department heads, assigned cases based on priority, and enjoyed lunches in the downstairs kids' lounge. James assured me Ozzy could join the daycare, but Teresa had trouble letting go of her grandson.

My best friend sat at her desk opposite mine and stared at the screen. I scrunched up a piece of paper and tossed it at Allie's head. "What's got you looking so pale?"

She looked up. "Cribs, bouncers, and diapers. Tristan's hiding something, and I don't know what it is."

"You're hiding a pregnancy from him."

"Shh, lower your voice. I'll tell him at the fundraiser this weekend. You're coming, right?"

"Yes. I can't leave James in the same room with Tiffany. Her claws come out at dusk."

"It would be easier if you told him the truth. We should make a pact to reveal their fatherhood at the fundraiser."

"We can't ruin the company's biggest night," I said.

"Stop thinking so negatively. James could be delighted."

"The operative word here is *could*. We're working for our boyfriends and the fathers of our children, and they have no clue. There's no hell pit deep enough for people like us."

Allie reached over to where our desks joined and held out her pinkie. "Let's make a reasonable pact."

My brows furrowed. "Define reasonable."

"We tell them as soon as an opportunity presents itself."

That could be anytime. Telling James I'd kept his son from him was a tough nut to crack, no matter how I cracked it. Point was, it had to be cracked.

I hooked my pinkie into hers. "Deal."

A light knock sounded from the door and Teresa stepped through, holding a potted plant in front of her.

"Knock, knock."

I waved her in. "Come in, come in."

"I brought a gift." She set a small tree with oval leaves on my desk. "It's a ficus ginseng, and it's said to bring good luck and harmony."

"Thank you. That's very sweet. Welcome to Laura and Allie's corner at Silver Securities."

"Why not Allie and Laura's?" Allie stood up from her chair. "Never mind. I gotta go to the bathroom. Morning sickness doesn't just happen in the mornings."

Teresa's eyes widened. "She's pregnant?"

"Tristan's baby," I said. "We're great at getting pregnant by the Silvers, but not so great at communicating the news."

"Does Wilma know?" she asked.

Allie grabbed the phone off her desk. "Emma's the only one. She found out before me, and I'm trying to tell Tristan. There's a lot going on with the Hartleys, too, but I gotta go before my bladder gives way."

She left, and Teresa sat down on the chair next to mine.

"How are you feeling, and why are you at work so soon?"

"I'm feeling fine. They removed the stitches, and the pain's gone. How's Kensi?"

"Nearly back to her bubbly self. She's down the hall with her mother. They came to visit James, and she'd doing amazing. You saved her life."

"I did what anyone would have done in my shoes. Where's Foxy?" I whispered.

"He's with his grandpa, which is why I need to talk to you. Jake wants to set up a tent in our backyard for a camping weekend with Foxy. Do you mind if he stays with us?"

"You're offering me free babysitting on a weekend and asking if I mind?"

"Is that a yes?"

"Yes, of course, it's a yes."

"Good. Now, when are you going to tell my son about his son?"

I knew this was coming. Teresa was one of the most amazing women I'd ever met and one of my biggest supporters. She was also a woman who always got what she wanted, and she wanted nothing more than to see James in Foxy's life.

"I was planning on this weekend, but I had no babysitter until now, so I guess this weekend is it." My heart hammered in my chest like the time had already come. "Just make sure James has no guns within his reach or my son will have no mother."

"Stop it. James loves you, and he'll love you even more when he finds out you bore his child."

"Loves me? Teresa, with all due respect, I don't think we're there. It hasn't been long enough."

"Since when do you put a timer on, love? Take it from a mother who knows her son better than he knows himself. James loves you."

He loves me?

My windpipe closed for too long, and I coughed. "I hope you're right, because I need all the help I can get to stay alive after the weekend."

"So it works out well we're having Foxy over for the weekend?" she asked.

"Of course. Thank you." I hugged her.

"Our pleasure." She stepped back. "You know, Laura, I can only imagine your parents would be as thrilled to know they're grandparents as we are. Maybe after you tell James—"

"They'll be next."

A wave of jitters flew through my body and settled near my stomach. If this worked, I'd officially name myself a leprechaun.

"All I know is they'll love Foxy as much as we do."

Someone cleared her throat behind us, and we turned toward the door. Tiffany was standing there with Kensi at her side, holding her hand. The girl looked better than when I'd last seen her. The jaundice was gone, and she'd gained weight. No wonder James was so happy. I would be too if it were my kid.

"Hi Nana." Kensi ran to her grandmother and threw her arms around her hips.

"Kensi wanted to see Mommy's new design. I hope you don't mind. Did I just hear you refer to Fox as Foxy? He told me you used to call him Foxy when he was a boy."

My face went ashen, and Teresa blinked three times before she began damage control.

"You misheard. I was talking about Laura's son, Ozzy."

"I was sure I heard…"

Tiffany froze mid-sentence as Kensi slid her hand into mine. "Can you show me all the gadgets?"

"Gadgets?"

"I know what they call my daddy: a double-oh-seven. You're the girl version of a secret agent, so you must have gadgets."

"We don't want to bother people at work, Kensi." Tiffany stepped closer.

I bent down as Kensi held onto my hand. "I don't have any cool ones here, but we have moon cushions your mommy set by the windows and they feel like clouds. Clouds help me think. Want to try those out?"

Her eyes opened wide. "Yes. I have a moon cushion in my treehouse."

"It won't be long, I promise," I told Tiffany, who stood openmouthed as she watched us walk away.

Kensi hopped on the largest oval pillow, sinking into its middle. The clear skies above gave the most picturesque view.

"Should you be jumping after your surgery?"

"I've got a super-liver."

"A what?" I laughed.

"The super-liver came from a super strong donor because I'm getting better. Did you know seven out of ten kids do well with super-livers?"

"I didn't know." I drew my brows together. "But even super-livers need rest, so it can settle in its new home. So not too much jumping. Okay?"

"Okay." Kensi slid off the seat like a pancake, but her hand caught a cushion's zipper near the floor, breaking the platinum bracelet around her wrist.

"Oh no!" Her eyes welled, and she covered her mouth with her hand. Tiffany and Teresa ran up to the window.

"What happened?" Tiffany lifted Kensi into her arms.

"My baby bracelet broke."

"It's okay, honey. I'm sure Daddy can fix it."

"I'm sorry. I didn't realize this would happen." I scooped up the bracelet, handing it to Tiffany.

"Don't worry about it," Teresa gave my arm a squeeze. "I'm sure James can fix it."

Kensi settled in Tiffany's hold and waved my way as they walked out the door.

I waved back.

"You would make a wonderful stepmother. You two are like peas in a pod."

"Thanks, but I don't want to step on another mother's turf. Tiffany looks like she has it handled. I'll tell James the truth about Foxy this weekend."

Teresa's eyes lit up. "Great. And I can't wait to make s'mores with my grandson over the campfire."

She hugged me goodbye, and I swear she had the power to infuse direct comfort into my bones. Eventually, James would find out the truth, and I preferred it came from my mouth.

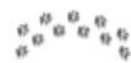

I PARKED my Wrangler in front of James's house and pulled in a long breath of courage. My hands, meanwhile, were shaking like maracas and my nerves were stripped bare. I walked out of the car and up the three steps on my trembling legs, pulling my trench coat together. Underneath was the sleek piece of lingerie Grace had gifted me through James. Tonight, I would pull every trick in the book to come out of this alive, with James not hating me.

The front door opened before I could lift my hand, nearly knocking me off my feet. James stood there in a pair of blue jeans and nothing else: no shirt, no socks, and, by the look of his thick cock at the side of his thigh, no underwear.

I swallowed thickly as a welcome smile stretched across his

face. He had trimmed his beard and cut his hair. The smell of his spicy cologne hit me, and I bit my lip.

"Hi," I said, tilting my hip to the side. "I'm here to make an arrest."

His eyes shone with wicked promises. "You brought your cuffs?"

"No. I'm role-playing," I whispered, and he chuckled.

"Oh, got it. That's okay, officer. I'll let you borrow mine."

He removed a pair of fluffy handcuffs from the back of his jeans and dangled them on his finger.

My mouth fell open, and a smug grin stretched across his face. I followed him into the pristine home. The girls were at their mom's, watching a new Disney movie. I'd conveniently left Foxy with Teresa and Jacob next door, in case James wanted to officially meet him.

"I brought something else." My voice cracked, and his brow lifted. I untied the trench coat belt at my front and let it fall off my shoulders. The fabric pooled around my feet.

James sucked in a sharp breath and drank me in from the bottom up. "Holy shit."

There was the reaction I'd been hoping for.

I spun around, and he hurried to close the door. Thrills bubbled inside me. He picked up my jacket and set it on a hook by the main door.

"I love your choice of clothing."

He walked the three steps back to me and took my hand, guiding me inside the kitchen. I grabbed a tiny, orange-flavored chocolate from a container and placed it on his tongue when he spun around to face me.

I wiggled my eyebrows and rested my forehead against his. "Now you know why the gift bag from Grace was tiny."

He lowered his mouth to mine and kissed me deeply. The taste of orange and chocolate spread along my tongue and I moaned, gently pulling away. He kept my body close to his, resting his thick thigh between mine, sending my arousal surging.

"It's perfect. Makes it easier to get you naked," he said into my mouth, flexing his thigh muscles enough that I felt it in my core. This was moving too fast. Being truthful would be easier with alcohol.

"We should celebrate my new job with champagne."

He backed up. "I don't have any." His forehead wrinkled. "But my parents do."

"I'm fine with whiskey, too."

Anything to ease my nerves.

He kissed me on my lips. "I'll be back in two and a half minutes to drink champagne from your belly."

Back from where?

The realization hit me too late, as he grabbed a t-shirt and was out the front door and over to his parents' house.

No, no, no.

I ran out the back and crossed the lawn barefoot. I hopped over a hedge and nearly slipped in a muddy puddle, which splattered to my thighs. Jake's tent, where Foxy slept with his grandfather, stood propped closer to the shore. I hurried up the back steps and opened the door before James could arrive at the front.

"Teresa!" I called her attention away from a magazine she was reading.

"Laura? What are you doing here?"

"Where's Foxy?"

"He's sleeping upstairs. Why?"

Oh, thank God I came.

"Not in the tent? James is coming."

"Now?"

"He's here for the champagne in your fridge. We only have a few seconds."

"Don't worry, I'll shush him away." She scanned me from the bottom up. "What are you wearing?"

"This is my trying-to-tell-James-he-fathered-my-child outfit."

She hoisted a shoulder. "Good choice."

The doorbell chimed, and I heard Foxy calling from upstairs.

"Don't worry. Jake will get him."

We waited, looking up to the second floor, but no sound came again.

"You should either hide or leave." Teresa nudged me to the kitchen, but it was too late. The front door swung open, and James walked through. I swiveled on my foot and stared at him like a deer stuck in the headlights while Teresa tried to cover me with her body.

Fuck, fuck, fuck.

"Laura? What are you doing here? Mom?"

I stepped sideways in my negligée, acutely aware of how I wasn't ready for him to catch me in this lie, but neither was James. He, too, stared like a deer in the headlights, with a thousand questions swimming in his eyes.

"What the hell happened to your feet?"

"I took a shortcut through the backyard."

"A shortcut? For what?"

"I, ahem, I came for some chocolate. Seventy-eight percent of people get nighttime cravings which result from an elevated level of hormones."

Oh, my God, did that just come out of my mouth?

His face drained of blood while mine heated like a crematorium furnace. I so wished I could step inside one right about now.

"I already have chocolate in the kitchen." He stepped in between me and Teresa and leaned into my ear. "You fed one to me earlier, remember?"

"Oh yeah." I breathed a strained laugh through my nose. "I forgot."

Please let the ground open up and swallow me whole!

"Are you going to stand there and chat, or get on with this romantic night?" Teresa wiggled her finger between us. "I'll get the champagne from the fridge, and you two can be on your way."

James turned to his mother. "How did you know I was here for the champagne?"

We walked to the kitchen. James removed a dishtowel from a rack and tried to cover me up.

"I mentioned it." I snagged the towel from his grip, but it wasn't large enough to cover everything. Or anything, really.

Foxy's squeaky laughter sounded from upstairs, and James's head flew in that direction. "What's that?"

"Your father's in bed watching television." Teresa removed the champagne from the fridge and handed it to James.

"Enjoy!" she said. "And don't go busting any stitches."

My cheeks flushed with more heat and embarrassment. There was nothing I wouldn't do to win him over because murder was always an option for a father who found I had kept his son from him.

"Thanks, Mom," he said.

I pulled on James's hand, guiding him toward the front door, leaving muddy footprints through the foyer.

Outside, a warm October breeze swept by, and I stepped out onto the porch. James set the bottle on the ground.

"You're crazy," he said. "You should have stayed home."

"You make me do crazy things." I shuddered as he pulled his t-shirt over his head and down my body. It smelled like him—pepper and a hint of rose. I swam in the thing, but it felt nice against my skin.

"I can't think when I'm around you, and then I make irreversibly stupid decisions, like taking shortcuts through backyards."

"Well, don't worry. I'm here to correct your stupid decisions for as long as you let me. Now, are we ready to go home?"

"I am."

I stepped off the porch and onto the dewy grass in the front yard. He picked up the champagne bottle and caught up to me, scooping me into his arms in one swift move. Laughter bubbled from inside me, and I leaned into his naked torso as he balanced the bottle and me.

"Let me hold the champagne, at least." I looked up into his blue eyes. Moonlight brightened the rims. His mom was right: Foxy looked just like his father. He swung the bottle over and into my arms and gripped me tighter. My offer to carry the champagne was a selfish one because his firm grip forced waves of heat through my body. His muscles bunched with each step, and I had the peaceful sense everything was going to be okay. He had to forgive me. I just needed a chance.

"You're lost in thought," he whispered when we reached his front door.

A dry patch resisted my swallow. "You can set me down now."

"You're not going anywhere in those dirty feet."

He opened the door and helped me set the champagne on the counter, then carried me to the upstairs bathroom. He lowered me to the bathtub's corner and opened both faucets, adjusting the water's warmth.

"I'm sorry for being so stupid," I whispered.

"There's nothing silly about chocolate cravings."

I smiled as he removed the showerhead from its hook. He switched the faucets and aimed the stream at my feet. He gripped one foot in his hand while pumping soap onto the other and washed it thoroughly up to my thigh before proceeding with the second one. A quick rinse later, I stood in the bathtub, facing him.

"Thank you." I stepped closer and wrapped my hands around his neck. His defined back was reflected in the mirror, taking my breath away. Columns of muscles and rows of more muscles stacked from his shoulders and down his back, narrowing near the waistline. I leaned into him and watched him curl himself around me, breathing me in. His arms held me like they belonged there. He gripped the shirt I was wearing and slid it over my head, leaving me in the skimpy negligee. He pressed his cheek against my chest and breathed me in, skimming his fingers over my ass cheeks. Arousal pumped through my veins. I raked my fingers along his scalp and he shifted, looking up.

"My bed."

I nodded.

He secured his arms underneath my ass and lifted me out of the bathtub, carrying me to his bed. He lowered me to the sheets, and I backed away. He knelt on the bed in his jeans and looked like a famished Greek god. Jesus, he looked hot. My insides quivered, and the heat consuming my body traveled through my limbs and collected between my thighs.

"I just realized I haven't been in your bed before," I whispered.

"Today, we correct that mistake."

He crawled on all fours over my legs and up my torso, forcing me to lie back. The weight of his muscles pressed me into the mattress as he hovered above me. I smoothed his hair to the side.

"James, there's something I need to tell you."

"No, no. We're not having any serious discussions before I have you."

"Why not?" I asked.

"It's a life lesson. The minute we talk about serious stuff, life and problems return. I don't want to think about serious stuff. Right now, I want to make love to you."

My breath hitched, but I had no time to reply as he kissed me hard. He tore through my thoughts with his tongue strokes, and I forgot how much I wanted to tell him that Foxy was his son.

Chapter 10

James

Laura was standing by the bar with Allie, and I waved her over to our table. She lifted her glass, hugged her best friend, and meandered through the maze of chairs. The deep v-cut in her sequined bodysuit ended at her navel, and drew attention from every man who passed. I memorized the face of each bastard and added them to my hit list. We were officially official, and I wouldn't let anyone steal her.

My parents approved of Laura more than Tiffany, but then again, how could they not? Laura was an ex-police officer and a single mother providing for her son. She was responsible and independent, beautiful and honest, both inside and out. And I was a lucky man to have her.

Her curly hair spilled down her shoulders, and she looked absolutely stunning in the revealing pantsuit. Dinner had passed in a haze as the family discussed Simone Hartley's miraculous return from the dead, but all I could do was think about how to get Laura into the suite I'd booked at the hotel. I stood up and pulled back her chair.

"Thank you." She sat down and clasped her hand over mine, grinning.

"I thought I lost you for a while."

"Just catching up with Allie. Tristan's not having a good night."

"No, he's not. It's never good when ex's come back to life."

"Ex's aren't good when they're alive either," she snickered, and I burst out laughing.

Across the room, my ex was salivating over Marc Leonardi, a young billionaire who'd inherited his name and wealth. She'd hang onto his arm until she figured out he was engaged. It'd be easier for me if he were single.

I cleared my throat. "We set the event up weeks ago. Tiffany's company furnished Hope for Hope and made a generous donation to the foundation. I should've mentioned sooner that she'd be here."

"No worries. We'll be fine, as long as she stays in her corner." Her beautiful mouth stretched wide, showing off her pearly whites.

"I couldn't agree more."

My father lifted his glass in a cheer.

"My parents are throwing a party for Kensi to celebrate her recovery. I would love it if you came with Ozzy."

"Me and Ozzy?" Her quick, high-pitched laugh threw me off, and I covered her hand with mine underneath the table.

"Come on—it's time you show off your cute boy to the family."

"How do you know he's cute? You've only seen him in a fox costume."

"I saw his photographs on the wall at your home. Don't be so modest, babe. Ozzy's a handsome boy."

My mother choked on water and I glanced over to find my dad patting her back.

"You saw his pictures?" Laura asked.

"Yes." I leaned in closer so only Laura could hear. "A few

weeks ago, after your surgery. That shower took everything out of you."

Her cheeks flushed pink.

"I left after you fell asleep. Point is, Ozzy and Laila are close in age, so they'll each make a friend."

"You should definitely come, Laura," my mother encouraged, and I gave her a grateful smile.

"And invite your parents," I added. "You know, since you've reconciled."

Her eyes flashed open wide, and she choked on her drink. Must be something in the water. I frowned, then passed her a napkin, and she dabbed her lips. What was going on with them?

"Are you all right?"

"Yes, thank you. I would love to come." She relaxed into a smile just as someone tapped me on my shoulder.

"Hi, Fox. Care to dance?"

I turned around as Tiffany sat down in the free chair my younger brother had left. She covered my hand with hers, and my skin immediately itched like an allergic reaction. I pulled my hand away.

"I don't think so, Tiff."

"Well, if you don't care to dance, then I need to speak with you privately. It's important."

"Let me guess—it can't wait until tomorrow."

"It's about Kensi, so no, it can't."

I let out a grunt and turned to Laura, kissing her cheek.

"I won't be long," I whispered in her ear, and stood up.

I followed Tiffany out of the gala room and into a side hall, where we found a bench against a wall and sat down.

"What's going on with Kensi?"

"Promise to keep this to yourself?"

"All right. What is it?"

"Promise?"

What the hell was this about?

"I promise," I said.

Her hand slid up my arm. "Get that worried look off your face. It's something good."

"Something good?"

"You know how I was away during Kensi's surgery?"

I bowed my head a touch.

"It's because I was having surgery. I'm the anonymous donor, James."

"What?"

"That's why I was away."

"But you weren't a match."

"My first tests were inconclusive, so I had them test me again. I was a match."

"So you didn't stay at your sister's during Kensi's surgery?"

She shook her head.

"Why didn't you tell me before?"

"You had enough to worry about with Kensi."

"You saved our daughter's life."

I couldn't believe this. If it were a different time and my heart didn't belong to a different woman, I would have kissed her. Instead, she plastered her mouth to mine and backed me against the wall. My arms flew sideways and my eyes popped as I held my breath.

"Get your fucking hands off my man." Anger blazed through the room, and Tiffany pulled away in slow motion. I shot off the bench and brushed off my suit like it was infested.

Laura walked right past me and faced the now standing Tiffany, who was completely surprised. The younger version of me would have expected a full-out, hair-tearing girl fight. The current version of me feared much worse.

"You roll through my office like you own it, flutter your

lashes and make sweet comments that taste like acid, and to top it off, you try to seduce my man. I believe it's time I made my intentions clear. James and I are together. We're dating, and he's not available. I respect the fact you share two beautiful children, but I will not stand for you disrespecting me, so keep your fucking mouth, hands, and everything else to yourself."

My Adam's apple bobbed.

I took Laura's hand in mine, weaving our fingers in solidarity. "I think she heard you loud and clear. Didn't you, Tiff?"

My ex gave an indifferent shrug.

"Thank you for your help with Kensi, Tiff, but we need to return to our table."

Laura hooked her arm into mine, and we walked away, leaving Tiffany by the bench. I couldn't believe my ex's selfless act, and I couldn't believe our luck. I was a grateful bastard to have two wonderful women in my life.

I lowered to Laura's ear and whispered, "That was hot."

"What?"

"You telling Tiffany off. It was fucking hot. I want to take you to the closest room and do things to you. Lots of things. Naughty things."

My chest rumbled, and she laughed.

"Really? That turned you on? Maybe it's time I cuff you to the bed?"

I had other things in mind and secured her arm underneath mine, taking a left toward the elevators.

"Where are we going?"

"Take a guess."

Her arms peppered with goosebumps, and we quickened our step. I spun her into my arms as soon as the elevator door closed and took her mouth. Her body fell limply into my hold and she parted her lips. My tongue swept along hers. She tasted like promises and irresistible temptation. I moved her up against the wall and roamed my hands over her body, swallowing her shallow breaths. My thumbs drew over her cheeks as I held her face between my hands.

The elevator dinged, and the door opened. I peeled my mouth away from her swollen lips and turned to the gaping couple at the entrance.

"This elevator is taken." The possessive grunt rolling through my chest surprised me too, but it worked. They stepped back. The door closed, and I returned to her mouth. I kissed her until we reached our floor. She giggled as we ran down the corridor holding hands, nearly tripping over our feet. I scanned the access card, grabbed her hand, and pulled her inside the suite and right against my body. My hands roamed over her silhouette in search of a fastening while my mouth couldn't get enough of hers.

"Under my arm," she said in between kisses, and I found the zipper.

The pantsuit swooshed to the floor, and she stepped out of the fabric. I kicked off my shoes, and she stepped out of her heels. Her tiny fingers worked the bowtie undone and moved onto the shirt buttons. She was swift and effective. The shirt opened, and I pressed my torso to her heated skin.

"Ouch! Careful," she hissed, and I pulled away.

"I'm sorry."

"No, no. Don't stop." She drew my hands back to her body. "The wound is still sore, but for the sake of my hormones and sanity, please don't stop.."

"You got stitches?"

I backed up again, wanting to see, but she pulled me in against her.

"I told you." Her lips vibrated over mine. "They cut me open, and the scar is not pretty, so I'm not sure—"

I shut her mouth with mine, kissing her deeply and hard,

robbing her of words and thought, the same way she had robbed my mind. I walked backward with her in my arms, keeping the seal between us closed. Her swift hands worked my slacks, and by the time we reached the bed, we were stripped to our undergarments.

She broke the kiss and hopped up on the bed, more agile than I would have expected.

"How rough can I be?" I eyed her. A red mark ran along her right side in the shape of a C.

A smile split her lips. "Why don't you test me?"

I shook out my hands. "I don't know. I don't want to hurt you."

She lifted to her knees, crawled on all fours to the edge, and climbed up my body, securing herself against me. My skin ignited at the touch as her soft curves melted underneath my hot muscles. I wanted to touch her and feel her all over.

"Then let me test you." Her seductive voice slithered into my mouth as her lips brushed over mine.

"What?"

"Do you trust me?"

"In theory."

She sloped her head to the left.

"All right, I trust you."

"How much?" she squealed.

"I want to say with my life, but you're making me nervous right now."

"I promise you'll come out alive. Lie down on your back and close your eyes."

This woman tested me in ways no woman had tested me before.

I shifted to the middle of the bed, and she rose and slipped off her panties one leg at a time. Her pussy glistened above me as she stood wide-legged at the side of my hips. She drew her fingers up her slit, over her stomach, and through the valley between her breasts. I watched as she slipped a finger between her lips and sucked off her essence.

Fucking hot.

She unclasped her bra and threw it aside. Her breasts spilled, and my dick went from hard to iron stiff.

"I like this so far." My breath rumbled.

She looked like a fucking temptress as she lowered herself down over my abs. Her wet pussy slicked against my skin. She bent down to my mouth, her breasts resting over my chest, and I wrapped her in my hold. Her thighs tightened around my ribs and she pulled away before stealing a kiss.

"Nah-ah. I said, 'lie back and close your eyes.' Arms to the sides."

"You're not making this fun," I lied, curiosity digging into my bones.

"I promise it will be worth it."

I closed my eyes, and she covered them with a smaller pillow.

"I'll let you know when you can look."

All right, maybe she was making this fun. I felt her get up off the bed with a squirm. Three breaths later, she gripped my wrist. The sound of a click registered in my ear, and I realized she'd used the cuffs I bought for her. She secured my hand to the bedpost, then the other one. My cock twitched. She removed the pillow from my eyes and straddled me again. I pulled on the restraints and my urge to touch her spiked. Blood rushed feverishly fast through my veins.

"Are you ready to watch me fuck you?"

I sucked in a sharp breath. "You have a dirty mouth."

"Something you should have known when you went for a cop."

She bent down, removed my boxers, and I sprang free and hot.

"Shut up and fuck me," I breathed. "There's a condom in my jacket—"

"Already got it." She twirled the silver packet between her fingers before lowering herself to my cock. I expected her expert hands to roll it down my length, but I got her hot lips instead.

"Fuck, Laura."

Her tongue circled underneath my crown as she took me all the way to the back of her throat and moaned on the way up, gently releasing my cock from her mouth. She tore the packet open with her teeth. I watched her grin in the dim light, pleased she was enjoying herself. She removed the condom from within, placed it over my cap, and skillfully rolled the latex down my shaft.

An urgent surge of need rushed through my veins as she rose to her knees and grasped my cock in her hand. She stroked me three times, testing my patience, and positioned herself above me. The head of my penis passed the pressure of her opening and she sank down in slow motion, gripping me from within. The deep penetration under her control made me lose my control. My ribs sank in and I pushed my hips higher, hitting her depth.

She lifted her hands to her breasts and started rolling her hips, back and forth, back and forth. The agonizing rhythm had me thrusting harder with every slide. The rigid texture of her walls rubbed down my length. She was warm, wet, and smooth: every man's dream combination. Then she pinched her nipples and let out a needy yelp, throwing me off a beat.

I yanked on the cuffs, but she clamped down around me. Every muscle in my body twisted and strained as her ass slammed down and she rode my cock. An ache built in my left side, yet I couldn't concentrate because my head was spinning, and my mind fogged as my control dimmed.

Her hair flew wild, and sweat glistened over her body. Her hand slid off her breast and into my mouth. She slipped two fingers in, pulled them out, and brought my saliva to her mound. A zap flew down my spine right to my balls. She tilted her head back, closed her eyes, and opened her mouth. I fucking nearly lost it at the sound of her moans.

"Fuck," I groaned.

She opened her eyes and watched me watch her touch herself. Her fingers circled over the spot I was eager to kiss.

"Laura…" I breathed, and she hastened her strokes.

I thrust harder inside her and she flew upwards. Her mouth opened, her eyes closed, and her head fell back as I pumped her while she lost herself to my dick and her touch. I lost it at the first spasm that flew through her body. Her thighs tensed and her body trembled. I gave in to the pressure and emptied myself to the tune of her scream.

Her breath settled, and she slowly rose off me and freed my hands. I slipped the filled condom off my dick, tied a knot, and tossed a three-pointer in the trash can. She collapsed on top of my chest. I smoothed my hand over her arm, deciding there was no better feeling than her skin against mine. Her cheek pressed to my chest, and her fingers danced over my chest hair.

"Next time, you're the one getting cuffed to the bed," I said.

"We'll see," she snickered.

"You like cuffing people?"

"It comes with the territory. Or, it came with the territory, since I'm no longer a cop."

"I'll tell you what: if you ride my dick like that every time, you can cuff me anytime."

She rose and looked up. "I can do better than that."

My brows rose in a slow arch. "You can, can you? C'mere."

I gently rolled her over and hovered above her, kissing her

forehead, nose, and lips. I kissed my way down between her breasts, then carefully around her right side.

"Your wound is healing nicely," I said.

"Doctor Hippo said it could take a few months for the scar to fade."

"Doctor Hippo?"

She froze. A forceful swallow worked her throat as her eye twitched.

"He was the on-call emergency doctor when I came into the ER." She shimmied from underneath me and pulled the covers over us both.

"Next time I see him, I'll have to thank him for doing such a good job on my girls."

She snuggled into my side. "Oh, there's no need. He's busy enough, and I'm certain my parents have thanked him a thousand times."

I took a deep breath in and released it in slow motion. I don't know what I would have done if I'd lost one of my girls. The sound of my drumming heart calmed in my head and I concentrated on her breaths.

"I'm sorry about Tiffany," I said, rubbing my aching left shoulder.

"She's still in love with you."

"I know. I'm not trying to lead her on, but it's difficult not to share time with her when we have the girls, and—"

"You did nothing wrong, James. I saw the whole thing, which was just short of her getting up on that bench and riding you."

"You know I would never let that happen. I love you, Laura."

She stilled. "What?"

"Why are you pulling back?"

"You said you loved me."

"Yes, I did."

"Why?"

A sharp pain flew underneath my ribcage. "Because I do. What's the big deal?"

"What do you mean, what's the big deal?" Her forehead creased and her body tensed.

"Are you angry because you can't tell me you love me back?"

"It's not that easy." She shot up and tried to get out of the bed, but I grabbed her before she could leave.

"Don't go. I don't want you upset." I pulled her back into my hold and whispered, "I'm not expecting an answer back. I just wanted you to know."

She shifted. "I'm not ready. My life feels like a mess, and I need to fix things before moving forward. Lots of things. I want to reconcile with my parents. I want to make things right."

"So, you make them right. Better yet, let me help you with whatever you need."

"It's not that simple. James, we need to talk."

Her voice cracked, and we sat up in my bed. She picked at her fingernails as her hands shook.

"That doesn't sound good."

She shook her head in a swift arc. "There's something I've been keeping from you. It's...it's about a baby—"

"I already know."

Her head flew up, and I took her clammy hands into mine.

"I'm so sorry about your baby."

"What?"

"Your parents told me you lost a baby when you were eighteen."

"They told you?"

"Yes, and it's not your fault. Ouch." I grabbed my left side and stretched my left arm above my head.

"What's wrong?"

"I... I don't know."

I lowered my arm, and the pain zapped around my ribcage. "Argh!"

"James? What's the matter?"

She shot up in the bed. My heart raced, my head spun, and my vision blurred.

"I'm losing consciousness."

A second later, everything went black.

Chapter 11

Laura

I paced up and down the hospital hall. The hum of patients' conversations carried through the room as I prayed for James's recovery. He'd passed out naked on the bed, and I'd called for the ambulance from my cell phone while getting the hotel doctor from the room's landline.

James remained unconscious, with a weak pulse and shallow breath. The two minutes before help arrived were the longest of my life. I covered him with a blanket and dressed in a haze, checking his pulse every thirty seconds. I rode with the paramedics, and I called Teresa and Jacob on the way to the hospital.

To top the night off, he'd told me he loved me.

The fogged glass door slid open, and a nurse came out with a chart. "Ms. Young?"

"Yes, that's me."

"You came in with Mr. Silver?"

"That's right. Is he okay?"

"His spleen ruptured, and they've taken him to surgery. He's lucky you were there when it happened."

"So he'll be okay?"

"He had internal bleeding and lost some blood, but he was

brought in quickly. We'll know more once we get in. I'll keep you updated."

"Thank you. Wait… He's likely to need a transfusion, and the blood needs to be irradiated. He has leukemia… Furry cell… No, hairy cell… Hairy cell leukemia."

"Thank you. I think I saw that in his chart, but we'll double-check."

The nurse left, and Teresa rushed through the door with Jacob right behind her. I ran into her arms, shaking. It was already three in the morning, and I was a complete mess.

"What's happening? Did you hear anything?"

"His spleen ruptured. They took him to surgery for a splenectomy."

"Thank God you were with him."

We sat down on the couch by the window, and I blew my nose into a tissue.

Jacob remained standing. "I'm going to get us some coffee. Laura?"

"Yes, please."

"Milk? Sugar?"

"No. Black." Because my soul felt like the black abyss in a cup. And I needed caffeine.

"I'll be right back."

Teresa wrapped her arm around me and brought me to her side. "He's a vigorous man. He's going to be okay."

"And what if he's not? What if he goes without ever knowing his son? I was about to tell him, but then he brought up my dead baby girl. My parents told him about my stillbirth."

She covered her mouth with her hand. "Oh, my."

"It threw me off, and then his spleen ruptured, and I never told him about Foxy."

"The good news is, he'll be bedridden, so you'll have another chance. And it will give us more time with Foxy. I've been toilet-training him."

"I've noticed. Thank you, but I can't tell James while he's recovering."

She gripped my hand. "Honey, if you're looking for the perfect time, there's never going to be one."

"I'm figuring that out. He also told me he loved me." My eyes doubled in size.

"I thought that fact was obvious. He's crazy about you."

"I'm crazy about him too, but I can't reciprocate when I'm a liar."

"We already had this conversation. Tell him the truth and move forward."

Gosh, I wished it were that easy. When I'd finally felt ready, everything fell apart. My shoulders drooped, and I checked my watch.

"I pick up Foxy in four hours. What if the surgery's not done by then?"

"Jake can pick him up, if you'd like. We're a family, Laura. You're not alone."

"Thank you." I lowered my head to her shoulder. Teresa's constant support made me yearn for my mother. We had been close before I lost the baby, but we drifted apart soon after. Over time, I'd realized I wasn't the only one resisting the relationship, and I couldn't figure out why. Although my parents called to check in with me, they kept their distance as much as I did. Maybe Teresa was right when she advised me to speak with them first.

As if on cue, I saw my mother passing through the hall.

"Excuse me." I stood up and caught up to her. "Mom?"

She turned around with a look of surprise on her face, but smiled. "Laura? What are you doing here? Is everything all right?"

"No. A friend of mine is in surgery. James Silver."

"Your boyfriend? Anything serious?"

I'd forgotten just how much he'd already told my parents.

"Splenectomy."

"It's not an unusually complicated procedure. He'll be fine. How are you doing after *your* surgery?"

"I'm almost back to normal, and the girl's transplant was successful."

My mother checked her watch.

"Mom, there's something I've wanted to talk to you and Dad about, and I was wondering whether we could have dinner? At home. Your home, in the Hamptons."

She smiled so widely I thought she'd lose her balance. "Come this weekend. Bring your boyfriend too, if he's well."

"No, he won't be there. I need to speak with you alone."

"Are you in trouble?" Her gaze skidded to the clock on the wall.

"Not at all. You should go. I don't want to keep you from work. But let me know what time works."

"Sounds good. See you soon."

My mother disappeared around the corner, and I let go of a shaky breath.

"You did great." Teresa smoothed her hand over my back. "They'll be ecstatic to learn they're grandparents."

I hoped she was right. We waited another two hours before the doctor told us the surgery was successful. Teresa agreed to pick up Foxy from Mrs. Brewer's, and I stayed with James in his room as he slept. I sat by his bedside, holding his hand and wishing he knew the truth already. His son needed him. We all needed him.

He stirred by nine in the morning. I lifted my head off the bedside and my eyes shot open.

"Hey, James." I touched his face. "There you are."

"What happened?"

"Your spleen ruptured. You had emergency surgery, but everything's okay. Hold on, let me get the doctor."

He grabbed my hand. "No, stay with me."

I sat by his hips, careful not to hurt him.

"Do I have a scar?" he asked.

"Not one as badass as mine. You're lucky they got you laparoscopically. Only three tiny incisions."

"Shoot."

"Surgeries are not a competition," I chuckled.

He pulled his hand across his eyes, as if clearing a fog. I lowered his arm back to the bed.

"Be careful with the IV. You scared me," I whispered. "I don't know what I would've done if I'd lost you."

"Is that a way of you telling me you care?" he asked.

"You know I care. I more than care—"

"You just can't say it." His brows narrowed. "Because something is stopping you."

He was hitting the nail on the head.

"Stop overthinking or you'll get a headache. Your parents should be back soon."

"You called them?"

"If you get to have private chats with my parents, I get to call yours when you pass out."

He grunted. "Fair enough. My mother will not let me out of her sight."

"Maybe that's a good thing. It's time someone took care of you for a change."

"I'd prefer my girlfriend's soothing hands on my dick. Now, that's care."

"In case you don't recall, the last time your girlfriend took control, she broke you."

He laughed and winced in pain. "Ouch. You didn't rupture my spleen."

"I don't know. We were pretty rough."

"Baby, that was only a prelude, and I excel at symphonies."

Warmth pooled in my nether regions, and my insides

tingled. But it would likely be a while before we could pick up where we left off.

"Then you better get well soon," I whispered, and kissed him on his forehead. "I'll go get the doctor and will be back this afternoon."

"You're busy. There's no need."

"I'll be back, James. I'm not subjecting you to hospital food."

"I don't mind."

"Then how about I come back for me, because I can't stand being away from you? The girls should be here soon as well. I let Tiffany know about the surgery."

"Thank you." He yawned and closed his eyes.

I left as soon as the doctor came to check on him, and drove to pick up Foxy from the Silvers. On my way home, I bought a potted hibiscus for my mother and my dad's favorite rum, but I didn't expect I'd be the one needing a drink.

THE WEEKEND ARRIVED TOO QUICKLY. They released James from the hospital, and he was recovering at home without complications. I stood in front of my parents' house in the Hamptons and shifted from one foot to another. Allie sat with Foxy in the car, waiting for my text to bring him inside. I lifted my hand to the doorbell and lowered it again.

"I can do this. I can do this," I chanted in my head. They couldn't disown me, and if Teresa was right, Foxy was missing out as much as his grandparents were. Maybe, so was I.

I pressed my finger on the doorbell and listened to the elongated chime. My mother opened the door.

"Hi, Mom."

"Laura, it's so good to see you. Come in."

"Is Dad home?"

"Yes, he's in the kitchen. We ordered sushi."

I stayed in my spot.

"Well, come on in, honey. This is still your home."

"I hope you feel the same way once you hear what I have to say."

She pursed her lips, looking over my shoulder to the driveway. "Is everything all right?"

"Yes, it is, but I didn't come alone. There's someone I'd like you to meet," I whispered, glancing back at the car.

My mother's attention followed my gaze. "Is that Allie in the car?"

"It is. She's waiting there with my son—your grandson."

My mother's face fell ashen, and time stood still.

"Did you say your son?" she whispered, and I nodded.

Her mouth opened and closed a few times before she composed herself. "Are you going to have them wait in the car or join us? Wait—kids don't eat sushi. I'll throw something in the oven—"

"Mom, it's okay. I have snacks. I… I just really wanted to see you and tell how wonderful and smart and funny he is, and—"

"Laura, stop. I don't want you telling me how great he is. I want to meet my grandson. Tom!" she called, unable to contain a smile. "Tom, you've gotta come out here."

Okay, I had to admit—Teresa was right.

I waved Allie over, and she took Foxy out of the car seat. My mother's hand flew to her mouth as she covered her shaky breaths. She hurried down the three steps and lifted Foxy into her arms, spinning him in the air. He laughed, open-mouthed, just as my father met us outside.

"Is that Allie's baby?" he asked. "I didn't know she had a son."

"No, Dad. This is Fox, and he's mine. He's your grandson."

"What?" He took a cautious step forward.

"I'm sorry, I didn't tell you."

"I have a grandson?" He let out a cautious laugh, and my

heart skipped a beat. I took in the moment as my parents passed Foxy back and forth, tickling him and showing him all the flowers he wanted to touch in the front garden.

"See? That wasn't so bad," Allie said.

"Yeah, who would have thought?"

"Teresa."

"You think she's right about James? That he'll grab Foxy into his arms and forget the past two years happened?"

"I doubt it, but good luck."

"Thanks," I puffed. "He must know how to forgive, right? I mean, he's related to Tristan, and the Silvers are all amazing—"

"And so is James. He may be upset when you tell him, but he'll forgive you. You're the mother of his child. Teresa's right, though. It will be better if he hears about it from you."

My father picked a sunflower and handed it to Foxy. Yellow pollen dusted his nose as he smelled the flower.

"He didn't forgive Tiffany for poking his condoms," I said.

"You're not her."

My mother picked Foxy up into her arms and joined us on the porch. "Let's go eat. I'm starving. Does Foxy like chicken nuggets? They're organic."

"He loves them."

We followed my parents inside, and I helped my mother with the food while my father played with Foxy in the back-yard. I'd forgotten how much I missed this home. We used to play badminton and pool volleyball all summer. Life was good —until prom night in high school. I didn't even know who attacked me.

"Laura?" My mother nudged my arm. "Are you all right?"

"Yes, just thinking."

"So, tell us more about Foxy."

I cracked a smile. "You want to know about his father?"

"I don't want to pry, but is he present in your life? I mean, I know you're dating. How does James feel about this?"

My father came inside to get a popsicle for Foxy.

"You're not prying, and you deserve an answer. I've complicated my life more than I wanted to. You know how I've kept Foxy from you?"

My father stopped at the door and turned back around. Air whistled through my mother's throat. "Oh, Laura, please tell me you didn't."

"I'm one heck of a smart daughter, aren't I?"

"But why?" she asked.

"I thought he was married, and I was mistaken. I jumped to conclusions."

"The apple doesn't fall far from the tree," my father grunted. He seemed off today, and I couldn't understand why. From the moment we came inside and he pulled my mother aside, I had the feeling they wanted to say something and didn't know how.

"Is he a good man?"

"It's James Silver."

"Laura—"

"I know, I know. I'm going to tell him."

"You gave his daughter your liver, didn't you?" my father asked, and grabbed a beer from the fridge.

I nodded. "How could I not? I was a perfect match."

My mother placed her hand over mine. "If James is as smart as I think he is, forgiving you should be easy."

"You're being nice. Why are you so nice? You hated me when I was pregnant."

"It wasn't *you*, Laura. It was the situation. The pregnancy flipped your life upside down, and you were supposed to go to medical school—"

"You know, if my baby girl hadn't died, she would be seven now. Foxy would have had a sister."

My father lowered his beer and coughed into his hand. "I can't do this anymore."

"We can't change what's happened." My mother's voice lifted.

"Maybe we can."

"Tom—"

"No, Alice. I think it's time."

My head flew from one to the other. "Mom, Dad—what's going on?"

"You should probably sit down." My father pulled out a chair.

During the next five minutes, my life was flipped upside down. That evening, I walked into James's home a complete mess and collapsed into his arms, sobbing. My makeup ran down my cheeks as I pulled in the sniffles and finally calmed enough to answer his continued questions as to what happened.

"You know how you said you'd help me fix things?" I asked.

"Yes?"

"I need your help to find my daughter."

Chapter 12

James

I browsed between screens searching through the adoption agency's database. Laura had only gotten a little information from her parents about her baby girl, and she couldn't stop crying for days. Her parents had lied to her about her baby's stillbirth and had given her up for adoption. For seven long years, Laura thought her baby girl was gone. They'd barely reconciled, and this broke Laura from the inside out.

I closed the laptop and stretched out my arms. Orange and red leaves decorated the backyard. We'd lucked out this fall with warmer weather, and carved pumpkins outside last night. The girls set them on the front porch. Tonight, we planned to add a scarecrow and a few ghosts and graves to the yard. Halloween was just around the corner.

Kensi laughed as her grandfather pushed her onto the swing. Laila squealed on hers. My father stepped between them and pushed one, then the other. I rose off the lounger and felt lightheaded, steadying myself by the railing. My surgery was successful, but healing dragged. The fatigue came in the middle of the day, and soon after I woke up. I recovered with a longer breath and dialed Laura's number. She picked up on the second ring.

"Hello?"

"Hey, how are you?"

"Getting better." She pulled in a sniffle. "Thank you for the flowers. They're beautiful."

"My pleasure."

"Did you find anything?"

"Not yet. I'm meeting your parents this afternoon and waiting for Axel's call."

"You think a lawyer can do anything?"

"It was an illegal adoption. They took your daughter from you. Lawyers will get the information they need from the agency."

She caught a breath and let out a sob. "There's nothing worse than knowing your child's out there all alone. Oh, James."

I pictured her tears and had the urge to drive to her house and kiss them away. My heart broke with each sob. I'd do everything in my power to return her daughter to her arms.

"I know, I know."

"You don't know. I've been so wrong," she cried.

"None of this is your fault. You didn't know, baby. Stop blaming yourself."

"All these months and years. Oh, my God, I'm a monster."

"Laura, I'm coming over."

She stopped crying like a switch went off. "No, it's all right."

"Are you sure?"

"Yes, I'll be fine." I heard her blow her nose through the receiver. "Ozzy just went for his nap and I could use a few hours of sleep."

"You'll still come to the barbecue this weekend, right?"

"I wouldn't miss it for anything. Your family is my family."

"I fucking love you so much."

The awkward pause between the time I told her I loved her and she spoke again lengthened every time, as if she were fighting an internal battle to tell me how we both knew she felt.

"Is it weird I still want my parents at the barbecue? We've missed out on so much already."

"You're not upset with them?"

"I'm angry they manipulated me, and I'm mad they gave up my daughter." She paused, gathering her thoughts. "But they also said they'll do everything in their power to help me get her back. If they had said nothing in the first place, I would be oblivious. Ozzy just got his grandparents back, and I should nurture that. Life is too short to be angry, and I'd rather spend the time looking for my daughter."

I was meeting with the Youngs this afternoon, hoping to get more answers. Mrs. Young had broken down on the phone. Laura was right: they needed each other now, more than ever.

"You're incredible," I said to her. "Just when I thought I couldn't love you any harder. Your parents are welcome. It will be a great day. The entire family will be here."

"Daddy, Mommy's here!" the girls screamed from the back as Tiffany strolled toward them through the side yard. They hopped off the swings and ran to their mother. Kensi sped like she'd never had surgery.

"Tiffany is here to pick up the girls," I said. "I should go. I'll let you know as soon as I find anything new. And Laura?"

"Yes?"

"You call me if you need me. I don't want to push, but I'm only twenty minutes away."

"Thank you, James. I mean it. I... I want you to know something, too."

"Yes?"

"It's on the tip of my tongue, but I can't say it until I fix things."

"So, until you find your daughter?"

"No..."

I pictured her shaking her head and closing her eyes as she sighed.

"I need you to know how much I adore having you in my life and how much I hope you'll be in it for a very long time. Once I clean up the mess of a life I've made."

"Hey, everybody's got a little bit of a mess in their lives. Go take that nap before Ozzy wakes up, and call me when you're up."

"I will. Take care."

We hung up, and I carefully stepped down the patio steps to the grass. Leaves swirled underneath my feet. I kicked through them, crossing the yard. Leaf raking was off the to-do list this year because I barely had the energy and strength. The girls piled them into heaps, which blew through the yard.

"Hey, Tiff. Are you ready for this weekend?"

"Can't wait to celebrate my girl's super-liver. That's what she's been calling her new liver."

"She's right." I messed Kensi's hair, and she giggled, running back to the swing.

"How are you feeling?" Tiffany asked.

"Much better with the spleen gone. The pills are killing my stomach."

"You should switch your diet. How's the pain?"

"Nothing I can't handle."

"You don't need to be sedulous. What can I do to help?"

I crossed my arms in front of me and put my head to one side in a questioning manner. "Are you okay, Tiff? I mean, after the transplant? You've been on your feet, barely recovering."

"What can I say? My vegetarian diet is paying off. You should try it."

I laughed. "I may. Glad to hear you're well. Tiff," I gently wrapped my arm around her and pulled her aside, "I want to find Kensi's birth parents."

She stopped. "What? Why?"

"Medical history. What if there's breast cancer in her family or melanoma or mental health issues? We need to be prepared."

"It was a closed adoption."

"There are ways. I talked to Axel Wagner, and he's going through legal loopholes. But if we find her parents, we won't have to worry about all the what-ifs."

"What if they want Kensi back?" She glanced back at our daughter, rubbing her hands over her arms.

"They can't have her back because she's ours. From my experience, biological parents are happy to share medical information when it will help their children."

"I don't want Kensi confused."

"She doesn't have to know until she's eighteen, or ready. When the time comes, we'll tell her everything she wants to know. We'll tell her everything we know."

She released the tension from her shoulders and shook out her arms. "All right. If you think we should do it."

"Thanks. Hey, I ordered a slide for the kids for this weekend, and—"

"Can I ask you something?" she interrupted, and I waited. "You and Laura… Is it serious?"

"Yes. I'm in love with her."

She nodded, and her face saddened.

"Tiff, you and the girls will always be important to me. That will never change. It's the real thing with Laura and me. She loves the girls and treats them well."

She let out a swoosh of air. "I'm happy for you. I'm not so happy for me because I, obviously, love you—"

"Tiff—"

"I can't change what I can't change, but I will be respectful. You mean too much to me to lose you, James, and you're the best co-parent I could have asked for."

Somewhere in my heart, there was a place where I did love this woman—just differently.

"Thanks."

"Hope for Hope has asked me to decorate a new wing they're adding. I have a meeting tomorrow."

"That's great. It should lead to new opportunities."

"Nah, I'm good with the clients I have. Need time for my girls. You'll let me know what you find about Kensi's parents?"

She waved the girls to come back.

"You'll be the first to know."

I hugged her and helped get the girls' backpacks. I secured them in Tiffany's pimped Hummer and grinned as they waved goodbye through the open window.

"Bye, Daddy."

"See you this weekend to celebrate your super-liver," I called out as they drove away. The wind picked up a heap of leaves, blowing through the front yard. I returned to my computer and happily clicked the submit button on Kensi's DNA history.

I SPUN A FORK OVER A NAPKIN. The front door opened, and the Youngs walked through the Marina's entrance. I stood up from my chair to greet them, shaking their hands.

"Thank you for meeting me here."

"Thank you for the flowers you sent," Mrs. Young said. "I appreciate the gesture." Her eyes were filled with worry and underlined with dark circles.

"These times can be hard on a family. Hopefully, they can bring a bit of sunshine to your home during these difficult times."

Mrs. Young smiled. "They have. You're very thoughtful. How is Laura doing?"

"She's determined to find her daughter."

"We thought she would be. Does...does she hate us?"

"No. She's sad and upset, but she doesn't hate you. She's asked me to invite you to our family barbecue this weekend."

"She did?"

"She loves you and has a good heart. That's why it's so important for me to find her daughter. Anything you can tell me about the day she gave birth would be helpful."

"The adoption records are sealed."

"We're working on those. Laura said she gave birth on June twenty-first, but hospital records show no stillbirths that day, or babies eligible for adoption."

The silence between them had me sitting higher. The air thinned into an uncomfortable string of unsaid words.

"Mr. and Mrs. Young?"

Her father drew in a long breath.

"We knew Laura would check all records, so we had the baby's birth registration delayed to the twenty-third. The records will show a stillbirth on the twenty-third."

That was Kensi's birthday.

"Except the baby was alive. The adoption agency has no record of Laura?"

They shook their head, and I knew Axel Wagner wouldn't be able to help me. The Agency would have no information to give.

"James, even if you get the adoption records open, you won't find any relevant information because there is none. The little girl left the hospital with nothing but a birthdate."

Mr. Young confirmed my suspicions.

"What about the father?"

"You won't find the father because Laura doesn't know who attacked her."

"Right."

"The agency was told the baby was found in a dumpster," Mrs. Young whispered. "I'm not sure how you'll find the girl. And if you don't, I fear Laura will never forgive us."

I lowered my hand to hers. "You forgave her for keeping your grandson to herself, and she'll forgive you for this. Time heals all."

She glanced over at her husband, and he returned her nervous look.

"We thought we were doing the right thing. We thought the baby would have a better future with a stable family. Laura had schooling ahead, but we didn't mean to rob our daughter of a child. This secret has eaten us from within over the years. We'll do anything we can to help you find our granddaughter."

Mrs. Young removed a rectangular box from a bag she carried and slid it over the table. "Can you please give this to Laura? We kept the baby's first clothes and a photo we took before we gave her away."

"Of course."

"And James?"

"Yes?"

"Should we get a lawyer?"

"Why?"

"Legally, we kidnapped a child and gave it up for adoption. Our medical licenses—"

"You think she would sue you?"

"She should."

I shook my head. "Laura has mentioned nothing about taking legal action. Like I said, she's upset, but she loves you. We'll find her little girl, I promise."

"Thank you, James. We'll come to the barbecue this weekend, and please let us know if we can help."

Mrs. Young hugged me goodbye. It was the first time I'd seen Laura's mother show deeper affection.

"Thank you."

The Youngs left, and my phone dinged with a message from my lawyer. As predicted, the adoption agency had no further useful information. I drove back to my aunt and uncle's, where my parents were having dinner.

"Uncle James!" Emma ran to my side with her two Rottweilers. "Where's Kensi and Laila?"

"They're with their mom today."

She followed me inside, where I poured myself a glass of cranberry juice and sat by the fireplace on the patio.

"How did your meeting go?" my mother asked. She set a plate of food in front of me. "Dig in."

"I didn't get as much information as I'd hoped."

"And you're feeling all right? You look a little pale."

"Just tired."

"Eat up. If you don't take care of yourself, who's going to take care of your girls?" She winked.

"Teresa? I can't find the apple pie," Aunt Wilma called out, and my mother went back to the kitchen.

Emma plopped on the seat beside me, pointing to the box. "What's that?"

"Laura's baby stuff."

"The baby she lost?"

"Yes. Some clothes and a photograph."

"Can I see?"

"Go for it, kid."

She opened the box and gently lifted the baby gown, the hospital bracelet with the name Jane Doe, and a photograph of a two-day-old baby.

"Uncle James?"

"Yes, Emma?"

"Why does the baby have Kensi's bracelet?"

Chapter 13

Laura

I refreshed my laptop screen as the digital clock switched from 2:59 to 3:00 in the morning. I'd sent my DNA to a lab the morning after I left James's house. The company would add the analyzed results to a match site where I'd created a profile. Eight hours passed, and there was no update.

I shut the screen and set the laptop aside. The sheets burned against my skin, so I pulled the covers off my body. It didn't help. I turned on my stomach and pressed my cheek to the pillow. Every time I closed my eyes, I saw my daughter's face, but when I opened them again, she was gone. Was she safe? Did she have a warm bed to sleep in? Frustration swam through my veins so fast, I had trouble slowing my heart rate. Sleeping pills didn't help, and I felt like I was losing my mind. Thank God for Teresa, who wanted to babysit Foxy again. The family fall barbecue was tomorrow, and I planned to tell James the truth about Foxy before the end of the day. I didn't want to do to him what had been done to me.

The clock switched to 3:01, and I hopped out of bed to take a shower. The house felt empty without Allie. She'd moved out to Tristan's and was hosting Thanksgiving next weekend, and I missed her. But she was dealing with pregnancy, a stalker, and a crazy fucking ex who'd come back from the dead, so I couldn't add any more to her plate. Besides, she couldn't help me do anything I couldn't do myself.

The shower trickled a few more minutes away. I dressed and drove to the office, picking up an extra-large coffee on the way. The brew at work tasted amazing, but the shit around the corner from our house would keep my eyes open much longer. Greg, the Silvers' secretary, was here already and loved the strong java just as much, so I dropped off an extra cup on his desk. At six in the morning, he was already sitting behind his welcome desk and clicking away in front of the screen.

"Good morning. What are you doing here this early?"

He looked up from his computer and pulled away from the keyboard. "I'm more than just a pretty face. Thanks for the brew. You couldn't sleep?"

"I don't know if you've heard, but I'm looking for my baby."

"I've heard. Everybody's heard, and everybody's looking. James is here, by the way."

I followed his outstretched finger to James' office. "Already?"

"Aha."

He hadn't called or texted in two days, and I was worried he had bad news or no news at all.

"You think he found her?" I asked Greg.

"He's certainly working hard. The bags under his eyes match my grandma's."

"I'll go say good morning."

He winked. "Sure thing."

I scanned through the secure entrance and walked down the hall to the corner office. The door had been left ajar, and James was sitting behind his mahogany desk with his head in his hands. I stood at the threshold and gently knocked.

"Good morning."

His head flew up and my eyes flew open; he looked like he'd stepped out of hell. His eyes burned like balls of fire, and dark shadows lay beneath them.

"Did you stay up all night? What are you doing here?"

He stood up and pulled his fingers through his hair. The move would have been sexy a week ago, but now it was tense and careless. "I couldn't sleep. Thought I would get a head start on the day. What about you?"

"Same. Could have told me you were here. I would have brought you coffee." I sat down across from his desk and set my coffee aside. "I haven't heard from you—"

"I'm sorry. It's just a lot."

"If there's anyone who can find her, it's you, James. I believe in you."

His eyelids dropped. "Laura, I will find her, but there's something you need to consider." He lifted his gaze to me in slow motion.

"What if your daughter is happy where she's at? If she's seven, it's unlikely the girl even knows she's adopted."

"You don't think I've thought about that? She'll think I'm nothing but a stranger. It will take time to build trust with the family—"

"The courts would likely prevent you from approaching her."

"Jesus, I haven't even thought the parents would mind, but they have no right. They got her illegally."

"Maybe they didn't know that."

"How can you not know you're buying a baby on the black market? Who doesn't do their due diligence?"

"You can't jump to conclusions. You don't know the situation."

"And you do?"

He stilled, and his eyes cooled from inferno to frost. "No, I... I don't."

"All right." I stood up from my chair. "I gotta get to the computer. My DNA results should be up on the matching site at any moment. Who knows? Maybe the parents are looking for me too, and I'll get lucky."

James gripped the corner of his desk and stood up, wobbling on his feet.

"Are you all right?" I asked.

"Tired." He breathed unsteadily. "I need sleep."

I got off my chair and hurried to his side, steadying him under his arm. I helped him to the couch where we'd first spent the night and covered him with a blanket.

"I'll close the door on my way out," I said, getting up, but he grabbed my hand.

"No, don't go."

I lowered to the couch beside him and snuggled into his body. My breaths instantly slowed, and my eyelids felt heavy. I'd had a long night and no luxury of a couch in my office, so his arms and body felt like the first peaceful moment since my parents' revelation. He held onto me like he was about to lose me.

"I'm looking forward to this weekend. I'm coming with Ozzy, and my parents will be there as well."

"Me too."

"It will be nice for the kids to spend time together."

Tomorrow night, my little boy would gain two sisters and a father. At the barbecue, with Teresa, Jacob, and my parents to support me, I'd tell the man I loved everything I'd kept from him.

"I'm looking forward to it." He yawned and loosened his grip.

"Imagine—by tomorrow, I could have a match with my daughter."

My phone vibrated, and I reached into my pocket and

checked the notification. I shot off the couch. "James, I gotta go."

He sat up. "What happened?"

"I have a match."

His phone chimed on his desk. "For your daughter?"

"No, for my chickens."

"You don't have any chickens."

"Exactly." I hurried out the door.

"No, Laura. Wait!"

But I was already down the hall, opening the staircase door. My legs sped of their own accord, taking me down the flights in seconds. I sat behind my desk, opened the computer, and logged into my account just as James pushed the office door open and ran over to my desk, nearly tripping. His disheveled hair flew in all directions, from left to right.

"There it is." I covered my mouth with my hand.

"What is?" His face was pale, and he was out of breath.

"It's the match. Hold on. Copy, paste, send. And there."

"There what?" He leaned over my desk.

"A personal note to the family about myself. Now I have to wait for a reply."

"Oh." His phone chimed with an incoming message, which he ignored.

"What do you mean, *oh*? That's great news. There's a match, James. This means she's in the system, so she's likely looking for her birth parents. It's the link I've been hoping for."

The lines on his throat tightened, and I sat back in my seat. His phone chimed again. "You don't appear excited about this, and it sounds like someone needs you. At seven in the morning."

He removed his phone from the back pocket, scrolled through his screen, and frowned.

"Is everything okay?" I asked.

His gaze lifted to meet mine. "I'm happy you found a match,

but I'm tired and I have work, so I'll leave you to yours. Let me know if you get a reply."

"Thank you."

He headed for the door.

"James?"

He stopped but didn't turn around again.

"I'm looking forward to the barbecue tomorrow."

"Me too," he said in a soft voice, and left.

Had I become too much for him? What if it was the leukemia? I popped open my coffee, took a sip, and refreshed the computer screen. My message had been delivered and read, but there was no reply. Patience was an expected skill for a cop, but difficult to maintain as a mother. The family, likely, needed time to think and reply, but it couldn't be long before they did —and hopefully, I could see my baby girl.

A DISTINCT AROMA of barbecue and fall carried in the air. The Silvers had set the event outside, and Emma had turned the backyard into a farm, complete with a petting zoo, a pony ride, games, and slides. The cloudless day one week before Thanksgiving carried a promise of good news in the air. I'd given Foxy a haircut that morning, arrived at the Silver's before everyone else, and retreated to the cove shore where we spent the afternoon on a blanket. Teresa brought out a bowl filled with lettuce, and we fed the friendly swans. I had just given Foxy another piece of lettuce when I turned at the shuffle of leaves behind me.

James strolled over in a pair of fitted slacks and a sweater. "Hey, what are you doing out here?" he asked. "I didn't see your car."

"I came earlier with my parents. F... Ozzy wanted to feed the swans. Your mother said they're friendly."

"These are, and they stay here all year. Is this the little man?" He crouched to the ground, and Foxy handed James a piece of lettuce. "Thanks. Want to feed them up close?"

"Quack, quack." Foxy pointed to the water, and James lifted him into his arms.

Oh, my God.

I held back the gasp as sweat dripped down my spine. I'd dreamt about this moment, but now that it was here, I wished it were different. I wished James already knew about his son.

James fixed Foxy's bowtie and carefully trod down the rocky bank. I let go of a long breath when he didn't make the connection. Maybe it would have been better if he had?

He bent down near the water, and the beautiful swans swam in closer.

"Swans mate for life," she said.

I stepped nervously over the rocks and crouched on Foxy's other side. James held him steady on the uneven terrain.

"What else can they do?"

"They're territorial and highly aggressive about defending their young. I should have been more aggressive when I had my girl. They didn't even let me hold her."

My throat tickled in the back, and I pulled my hand across my eyes.

"I'm so sorry, Laura. It's not—"

"Not fair? It's F.U.C.K.E.D. Up. I'm going to find her, James, if it's the last thing I do."

His Adam's apple bobbed.

"You haven't found anything yet?" I asked.

"Laura! James!" Jacob's deep voice boomed from the back-yard. "Food's ready!"

James lifted Foxy in his arms. "Come on. You must be starving."

I followed him up the stone bank. He set Foxy on the ground and took his right hand while I took his left. We crossed the backyard to the sitting area. As if on cue, the entire family turned around, and the patio was silenced. I saw what they all saw: a happy family walking hand in hand, except the picture was so wrong. The secret was eating me from within and after dinner, when Foxy went down for his nap, I would finally tell James the truth.

Allie arrived with Tristan and sat near the end of the table. I couldn't wait to catch up with my friend. The long wooden table underneath a pergola overgrown with vines extended at least twenty feet, seating three large families. My parents gaped, along with everyone else in on my secrets, and I avoided eye contact. Emma sat with Kensi and Laila, helping them to a smaller table. They had set sunflowers and candles in the middle, igniting a warm family ambiance. James pulled out my chair.

Foxy squeezed my hand. "Mama, pee-pee."

"Excuse me for a moment. I'll be right back."

"The powder room is being fixed. You can use the upstairs bathroom," Jacob said.

I lifted Foxy into my arms and went inside, heading to the second floor. We hurried to the end of the hall, and I knocked on the bathroom door.

"Sorry, it's taken," Wilma called out. "There's another one near the boy's old room."

"Thank you."

We turned around and crossed the hall to the other end of the house, but stopped at one room where Tiffany was standing, facing a wall. She turned around when she heard us.

"Hey, I'm looking for the second bathroom," I said.

"Your parents call your son Fox." She stepped closer. "I heard them talking to Teresa."

"I don't know what you heard." I turned my son in my arms so he wouldn't be facing her, and she flipped over a picture frame she was holding.

"This is Fox when he was a baby. At first, I thought to myself, why would Teresa keep a picture of Ozzy in Fox's room? Then I realized it wasn't a picture of Ozzy, but of his father, who looked just like him when he was a toddler."

I kept silent as my throat screamed for water. Foxy came closer to my ear. "Mama, pee-pee." I rubbed over his back and stepped back out into the hallway.

"He said he met someone in Colorado, but she left. It was you, wasn't it?"

"I wanted to stay out of the way. You were pregnant, and I didn't know you weren't together, so I stayed away."

"And kept his son from him? James doesn't know about him, does he? And his name isn't Ozzy, is it?"

"Tiffany—"

"How could you?" She pushed past me.

"Tiffany, wait!"

I rushed after her until a warmth dripped down my shirt and jeans.

"Mama, pee-pee."

We didn't make it to the bathroom. I stopped and turned around to Teresa's room, where she kept a change of Foxy's clothes for his sleepovers. I laid him down on the bed and undressed him in a hurry. My heart battered my chest and my hands shook, making dressing a giggling toddler nearly impossible. An argument from the backyard drew my attention to the window.

Fuck.

I pulled up Foxy's pants and took him back into my arms, peeking through the curtains. Tiffany hadn't made it down yet, and James was standing by the barbecue, talking to my parents. My father waved his hand up and down as they argued.

"What the hell is going on?"

Holding my son tightly in my arms, I ran downstairs and stepped out onto the patio. Everyone's attention turned my way, and the backyard fell quiet. Tiffany was standing beside James, and my heart stopped.

My mother and Teresa walked up with the girls.

"We're taking the kids inside," Teresa whispered. I handed Foxy over and walked three steps forward before I froze. James strode toward me, nostrils flaring and fury raging. He stomped through the foliage like an animal.

"Is it true?"

I startled, tears welling in my eyes.

"Oh, my God. It's true. Ozzy… I mean, Foxy is my son?"

It was over. While the tightness released from my chest, I couldn't breathe. James was fuming. His face turned beet red and sweat dripped down his forehead.

"You can't even fucking admit it!"

I struggled to answer before Jacob's booming voice sounded from across the patio. "James!"

"How could you do this to me?"

"You had a family," I stuttered. "I didn't want Foxy with someone who couldn't be there full-time."

He leaned forward, spewing breath from his nose. "And what gives you the right to decide whether I'm a fit father? You don't even fucking know me!"

"James!" Jacob's heavy steps boomed across the deck as he approached us.

"I'm sorry." My vision blurred, and I wiped the tears away.

"You've stolen my son's first two years from me. I trusted you like I never trusted anyone before."

"James—"

"I can't stand looking at you. I will never forgive you for this."

Jacob grabbed his son's arms, pulling him away, but James ripped out of his father's grip.

"And you want my help to find your daughter? You make me sick!"

"James, that's enough." His father stepped between us and physically pushed him inside the house.

I collapsed to my knees. Allie rushed to my side, helping me up.

"I want to go home." I looked up.

"All right. I'll get you home, honey."

"No. I need to be where James can't find me and Foxy. I'm going to the Hamptons with my parents."

"You're sure?"

I nodded. "I'm going to work online for a while."

"Yes, of course. Take your time."

"Thank you."

She hugged me goodbye while my father secured Foxy in the car seat and my mother packed his bag. Teresa enclosed her arms around me like she never wanted to let go. "He'll come around, Laura. Just give him some time."

I hoped she was right, and prayed James had learned forgiveness from his mother. The question was, could I forgive him?

I tilted back in the chair, watching the stars, fighting insomnia. Water sloshed underneath the dock where I'd parked my foldable chair. The nearly empty whiskey glass in my hand provided little comfort. I sat up, reached to the dock for my bottle, and refilled my glass.

The first swig drew my senses to the burn in my throat enough to blur the ache. I had a beautiful son, and Laura had kept him from me. She'd had so many opportunities to tell me the truth, yet she'd kept him a secret. He was sweet and curious, and he'd occupied my heart the moment Tiffany told me he was mine. Actually, he'd had it before we met, because I'd wanted Laura and her son...*our* son, to build a life together, even before I knew he was mine.

Our son.

I pulled my fingers through my hair and coughed out cold air. Tiffany left with the girls before the Youngs approached me about Kensi and all hell broke loose. They said Laura's resemblance to my daughter was unmistakable, and now that I knew the truth, I couldn't deny the likeness, and confirmed their suspicions.

But how could I tell Tiffany that her daughter's biological

mother wanted Kensi back? I was a coward; I never told Laura about her match. Every time I read the profile letter she'd posted to Kensi's parents, my anger waned. Logic guided my mind toward forgiveness, but the rage burning through my veins also burned through all that logic. Drowning it all in a glass of whiskey was even better.

I took a long swig and swept my finger over the phone, opening the message.

To my seven-year-old daughter's parents/guardians:

My life changed when I found out I was pregnant at seventeen. People around me had opinions, but I only had one: I loved my baby girl, and I couldn't wait to meet her. I couldn't wait to kiss her tiny hands, soothe her first hunger, and hold her in my arms, next to my skin, but I never had the chance.

The doctors took her away from me and told me she died.

I am now blessed with a two-year-old boy, and he has the sweetest and kindest soul. One day, I hope he gets to meet his big sister. This match is the chance I've been waiting for to meet my baby girl and have the opportunity that was stolen from me to watch her grow. I hope you will find space in your heart and life for an extra family member.

With love,

Laura Young

"What are you still doing out here?"

I startled at my mother's voice and set my glass underneath the chair before she saw through the darkness.

"You're going to freeze."

I stood up, turned around, and she waved her hand in front of her nose. "Oh, God. By the smell of it, maybe you won't freeze."

I retrieved the glass from underneath the chair and finished the remaining quarter in one swig.

"Is that how you solve your problems? Drown them in a glass of whiskey?"

"What do you want me to do?" I threw my hands up in the air.

"Be the man I raised you to be." She smacked my arm. "She came back for you, fool. And you threw her away at the first challenge you faced."

"What are you talking about—she came back?"

"She came back to tell you she was pregnant. Laura drove to your house and saw you and Tiffany through the window. Kensi was coloring and Laila was in a swing. She saw a happy family, and she didn't want to break you apart. Don't you see? You were meant to adopt Kensi, and Laura was meant to find you. Fate brought you together. Maybe not then, but definitely now."

A colder wind swept through, and she pulled her sweater closed.

"You're not upset she kept your grandson from you?"

"How can I be upset? I have a grandson. I'm grateful she opened her heart to our family and gave us a chance."

"She didn't choose to tell me."

"But she wanted to, James. Do you know how many times she tried? Even before your splenectomy."

"Wait a minute. You've known about this? You knew and didn't tell me?"

"It wasn't my place, especially since Laura's intention to tell you herself was clear. She may have made a mistake, but you didn't even give her a chance to explain. You tore through that girl and embarrassed her. You owe Laura an apology, if not much more."

Three-quarters of a bottle of whiskey swam through my veins, coursing through my blood and my head. The memory of her stricken face as I yelled flashed through my mind. Tears streamed down her face, and Laura couldn't get a word out. She stood on the patio, her eyes begging, while I spewed filthy words her way.

"I'm a fucking asshole."

"And a hypocrite. You're keeping Kensi away from Laura."

My head flew up. I rubbed my stiff fingers and puffed a breath into my hands.

"Who told you?"

"Emma. She had to cry on somebody's shoulder. Tom and Alice Young confirmed it. Come into the house; it's nearly freezing."

I took my mother under her arm, and we walked across the backyard.

"We fought about Kensi during dinner, while Laura was in the house with Foxy, before Tiffany came downstairs."

"I saw."

"They said Kensi looks just like Laura when she was a little girl."

"And you said nothing to Laura. Isn't it hypocritical to keep the girl from her mother? A mother who never wanted to give up her baby?"

Fuck.

This couldn't be happening right now. The way out of this mess was definitely not with the heavy head full of whiskey I was carrying.

"Tiffany is her mother," I said, pushing open the back door for my mother.

She filled the kettle with water and lit the stove. "We both know what Tiffany did. She purchased a child on the black market."

"I didn't know that at the time."

"Don't give me excuses. It's a child, and you should have looked over the paperwork."

"There was no paperwork." I rubbed the back of my neck.

"Well, that should have been your first clue."

For nine months, Tiffany had pretended to be pregnant. We weren't living together anymore, so it wasn't like I ever saw her without her clothes on. One day she came home from the hospital without a stomach and with a baby in her arms: my baby. I never questioned whether Tiffany had given birth, and I didn't find out the truth until Kensi became sick and the doctors asked us about family history. By then, I loved Kensi like she was mine and wanted to give her the family she deserved.

"If I'd reported Tiffany, the only one who would have suffered would have been Kensi. She needed a family, and I already thought of her as mine. I couldn't give her up, Mom. I can't do it now, either."

My eyebrow twitched. My mother passed me a cup of cooling tea.

"Tiffany gave Kensi her liver," I said.

"Who?"

"Tiffany. She was the anonymous donor."

My mother puffed out a frustrated breath. "And you call yourself a private investigator? I thought your father taught you better."

"Let me guess. Tiffany's not the anonymous donor?"

I watched as my mother's face brightened. "And you know who it is."

At my obvious confusion, she added, "It's Kensi's biological mother."

Laura.

"She never had an appendectomy?"

"No. She tested for compatibility the moment she heard about Kensi, and donated her liver without a second thought. Laura didn't tell you because she didn't want to win her way back to your heart with a liver."

"Fuck. She saved her daughter's life."

"That's right."

And I crushed her in the most fucked-up way. "Fucking Tiff," I growled.

"Drink your tea and get some sleep. We're leaving for Austria in three weeks."

"I can't leave. Not with everything that's going on."

"It's your brother's wedding."

"The girls—"

"The girls will come along on the trip, and they won't know what's happening until you, Laura, and Tiffany figure out your shit and give them the family they deserve."

My face hardened, and my shoulders drooped. "I don't know if I can do that, Mom."

"You're drunk. Sober up, get some sleep, and make a plan. And it better be a good one, Fox Silver, because I want all three of my grandchildren in my life."

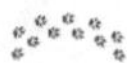

I HIT the pavement at five in the morning, and pushed my feet along the shoreline path until my muscles ached and my lungs burned. My father had always said actions speak louder than words, but the conflict in my chest held no amicable resolution. I didn't know what to do. I'd promised Tiffany submitting Kensi's DNA to the match site was a good thing, but I doubted she'd see it the same way when she found out Laura was Kensi's mother.

I showered after my run, gathered myself, and went over to see my girls for breakfast.

Tiffany opened the front door with a wide smile. "Good morning. I didn't expect you here after the fiasco last night."

I cleared my throat. "I didn't expect to be here either."

"Come in. We're about to sit down for breakfast. Martin made pancakes and omelets this morning. It's like he knew you were coming."

Tiffany's butler made an extravagant breakfast every morning. He'd been with the family since Tiffany was a young girl.

"No need to worry him. I'm sure there's enough. Good morning, girls."

"Daddy!" They each gave me a hug, and I poured myself the third cup of coffee this morning. I shared a plate of pancakes with the girls and waited until they went outside to play.

"You're giving me bad vibes, James."

"Rightfully, so."

She set her coffee aside. "Are you going to sue her for custody of Foxy?"

"I'm not here about Laura, or Foxy. Well, actually, I am here about Laura—and you."

"Okay…"

"How's the wound healing after your surgery?"

Her gaze skidded to the backyard before she made eye contact.

"Great. It's a super-liver."

"Let me see the scar."

"What?"

"I want to ensure it's healing well."

"I already told you it is."

"Because you don't have a scar, do you?"

Her neck went taut.

"Truth, Tiff. I want the truth."

Her eyes glistened. "I wanted you to value me. That's all."

I pinched the bridge of my nose. "You're lying the same way you have before, Tiff, and if I can't trust you… We had an agreement. Full truth and nothing but the truth as co-parents. Your lie about Kensi was supposed to be the last one—"

"This lie was a white lie, and no one got hurt. Kensi still has a super-liver."

"That's not the point I'm trying to make."

Her chin dropped. "I know. I'm sorry."

I drew air in and out of my nose, choosing my words carefully. "We got a match on Kensi's DNA," I said.

"We did? That's great, isn't it? You said it would benefit Kensi."

"I did, and it does. Her birth mother reached out. She asked us to find space in our hearts and lives so she can get to know her daughter."

"What? James, you know what this means, don't you?"

Shit.

My brows twitched toward each other.

"The mother wants her child back."

"She's not like that."

"You know who it is?"

I released a strangled breath. "Her mother was the anonymous liver donor. They took the baby from her at birth and told her the child was stillborn."

Tiffany covered her mouth with her hand. "Oh, my God."

"I know. She's only recently found out her girl is even alive."

"Oh, my God."

"It's messed up. I can't even believe how messed up it is, Tiff. I… I don't know what to do."

"Wait—so who is it?" A worried look coasted over her eyes.

"It's Laura. Laura is Kensi's biological mother."

Tiffany must have held her breath for at least a minute, and when she let it go, she gasped and held it longer.

"How is this possible?"

"I don't know."

"You're sure?"

"Yes."

"How…how did you find out?"

"Laura was told her baby died at birth, like I said. But Kensi's baby bracelet that she had when she was adopted is identical to the one in a photograph I got from Laura's parents. I haven't verified the records yet, but Laura's the anonymous donor who gave Kensi a piece of her liver. I'm confident they're a match, and…"

I rested my elbows on the counter.

"And?"

"And I got a match on Kensi's DNA profile. It's definitely Laura."

"Oh, my God," she whispered again. "Does Laura know?"

"No. I stormed out after you told me about Foxy. I couldn't think about anything else."

Tiffany poured herself a heavy glass of wine and knocked back a few healthy sips. She set the glass down, looked at me, and lifted it back to her lips, taking a few more swigs.

"I'm not losing my daughter," she said. "She may have your son, and you should fight for him, but I'm not giving away my daughter."

"No one's asking you to give Kensi away. You're her mother. We'll always be a family. But I can't keep this secret from Laura for long. And when you look at things from a legal perspective—"

"No, James. No. It's not happening."

"Tiff, you bought a baby on the black market. If this goes to court and they ask for papers, we could lose Kensi. We could gain so much more if we talked to Laura."

"You've already forgiven her for stealing your son?"

"Foxy's a different issue. I'm going to Austria for my brother's wedding this Christmas. Let me take the girls."

"No."

"You can come with us."

"I'm not taking Kensi anywhere near her."

"Sooner or later, we'll have to tell her the truth."

"Make it later."

"If she gets a legal team, she will win her case, and I don't want to involve lawyers. We have to solve this on our own. Tiff, please. Don't you get it? I'm in love with this woman."

The girls laughed outside, blowing soap bubbles into the air.

"Despite what she's done?"

I nodded, and she rose higher in her seat.

"I need time to think. Give me this Christmas with Kensi. I want time with her before everything changes. I'll take her to my sister's."

"The girls would be separated."

"Kensi will be with her cousins. My sister's kids are closer to her age. She'll be fine, and I already saw Laila playing with Foxy, so they'll get along."

She reached for a tissue and blew her nose.

"Tiff—"

"If you're asking me to reason right now, it will not happen, James. I'm not giving up my daughter, and I need time. That's my final offer."

"All right. I'll give you Christmas, and then I'm telling Laura the truth."

I said goodbye to the girls and drove home to decompress. My head was pounding, making concentration impossible. Clouds drifted from the south. The storm crossing the country hit the coast in the evening: rain, followed by freezing rain, followed by snow. All transportation stopped, sealing us in the city. A week passed before I found the nerve to drive to Laura's, but it was Allie who opened the front door.

"Hey, what are you doing here?" I asked.

"Picking up some of my stuff. I assume you're looking for Laura?"

"How is she?"

"Hurt. And she's not here."

"Where is she?"

"With her parents."

"Can you be more specific?" I leaned against the doorframe.

"I thought you were an investigator."

Her words hit me like a punch. She was the second person to question my abilities, and it was pissing me off.

"Laura needs space right now. She's working remotely, and I don't expect her back in the office until after the new year."

Fuck.

"And my little boy? How is he doing?"

"Laura's a wonderful mother, so I'm sure he's fine."

"Are you upset with me, Allie?"

"Yes. You hurt my best friend."

"I know. And I'm sorry. I'm going to do everything I can to get her back."

Her shoulders relaxed. "You need to make things right because I love you both."

"Thank you. I will."

I would move mountains, cross seas, and beg on my fucking knees for forgiveness. I wouldn't give up on the family we all deserved.

Chapter 15

Laura

Thump... thump... thump....

The sound of my beating heart drummed in my ears, deafening the world around me. I sat by the fireplace, sipping hot cocoa. Foxy sat on the rug, playing with the new train set my father had bought. I pictured James beside Foxy every time my son giggled or laughed, and my heart ached. The barbecue was supposed to be our beginning, and now I didn't know how to move forward.

With Christmas one week away, my parents were rushing between work and surgical obligations, but there was never enough time. Though my mother was going on sabbatical, it wasn't happening until the new year, and it looked like I'd be spending Christmas with Foxy, alone. Most of the Silvers, along with Allie, had already left for Austria for Sam and Gabe's wedding. James was his best man. Three weeks ago, I'd been confident we'd spend the holidays together; yet here we were, further apart than ever, and I couldn't find it in my heart to forgive him. I wanted to, but I couldn't. Grudge and stupidity were bitches.

A rare thunderclap broke through the snowstorm and my thoughts. Foxy jumped up.

"What was that?" I opened my eyes wide and gave him a mysterious look.

"Boom." He pointed to the window.

"Say *thunder*."

"Boom," he repeated, and my father entered the room.

"Laura? James is at the front gate."

"What?" I shot off my chair.

"Should we let him in?"

"No. Tell him to leave. I don't want to see him."

"We did that an hour ago. He's still there. He won't leave unless you talk to him."

It's freezing out there.

I puffed out a frustrated breath. "It's not happening."

"He's there with flowers."

"Flowers? He thinks *flowers* will fix everything? I won't have a man treat me the way he did."

"You're just being stubborn and unreasonable."

"Am not."

"Of course you are. Laura, you forgave us an unforgivable mistake. James was angry, rightfully so, just like you were when—"

"I'm not ready."

My mother hopped into the conversation with even more bad news. "I opened the front gate."

"What?"

"I couldn't let him freeze out there, and it's time you two talk. If not for you, do it for Foxy."

The doorbell rang, and my parents stepped aside.

I set my cocoa on the table and stood up, shaking out my arms to get rid of the tension. It wasn't working. I tightened my robe and slipped into my fluffy slippers. My hair resembled the same mess I was inside, but I cared little at the moment.

I lifted my chin just as the doorbell rang again. "Fine. I'll see him. Stay with Foxy?"

My parents nodded, and I went to the front door.

James stood there holding an enormous bouquet of seasonal flowers in his arms, and another one was propped on the ground beside him. I mistakenly drew my gaze over his perfect look, and my knees softened. The long charcoal dress coat over a white sweater carried a vibe. A checkered scarf hung loosely around his neck. His beard was trimmed, and his hair fell to the side. For a moment, I forgot why I was so angry with him and remembered how much I'd missed him.

I pulled the door open wider and cleared my throat. "Come in."

"Thank you for seeing me. These are for you." He handed me the bouquet in his hands, and I set it on the hall table.

"And these are for your parents." He placed the other arrangement on the floor underneath, followed by a few bags filled with what I assumed were Christmas gifts. I held back the smile.

"I thought you were in Austria."

"I'm on my way to the airport right now. The pilot is on standby. I didn't want to leave for Christmas without seeing you. Laura, thank you for what you did for Kensi."

I held my breath.

"My mother told me," he said.

"Right. You're welcome. I'm happy the super-liver is working."

The corner of his mouth lifted. "It's more than working. You saved her life. It's the best Christmas gift I could have received."

"Technically, it happened around Halloween, so—"

"You know what I mean."

My laugh dissipated into awkward tension. James rubbed his hands together and stepped closer. "I'm also sorry for the way I spoke to you and the way I treated you at the barbecue. I had no right. You didn't deserve the hate, and I'm so sorry."

"Thank you."

The deep tone resonated in my bones, and I shivered.

"I never want my son seeing me like that," he whispered.

"Foxy was inside."

The bulge of his throat inched up, then down.

"I also never want the woman I love seeing me like that. I'm not that man. Is Ozzy… I mean Foxy okay?"

I glanced back over my shoulder. "Of course, he's okay. He loves spending time with his grandparents."

"Okay."

"Would you like to see him?"

He smiled. An instant spark of happiness lit up his eyes and my heart. He removed his jacket, and the smell of him hit my lungs. The light scent of pepper and rose sent a delightful reminder through my body.

I hung his jacket on the coat rack and gestured him inside.

He turned around, rubbing the back of his neck. "I don't have long, and I do wish I could stay, but it's my brother's wedding and I'm the best man."

His nerves were cute.

"It's all right. Hey, Foxy." I stepped into the living room, and my parents left to give us privacy. My son turned around, his two front teeth shining brightly, and I picked him up.

I walked over to James, who couldn't stop staring. "Baby, this is your daddy."

James's gaze caught mine, and I whispered, "He likely won't understand."

"You think it would be all right if I held him?"

A sudden warmth filled my chest.

"Yes, of course." I gave him to James, and that warmth turned into something else. This was the moment I'd been waiting for. Maybe I didn't get here the way I'd fantasized, but seeing Foxy in his father's arms was definitely special and worth every heartache.

"Come to Austria for Christmas with me." James held Foxy at the side, over his hip. Seeing them close together like this was nice.

"I can't. My parents are here, and it's their first Christmas with their grandson. And I'm closing a couple of cases while Allie's away."

I didn't tell him about my parents' Christmas full work schedule, or the fact I would finish my work by tomorrow night. The holidays would be quiet and lonely, but I wouldn't be alone. My son reached out to me, and I took him back into my arms, setting him in the playpen. The spark James held in his eyes vanished, and he lowered his head.

"If that's the case, then I'll miss you. I'll miss both of you. Merry Christmas, Laura."

He wrapped his arms around me, and I melted.

"Merry Christmas, James."

I didn't want to let go, but since he had, I did the same.

Feeling like a mess on the outside and inside, I pulled my robe together and walked down the hall, leading the way to the front door. He mentioned nothing about taking Foxy away from me, nor about my lies.

"You look like a hot mama."

The rumble from his chest caught my nape, sprinkling shivers down my back.

"A total MILF."

I turned around before opening the front door, and gripped a clump of my hair bun. "You should have told me sooner you're into hot mess mothers. Have a safe flight, James."

He smiled gently before he turned around and left. The car pulled away, and my inner anger turned into a yearning for more time. I closed the door and picked up the bag of Christmas gifts James left behind. I picked up an envelope with my name written across in neat handwriting and removed two plane tickets for me and Foxy, leaving for Austria in four days.

Cold mountain air filled my lungs, and I squeezed Foxy's hand. When we'd arrived at the airport to check in, I hadn't expected to be flying on a private jet with James's cousin and his girlfriend. Foxy slept through most of the flight, but I could barely close my eyes. Four days ago I'd thought we'd be spending Christmas alone, and now, we were standing in front of Gabe's mansion in the Austrian Alps.

Julian pushed through the door and yelled out, "Surprise!"

I followed Kendra inside. Foxy let go of my hand and ran past the twelve-foot Christmas tree in the foyer straight to his grandmother's open arms. The cabin-styled home was on a smaller scale than the one in Colorado, but just as exquisite, decorated in a winter wonderland theme.

I lowered the bag ffom my shoulder and looked up to the second story, where James was standing beyond the railing. Ice and fire consumed his eyes as I held his gaze. I went further inside and found Allie.

"Oh, my God. I'm so happy you came!" Her eyes flew up to the second story and back to me. "How's everything going?"

"I don't know. I hope I didn't make a mistake coming. Is Tiffany here?"

"No, she's staying with Kensi and her family back in the States."

Someone flicked on a switch, and the fairy lights hung underneath the beams lit up. Evergreen branches with giant red bows hung on the fireplace mantle. Christmas music played in the background, and the smell of cinnamon, pine, and peppermint carried through the air.

"This house is beautiful," I said. "I can't believe I'm going to a wedding tomorrow. I barely had time to pack."

"It's casual and family only."

"There must be thirty people here, at least. How are you feeling? You're showing already." I pointed to her stomach.

"The morning sickness is gone, and the baby's kicking hard."

"I'm so happy for you." I hugged her again.

"There's Mommy." Teresa's voice chirped behind me, and I turned around. My son was gripping a toy bear and a new fox stuffy. His cheeks were flushed, and he was grinning from ear to ear, but with the time change, it was way past his bedtime. His long nap on the plane and the calm ride from the airport had paid off, but my gut told me the crankiness loomed. He let go of his stuffed toys and reached up.

I took him from Teresa's arms. "He's tired. Can you show me where I can put him down?"

"Yes, of course. Come with me. Your bags should be inside the room."

I turned on my heel toward the staircase, scanning for James, but he was no longer on the second floor, and I couldn't find him. I followed Teresa up the stairs and through an extension to the house. We walked across a bridge enclosed in glass. Below us, the outdoor pool glowed bright blue, steaming.

We crossed to the other side, and she pushed the third door open. "This is you and Foxy."

I walked inside, gaping at the beautiful accommodation. A king-sized bed was centered against the wall, leaving enough space for cartwheels. The most beautiful mountain landscape lay beyond the glass window that spanned the wall.

"Your bathroom is past that door. The kitchen fridge is full, toddler snacks are on the counter, and… Well, if you can't find something, just ask. Please make yourself at home."

"Thank you, Teresa."

She hugged me tightly and left. I unpacked our suitcases, bathed Foxy, and put him to bed. He fell asleep in an instant. I took a long, hot shower and slipped into the fluffy robe. I walked out to the bedroom and jumped when I saw James sitting in the chair.

I grabbed the middle of my chest. "Jesus, you nearly gave me a heart attack. You're lucky I don't have my gun with me."

Partially illuminated by a night lamp, he was sitting cross-legged. He dragged his gaze up my body. My skin seared underneath the robe, and I wasn't sure whether it was from the shower or him. Likely, the latter.

"I'm sorry. I didn't mean to scare you." He stood up and crossed the room toward me. "I knocked, but you didn't open the door. And yes, I'm very lucky you don't have a gun."

"I was in the shower." I pulled the robe tighter around me. "What...what are you doing here?"

"I didn't say hello when you arrived. I didn't want to over-whelm you. The family can be a little...overwhelming."

"No." I smiled. "They're perfect."

"Thank you for coming."

"Thank you for inviting me."

"James..."

"Laura..."

We chuckled at the same time.

"You're stressed, and I want you to relax. It's Christmas."

"I'm trying. It's a lot to take in. I'm in a new country with Foxy, and your family's here, and you're here." I shut my mouth to stop the babbling, and turned to observe James focusing on his son.

"He's really mine?" he asked.

I nodded. "He's amazing and bright, and you must hate me for keeping this from you."

"I could never hate you, beautiful." He turned back my way and brushed my hair off my cheek to behind my ear. "I'm just so sorry for the way I reacted and treated you. I never gave you a chance."

"I've wanted to tell you for a long time. Even before the

arrest. But I never found the right time." I sighed. Teresa was so right.

"We have the time right now."

I yawned. "What time is it?"

"About eight o'clock."

"Feels like it's past midnight."

"It's two in the morning back home. You can cure jet lag if you stay up your first night."

"So you're saying I shouldn't go to bed?"

He glanced over my shoulder. "Definitely not that bed."

I bit my lip, and he bent down to my ear. "I don't want Foxy waking up when I fuck you."

His hands snaked down my back to my behind, and my body pressed flat against his. Could this be true? Was this the prequel to makeup sex? If so, I welcomed his forgiving hands squeezing my ass because nothing felt better than his fingers digging into my skin. I closed my eyes, and his lips gently touched mine for a slow, drawn-out kiss. He pulled away, leaving me breathless.

"I love kissing you, and I love having you in my arms."

I loved forgiveness. It closed wounds and opened new doors.

I placed my hand over his heart. "I need you to know I've wanted nothing more than for Foxy to have his father in his life. I just didn't know how to make it happen, and—"

"Allow me to make it happen." He lowered his mouth back to mine for another sensual kiss. My heart felt fuller than ever. So many wrong words had been said, and so many right ones had been stuck in my throat. I pulled away from the kiss and took hold of his face.

"I love you, James," I whispered.

"I love you too, Laura."

Our next kiss intensified. The deep longing inside of me

was soothed by his lips. I couldn't stop kissing him, wanting more and needing more, until he pulled away.

My mouth lifted at the corner. "How will you fuck me without waking Foxy?"

He pointed to a barn door behind him I had thought was decorative.

"My bedroom's behind that door."

"You planned this?"

"It's the perfect setup. Our son has his bed, and we have ours."

"What about the girls? I haven't seen Kensi."

"Laila's in her grandmother's room, and Kensi's spending Christmas with Tiff and her family."

I bit my lower lip. "So, why are we still standing here?"

He relaxed his hold on my hips. "My family wants us for dinner in five minutes."

"More than you want me for dinner?"

"Definitely not, but it's a pre-wedding thing I can't miss. Also, my mother insisted you come."

I loosened my robe tie. "I guess we're doing dinner with your family."

The fabric came apart, and cool air touched my exposed front.

"Laura? What are you doing?"

The robe slipped down my shoulders and fell to the floor, leaving me naked.

"Getting ready," I said. "For dinner."

I strolled to my suitcase and bent over for a pair of panties. Eighty-seven percent of couples failed in the foreplay department, and I didn't want to become part of that statistic.

"Do you want us to be late?"

"Of course, not. I want to make sure you don't lose your appetite after dinner."

"I doubt that will happen. For the love of my dick, get dressed," he said in a hushed voice, adjusting his hard-on.

I picked a pair of sexy panties, James fastened my bra, and I slipped into a zip-up dress. I applied a dusting of blush to my cheeks. The charcoal mascara brought out my eyes, and the new coral blush I'd bought for the occasion plumped my lips. I walked out of the bathroom in my high heels.

"You look stunning," he said.

"Wait—I can't leave Foxy."

"Lucky for us, I installed a camera." He pointed to the room's corner ceiling. "We'll have eyes on him the entire time, and Emma's promised to stay here after dinner. It's a twenty-second walk to the dining room. I timed it. If he opens his eyes, I'll be here in five through a shortcut."

I glanced over to Foxy, then back to James.

"I promise he's safe."

"You've really thought this through."

Joy welled in my heart, and the warmth swimming through my veins was replaced with love.

"You have no idea," he said.

We walked into the dining room holding hands. They had set up a long U-shaped table with our hosts in the middle. A unanimous family cheer greeted us at the entrance, and we took our seats. James set up his phone with a live video of Foxy sleeping, and I relaxed.

"Welcome to Austria." Gabe poured me a shot glass of vodka.

"I don't hold my liquor well," I said.

"This stuff is good. And you're only having one. For Sam's and my health. She can't drink and neither can Allie, so you're it."

I lifted the glass so he could pour. "Atta girl. You're going to fit right in. James, I already love her."

"Me too," James said openly, and Teresa smiled from across

the table. Laila sat beside her grandmother, who plated her dinner.

We clinked our glasses to Gabe and Sam's health, and I threw back the shot. The vodka flew even more smoothly than Gabe had promised. Over the dinner hour, he convinced me to have three more shots, but it could have been four because the room was spinning when I stood up after the last one.

"Whoa."

James held me by the elbow. "Are you all right?"

"I have to pee-pee."

I thought I was whispering, but apparently, I wasn't, because a few chuckles resonated around me.

"I'll go with you. See you all in the morning. Don't stay up too late, Gabe, or you'll miss your wedding."

"I'll drag him out of bed if I have to," Sam replied.

James took me under my arm and led me through the maze of a mansion he said he could run through in five seconds. It felt like forever until we reached our room. Foxy was sleeping soundly in bed. James covered him, and I went to the washroom.

Thankfully, my bladder held the liquor better than my head. I washed myself and returned to the bedroom, where James was sitting in his boxer briefs beside Foxy, convincing me there was nothing sexier than a half-naked father sitting on the bed with his son. Soft light glowed over his yummy muscles. I dragged my gaze over his body, slithering over the V-cut between his hips. The path up took even longer until I found his blazing blue eyes. Jesus, was I ever grateful I'd agreed to this trip.

"Does he always sleep so peacefully?" he asked. "I can't stop staring at him."

I stumbled forward, grateful that one of us was sober while in the same room with our son.

"The solid sleeping is recent, which is great news for us." I yawned and turned around. "Can you unzip me?"

"My pleasure."

The dress loosened, and I slipped out of the fabric, turning in the spot. "I can't find my pajamas."

James chuckled. "Here, let me help. Stay still."

He flicked my bra clasp open, and my breasts spilled out. The touch of his fingers seared along my skin, but I couldn't concentrate on their igniting path south because James slipped his t-shirt over my head. His spicy scent brought an overwhelming comfort, and the next thing I knew, I was in his bed and in his arms, falling asleep.

Chapter 16

James

"Say *Dada*," I whispered to Foxy as I held him in my arms on the chair by the window. "Dada. I'll take *Daddy* as well."

He traced his finger over the fog in the window's corner. I took his little finger and outlined a heart. Hot coffee was steaming in the cups behind us and fresh croissants waited at the side. Foxy had woken up at four in the morning. I changed him and made him oatmeal in the kitchen. The great thing about a large family was that everyone was eager to help, especially the two pregnant women, Sam and Allie.

"Let Laura sleep. It's about time she had a break. Do you know how many cases she closed between Thanksgiving and now? Twelve," Allie had said in the kitchen earlier.

"What? Why didn't she tell me?"

"Laura doesn't brag, and she doesn't ask for help when she's with Foxy. You two make up last night?" She'd wiggled her brows.

I wish we had.

I glanced at her sideways, then ignored her question and headed back to the room with Foxy.

Unfortunately, Laura had a few too many shots last night

with my brother and passed out in my arms. I held her like I'd held no woman before, promising myself to never let her go. Looking at her now, curled underneath my covers, was a Christmas wish come true.

Foxy hopped into my lap, and I gave him a piece of a croissant. He was one of the best fucking things I ever made.

"Say *Dada*. Da-da."

"Mama." He pointed to the bed, and Laura stirred. She pushed the covers away and shifted to her side, hugging my pillow between her legs. The sun shone over her naked ass, and I got an instant hard-on.

It was the third time she'd flashed me that morning.

"Mama," Foxy said louder, and she shot up, scanning the room, trying to get her bearings, then checked her clothing, which was nothing more than my t-shirt. When she saw me with Foxy in my lap, her fear settled, and she bit back on her wide grin.

I stood up with our son in my arms and walked over to the bed.

"Good morning, Mommy," I said.

"Good morning." She reached for Foxy, and I set him beside her. "Good morning, sunshine. How are you?"

"He had breakfast three hours ago."

"What? What time is it? The wedding—"

"Don't worry, we'll make it. The back yard isn't far."

"How long do I have?"

"A couple of hours."

She fell to her pillow with relief and then shot back up. "Does he need changing? He's been potty training, so he's usually good—"

"Laura, relax. He's fine. He woke up a few hours ago and climbed into our bed. It was cute."

I lifted him out of bed and turned him so he could see his

new toys in the play area I'd set up. I might have gone over-board, but then again, I was catching up.

"Choo-choo." Foxy pointed to the train set I'd bought him for Christmas and which we'd set up after breakfast, together. I set him down in the play area and returned to Laura's side.

"Looks like Santa came early," she said.

"I couldn't help it, but if we play it right, Santa can definitely come again."

"Will I get to sit on his lap this year?" she murmured, writhing against my cock.

"Only if you promise to sit on his face."

Her cheeks flushed a beautiful pink, and she pulled her hand through her hair. "I'm so sorry about last night. I warned Gabe about the drinks."

"It was nice seeing you relaxed."

"I can usually hold myself better than that. Thank you for helping me to bed, though I don't quite remember how I got here."

"Jet lag and alcohol don't go well together. Do they, Foxy?"

Our son looked up grinning. "Choo, choo."

"Thank you for making him feel so comfortable. James," she said, curling her lower lip inward, "are we okay?"

I took her hand in mine. "You tell me."

She smiled. "Yeah, I think we're okay."

"If we don't want to be late, we'd better get going. Also, my mother brought a new outfit for Foxy for the wedding. He'll match Laila."

She pushed her hands underneath the covers and checked around her mid-section. "Where are my panties?"

"You took them off."

"Oh, my God. I think I had a wet dream. Sixty-eight percent of women have wet dreams."

"You quote stats when you're nervous. Don't be. By tonight, you won't need wet dreams."

Her eyes popped out like two saucers. "I'm going to your brother's wedding. I didn't even bring a proper dress. Why didn't I bring a proper dress?"

"Relax, Laura. Anything you wear will be fine. It's casual."

"Silvers don't do casual."

I laughed. "Yes, we do. Now get dressed. We'll be in the family room for breakfast."

I kissed her once more and left with Foxy. He held my hand, hopping across the glass bridge with a giggle. God, he was such a good kid.

My father set Laila down and she ran to my side. "Daddy."

I lifted her high in the air and Foxy tugged on my shirt. I crouched to the ground, secured him in my other arm, and stood up with both kids.

"Well, isn't this a nice picture? How's Laura?" my mother asked.

"Getting over jet lag."

"I just spoke with Tiffany and Kensi. It's snowing back home. They're taking the kids for a sleigh ride."

"Have they left yet?"

"No, she's waiting for your call."

"All right. Thank you." I set the kids down in the play area and excused myself to make a call to my daughter.

"Good morning, sweetheart," I said after Tiffany handed her the phone.

"Mommy's taking me on a sleigh to see Santa, and she says he has a big bag of toys this year because kids with super-livers get special gifts."

"Is that so?"

"And we're going to feed Rudolph, Dasher, Dancer, Prancer, Vixen, Comet, Cupid, Donner, and Blitzen."

"You're not giving them your breakfast, are you?"

"No, Mommy made me a big breakfast because other mothers can't cook."

"What?" I'd never seen Tiffany cook in her life.

"My mommy's the best, and there's no other mommy I want in the world."

Wonderful. Tiffany must have been whispering into Kensi's ear. Her insecurity unnerved me. I had yet to figure out how to introduce Laura to her daughter without my ex losing her shit.

I missed Kensi, but it sounded like she was having a wonderful time.

"You make sure you eat all your veggies to keep up with that super-liver."

"I will, Daddy. I love you."

"I love you too, my bug. Merry Christmas."

We hung up. I looked out the window at the picture-perfect day. Blue skies, snow-covered mountains, and no wind. Today could be perfect if Kensi were here. Maybe one day, we could all spend Christmas together.

I turned around as Laura entered the room.

"Holy crap."

She was wearing a hip-hugging white sweater with matching leggings and looked absolutely stunning. She'd pinned her hair halfway up, and I couldn't take my eyes off of her through my brother's wedding. The minister prompted me twice for the wedding bands. I barely remembered the ceremony.

We spent the day eating and dancing. Laila fell asleep in my arms as I danced with Laura and Foxy napped on the couch by the fireplace. My mother sat beside him reading a book. I set Laila down by my mother's other side and took Laura back to the floor.

"I didn't think I would spend Christmas with you," she said. "I had an amazing day today."

"The day isn't over yet. Unless you're tired…"

"Not at all. There's so much adrenaline in my veins, I couldn't sleep if I tried."

Her admission sounded like the perfect invitation and opportunity.

"That's good. We're going tobogganing when the kids wake up."

"And after?" She drew closer in my hold, pressing her body against mine.

"Christmas Eve dinner." My chest rumbled.

She lifted to her tiptoes and whispered in my ear, "And after?"

Her seductive voice held carnal promises.

"Christmas Eve dessert. In our bed."

"I better not miss that."

"I won't let you."

The song finished, and we continued dancing until chattery gossip caught my ear.

"James and Laura are next," Emma squealed. "There are so many weddings to plan, I'm losing count."

I took Laura under my arm, and we sat by the windows. Heavy snowflakes fell from the sky.

"Don't worry, Ems, I'll give you a long heads-up—because I'm not getting married anytime soon."

An unexpected sting pierced my chest. "You wouldn't marry me?"

She looked up. "Are you asking?"

"No. It's hypothetical."

Her eyes softened, yet my heart still ached at her words.

"I can do better than hypothetical. I love you—"

"But?"

"I was going to say, I love you, *and* I want you and Foxy forever in my life. I also have a little girl missing out there, and I can't imagine concentrating on anything else before I find her. Have you found anything?"

I swung my head in a swift *no*, the lie burning through my bones.

"I can't believe the match didn't reply." Her shoulders drooped. "What's the point of matching if you don't reply?"

"Don't give up so soon. It's Christmas, and it's the season of miracles. Let's not be sad. Santa's coming this evening."

She checked over her shoulder, and her eyes glazed over with desire.

"Does that mean I'm coming too?"

"Hypothetically, it's a definite yes." I kissed her.

The sound of her chuckle eased my guilt, but only the truth could erase it. I pulled away.

"The kids are getting dressed to build a snowman."

She stepped away but kept my hand in hers. "Are we in an avalanche zone?"

"No."

"Then let's build a snowman."

Thick snow fell from the sky as we rolled heavy balls throughout the powder. I pushed the spheres while Laura made snow angels with the kids. Foxy came up to the last one and helped me build the snowman's head. His cheeks were red and his eyes shone brightly as he grinned from ear to ear.

"Say *Dada*," I whispered.

He stopped, looked up, and repeated, "Dada."

My heart nearly ripped out of my chest.

"Laura, did you hear that? He said Dada."

I lifted him into my arms and spun in a circle. He tilted his head back and squealed, catching snowflakes on his tongue.

"Dada, Dada!"

I couldn't wait for Laura to reunite with her daughter.

Laura got up from making snow angels with Laila, and they trod through the snow. We finished making the snowman, with a carrot for his nose and charcoals for the eyes and mouth. I cut off two lower branches from a spruce for the arms.

The kids jumped up, clapping, and my parents opened the

front door. My father wrapped his arm around my mother as she took in the scene with her hand placed over her heart.

"It's almost suppertime," she called out.

I lifted Laila and Foxy into my arms, and we went inside. We changed the kids out of their snowsuits, dressed, and joined the family for a beautiful dinner. They had set the long table with poinsettias and flickering candles. My mouth watered and my stomach grumbled. I patted Olivier on his back, thanking him for the beautiful dinner. The chef was truly a master. Joy and love filled the room. After dinner, I changed into a Santa suit for the annual reading of the Christmas story, then listened to everyone's wishes as they sat on my lap. I winked across the room to where Laura was sitting beside her best friend, and she lifted her glass of eggnog in a cheer.

I wiggled my finger for her to come hither. She whispered something into Allie's ear and strolled straight to my lap. I secured her in my arms and nuzzled my white beard against her ear.

"Merry Christmas, Laura."

"Merry Christmas, sexy Santa."

"Do you remember what happened last time you had spiced eggnog?"

"Of course, I do. That's why I plan to stay sober. This one's alcohol-free, and please tell me you're bringing the Santa costume to bed."

"Maybe another time. Tonight, Santa intends to stay very naked."

She shifted in my lap, and my dick hardened.

"Remember what you asked for the last time you sat on my lap?"

"I believe that was a long and naughty list."

"Maybe this year Santa can cross some of those things off."

She covered her mouth with her hand as if someone could

read her lips. Emma was a lip reader, but she was the only one in the family.

"Like me licking melted orange chocolate off your dick?"

"I'll take anything that has to do with my cock and your mouth, Ms. Young. Consider the wish granted. Anything else you'd like to ask of Santa?"

"Yes." Her face fell serious. "Please give me an answer about my daughter."

My jaw set hard underneath the beard, and I was grateful for the coverage because the guilt must have been painted on my face.

"I'll do everything in my power to get you an answer."

I checked whether the kids were looking, pulled my beard down, and kissed her hard. She jumped off my lap and strolled back to Allie's side with a spring in her step.

I couldn't fucking wait to devour her.

By nine o'clock, the party had moved to the platform over the outdoor pool. We took the kids to bed in Laura's room and she went to the bathroom to shower. I shed the Santa suit and typed out the message I'd been constructing on my phone. I removed my boxer briefs and joined her underneath the stream.

"What if they wake up?" she asked.

Steam rose, and I submerged underneath the water.

"I left the door open. We'll hear them."

I slid down her body to my knees, my hands grazing along her sides. She gripped my shoulders when I reached for her belly button and held her breath. I kissed back up over her healing scar. The red line would fade with time, but it was the most beautiful mark I had seen on any woman in my life. I kissed a line down her belly, along the water's flow.

She braced her hands flat against the wall. I squeezed her ass tight in one palm and parted her waxed pussy with my tongue. Her essence flowed over my lips, and I closed over her clit. Her beautiful moans fed my hunger as I balanced her desire between flicks and kisses.

I'd told her I'd fuck her, but I couldn't. Not yet. I took my time kissing her, touching her skin, and testing her limits. I took much more pleasure in discovering her body all over again. I traced over her soft skin with my tongue as water dripped over my face. The floral soap scent blended with her sweet arousal.

"Please, James. I... I need to... Oh, my God."

Her moans encouraged my tongue strokes as her pussy swelled between my lips. The first jitter spasmed through her body, and I sealed my mouth around her clit. Her flesh pulsed against my tongue. I looked up over the streaming water as she clasped her hand over her mouth, holding back the scream. She shook in my hold and I closed my eyes, allowing her pleasure to float over my tongue, sucking the last tension held by her orgasm until she let go again. Five tongue strokes later, her knees softened, and she fell into my arms.

"Hey there, beautiful. You all right?"

Her eyes held a dreamy look. "I think I just had one of the best days of my life."

"But Ms. Young, we haven't even started checking things off your list. Besides, I would love to invite you to an orgasmic symphony."

Chapter 17

Laura

A symphony: the strumming of a man's finger along your skin to the tune of an orgasm.

I tingled all over as James carried me across the room. Our kids were peacefully asleep in my bed. He set me naked over the cold sheets of his bed and took my lips in a drawn-out kiss. His hands ventured over my body, memorizing every inch. He kissed each freckle, the scars from my surgery, and old bullet marks. The tender kisses he scattered over my skin danced like flickers of fire. I closed my eyes, enjoying the teasing build and the warmth swooshing through my veins, but I needed more. I wanted him inside me. I needed him inside me.

"How long does a prelude last?" I purred, my voice getting lost between heavy breaths.

He pulled his mouth away from my nipple and looked up. A sly smile stretched across his face as he reached between my legs. "Let me check."

His fingers slid through my folds to my soaked opening and deep inside my pussy. My lower back arched. "James—"

"We're almost ready."

"Almost?"

I writhed over the sheets as the rhythmic pumping of his

fingers intensified. His experienced lips played over my mound, hovering awfully close to the throb.

"Ready, swollen, and wet," he murmured over my pussy, and I trembled with fresh arousal.

"No, not this." I pulled on his head. "I want you inside me."

But he kept steady over my clit, slowly licking around the swell.

"I need more of… Oh… Oh, my…"

What was he doing?

He withdrew his fingers and lifted my feet to his shoulders in a position more suitable for a gynecological visit. I resisted until his tongue rimmed my opening. I gave into his skilled mouth.

Jesus Christ. He was doing it again. He was going to make me come.

"James, please."

He pulled away, set my legs down on the sheets, and sat up.

We weren't done, were we? "What are you doing?"

He opened the night table drawer and removed a container. The jar released a delicious aroma.

"I infused the Nutella with orange flavor. Your favorite."

He stuck a finger inside, scooped up a dab, and brought it to my mouth. I parted my lips and licked off the chocolate, sucking off his finger like it was his dick.

"Naughty." His crooked smile hid promises. He lowered his lips to mine and kissed me deeply.

"You just want the chocolate," I giggled against his mouth.

"Wrong answer. I just want you."

James scooped another dab and circled his finger around my nipples. I writhed on the bed as he painted my body in beautiful patterns. The left nipple became the center of a flower, and a heart decorated my navel. The touch of his finger sizzled, yet it wasn't enough. I wanted his hands on me and his dick inside me. I wiggled over the bed with impatience.

"James…"

He finally lowered the container and lay back.

"We're done?"

"No, baby. We're just beginning."

He flipped me over to straddle his face so quickly, I barely had a chance to catch my balance. As my knees sank into the sheets near his head, I braced my hands on the headboard. I looked down at my body and the chocolate smears until I found his grinning face below my pussy. He pulled his tongue over my slit, and I quivered with pleasure. He circled his tongue over my flesh, watching my reaction. I dug my knees into the sheets, opening myself.

His mouth returned to my spot, and I grasped my breasts, pinching my nipple on the chocolate-free breast. The air thickened with the scent of chocolate, us, and sex. The sound of his slurping mouth and the timing of his licks had my hips gyrating above his face. A sudden burst of pleasure shot through my body, and I clasped my hand over my mouth, holding back the scream. My eyes flew wide open, and my whole body trembled as James licked through my growing orgasm. I needed him to stop so I could catch a breath, but I wanted the bliss to continue. Dazed and bubbling with satisfaction, I pulled away and lowered myself to his body, smearing the chocolate over his skin. I lay over his chest with my legs parted at his hips.

"Slide lower," he breathed into my ear.

"What about a condom?"

"Condom? I'm gonna fucking cum in your sweet pussy until you drip, so we can make more beautiful babies like Foxy. Maybe we can make a little brother for him?"

God, he was so hot. I couldn't say no to this man now…Or ever. He'd forgiven me and loved me as hard as I loved him.

He nudged my opening, and I parted my legs, sliding onto his cock. He brought me close and rolled us over. Skin to skin, we held each other as his hips moved back and forth. The melted chocolate between us was a mess, but it was a beautiful mess. His lips completely took over my mouth, his tongue dancing along mine with seductive strokes. A harder thrust of his hips freed my mouth, and I sucked in air. His fervent jabs hit my depth and his lips parted, releasing a low grunt every time. He was getting close, which turned up my heat. Arousal tore through my blood and he flipped me to the side, plunging deeper and rougher, the friction igniting my clit.

My leg flew over his and he scissored me, trapping my crotch between his thighs, and thrust at an angle that pushed us both over the edge. He stilled inside me, his cock pulsing within me while I trembled through my orgasm. I bit on the sheets. His grunt echoed through the room as he settled deep inside me, finding his release. Five breaths later, he withdrew and lay back on the bed. Short orgasms sucked for men.

The drip of his semen along my thigh put me on high alert. This need for him to remain in my life forever warmed my chest. I wanted to raise a family with him, and if we were lucky, Foxy would have a little brother or sister. I turned around on the bed, lifted my legs high in the air, and propped them against the headboard.

"What are you doing?" He laughed.

"Making beautiful babies. Twenty-three percent of couples struggle with fertility."

Our kids stirred in the bed in my room, and James rose to check on them. I watched him walk in the dim light—a fine specimen. His calves flexed and his ass tightened with each step. The muscles on his back twisted, and my belly stirred with fresh need. I didn't want this night to end. James washed the chocolate off his hands, covered Foxy with his blanket, shifted Laila closer to the middle of the bed, and then walked back to our room. His frontal stroll, as impressive as his back, had me twisting in the sheets again. I gripped the covers as he strolled my way. He held his head high and his shoulders wide. I admired his beautiful body from the top down, his strong abs supporting the narrowing rack of ribs and the V-line of hair leading straight down between his hips. I licked my lips.

"We made a mess." He pulled on the chocolate-smeared sheets. "You know, you don't have to do that. My swimmers are strong. Foxy took one shot, without trying. And if it doesn't happen the first time, we'll have fun trying again."

I lowered my legs and lifted myself to a sitting position.

"Why don't you go shower? And I'll change the sheets," he said.

"Are we going to sleep?"

He bent down until his mouth hovered above mine. "There's always an encore, my love. Always."

He kissed me, sucking on my lower lip, and the first wave of fresh arousal trickled between my thighs. Or maybe it was his semen? I got up off the bed and he gently slapped my ass. I hastened to the shower, grateful the kids slept like rocks. We'd be zombies by the morning, but it was worth it, and strong coffee cured everything.

I stepped underneath the shower stream. Chocolate dripped down my body, its sweet aroma rising on the steam. I washed my hair and was just rinsing when James stepped inside, in his godly chocolate glory.

I removed the showerhead from its handle and aimed it at his chest. More chocolate flowed down the drain, revealing his glowing tan. I pressed the soap dispenser and brought my hand to his chest, slowly circling over the pecs, washing the last of the chocolate away. I continued down his torso before crouching. His cock stood tall, heavy, and inviting. I wrapped my fingers around him, pumped twice, and looked up to meet his hooded eyes. I kissed the tip and watched as he sucked in air. His ribs rose and his jaw tensed. He pushed his cock into my mouth and I took him to the back of my throat. The thick vein running up his length pulsed along my lip. The rippled flesh was smooth and warm, with chocolate essence on his skin.

He held my head steady, his fingers gripping my hair. I drew my hand up his inner thigh and cupped his balls. Pleasure vibrated off his lips, followed by an aching grunt for more. I held him firm, bobbing my head and tightening my lips. His taste dominated my mouth as I found an irresistible rhythm.

"Fuck." He spat shower water through gritted teeth. His dick pulsed once more in my mouth, and his hands stopped my head movement. A jerk later, he found his release.

Was that our encore? Because it sure felt like it.

I drained his last drops, stood up, and tilted my head back to the shower. Water streamed down my face, rinsing him from my mouth. James joined me underneath the stream and kissed me in that torturously slow way he began his preludes.

Oh, God, he was getting hard again, and I, too, was becoming tingly. His hands grazed over my body as he kissed me. The tingle flowing down my spine spread through me as I realized I could never get enough of him. He dragged his lips away and braced his forehead against mine.

"Let's go back to bed. I can't get enough of you."

"Sounds like a perfect plan. I can't believe the kids are sleeping through this."

"We've trained them well."

I snorted.

We stepped out of the shower, dried ourselves, and slipped underneath the fresh sheets, where we did everything James had promised… And a little more. He strummed on my instruments like he was solely responsible for an orchestra. I dozed off early in the morning when the sun showed its first light in the night sky.

"We should get dressed. The kids are going to wake soon."

"We pulled an all-nighter?"

"Apparently so, Ms. Young. Come with me. I have a surprise for you."

"A surprise?"

"It's Christmas morning, and this family gets gifts on Christmas Eve and Christmas Day. We're going to need a lot of coffee."

He kissed me, and I followed him out of bed to the closet. He took out four matching outfits for us and the kids, all white and silver-gray, and handed me mine.

"Merry Christmas, Laura."

I took the hanger with the lovely sweater and pants.

"Thank you. They're beautiful."

When I lifted my gaze, he was holding another gift bag. I laughed. "I get the feeling you enjoy this?"

He grinned. "I love it. There's something in there from Grace Wagner. It will go well underneath the sweater and pants. I picked it out. If you don't like it, I have another one under the Christmas tree."

"The giant one in the foyer?"

"I recommend opening the gifts in private. We should get going. The family likes to start things off early on Christmas Day."

I loved the excitement in his voice. I adored his efforts to involve us all in the family activities. They restocked a table with snacks and drinks from morning to night. Long gone were the days of burnt turkey dinners and over-salted green beans because the gourmet food the Silvers prepared was of MasterChef quality.

I yawned. "I'm starting things off with a coffee. Double espresso."

"Note to self: infuse Nutella with coffee."

I snickered. At least, my fatigue gave him a chuckle.

The kids woke up, and we dressed them in matching snowflake pajamas and walked hand in hand to the family room. Foxy held my hand and Laila's, who was also gripping her dad's fingers. Everyone turned as we entered. Someone snapped a picture of our family by the fireplace. Teresa wiped away a few tears, and Jacob stood tall with pride. Flames crackled behind us, and the smell of freshly-baked cinnamon rolls filled the room. The family gathered around the Christmas tree, and Emma dug underneath the branches, pulling out gifts. The merry chatter and excitement, warmth, tears, hugs, and love nearly completed me. I'd heard about this kind of Christmas since childhood, and now Foxy would have it all. Only one thing could make this day perfect: my missing daughter.

"James, I didn't get you a gift."

"Are you kidding me? You brought back my son. I couldn't have asked for anything better."

He wrapped his arm around my shoulder and brought me to his side. Laila and Foxy joined their grandmother by the tree and began opening the mountain of gifts. Sam and Gabe had already left for their honeymoon, and we had a day filled with charades and sleigh rides. Hopefully, somewhere in between there, I could find a moment to nap.

I never found that moment. James kept us busy until night-time, when we fed the kids, bathed them, and I collapsed on the bed beside them. He disappeared into the bathroom. Somewhere in the distance, I heard the distinct sound of a new phone notification, but I couldn't open my eyes. My eyelids felt too heavy, and my body was so spent I couldn't lift myself off the bed. I was paying the price for staying up for over forty hours, and my brain was barely working.

I don't remember how I woke in his arms, wearing his t-shirt and secure with his warm body behind me. He draped his arm over my front and cupped my breast. He pinched my nipple, and I moaned, wiggling my behind over his hard dick. I parted my legs, and he slid inside me from behind. He pumped slowly and steadily, our bodies in sync. His hand roamed over my skin, caressing my breasts and keeping the arousal on fire. We made love until I fell asleep with his dick and cum inside me.

I woke up at noon the next day in an empty bed. The kids were gone, and the other bed had been made. The man was a superhero. I hopped out of bed, cleaned myself up, and dressed before calling my parents with Christmas wishes. Today was the only evening they had off work.

I turned on my phone, and a new notification pinged for my email. I opened the app, and my hands began shaking as I opened the link and read the most beautiful message. My legs ached as I raced to the family room, covering the twenty-second walk in five, the way James had said he would. I stopped in front of him and gasped for breath. The room spun, and my vision blurred. I pulled my hand across my eyes.

"Laura? What's the matter?" He gripped me by my arms, and I let the sobs break through my breaths. Tears dripped down my cheeks in streams.

"Talk to me, Laura." His hold tightened.

I caught my breath and straightened. A beautiful wave of relief spread through my body.

"I don't know what you did, Santa, but it worked. I'm going to see my daughter."

Chapter 18

James

Laura handed me her phone, her hands shaking. I read over the message I'd written to her on the DNA match site.

Dear Laura,

Thank you for reaching out to our family about our daughter. We're sorry to hear your baby was taken from you. We are currently away on Christmas holidays with the kids, but we're looking forward to meeting you early in the New Year. When we return to the country, we will reach out.

Merry Christmas.

Sincerely,

The Millers

If I did things right, maybe Laura wouldn't bring charges against Tiffany for buying Kensi on the black market. Maybe Laura wouldn't sue for damages, or worse, custody. Putting my daughter, our daughter, through the courts wasn't an option; just the idea made me sick to my stomach. I didn't know if I could pull it off. I just knew that I had to. The resolution between Tiffany and Laura would simply have to be an amicable one.

"I thought I was dreaming. This isn't a dream, is it?"

She paced along the wall of windows, chewing on her nails. There was so much I had to tell her. I'd made a mistake supporting Tiffany's lies. Had I spoken up sooner, perhaps Laura would have found her daughter earlier and had a chance as a mother. But Kensi loved Tiffany. She looked up to her mother like all seven-year-old girls did. She was the only mother my girl had ever known. Still, Laura deserved the truth.

"No, you weren't dreaming. The message is there."

"We should fly back home now. Tomorrow. Please, make it happen tomorrow." Her hollow eyes begged. I would lose this fight if I lost her attention.

"You don't want to miss your best friend's wedding, babe." I walked up behind her and wrapped my arms around her waist, staring at the snow-covered valley below. "How can I make you relax? We have time."

I grazed my lips along her ear cartilage and down her neck, kissing the soft spot underneath her jawline. Emma was doing crafts with the kids. My mother was helping Olivier, a family friend who catered our Christmas and wedding, in the kitchen, and my father was smoking a cigar outside with my uncle. Tristan had taken Allie out skiing. Laura's best friend had no clue they were getting married on New Year's Eve, and we had time alone.

"Is that a bruise?" She pointed to my arm.

"You roughed me up last night and the day before."

"Me?" Her eyes twinkled.

"Yes, you." I swept her hair off her neck for better access, but she pulled away.

"You can find the Millers, can't you?"

It seemed my lips no longer worked on my woman.

"We should wait to hear from them and set up a meeting. What's the point of finding their empty house while they're on vacation? Besides, do you know how many Millers there are?"

She chewed on her fingernails, and I gripped her hand, cutting off access.

"Maybe you're right. I just can't wait."

"You've been patient so far."

"It's a façade. Sixty-seven percent of people have a façade."

I turned her around in my arms and lifted her chin. Her beautiful eyes met mine.

"I'm not used to being this broken."

"The Millers…" I swallowed past the scratch in my throat, wondering whether she'd connected the last name to Tiffany. "They replied, which shows they have good intentions. Yesterday, we didn't know if your girl was even alive…" My fucking throat tightened. I couldn't wait to get rid of my own façade. "… and today, we know she's with a good family and they take care of her. They're on Christmas holidays."

My heart hammered in my chest, but she let go of the tension in her neck. "I guess that's a good thing. Maybe you're right, but you're going to have to hold my attention, which won't be easy—"

"Will my dick not do?"

She squirmed in my hold. "Alcohol and dick. Sounds perfect, but you need to be more creative."

"More creative than orange chocolate?"

"Way more. Hold my attention."

"Challenge accepted, Ms. Young. The kids are feeding the reindeer with my parents today. Julian's out shopping with Kendra. Tristan's romancing Allie, and… I'm just trying to say you'll be able to scream."

Blood rushed south at the thought of her voice singing as I brought her undone. Someone should have handcuffs in this house.

"How are your parents?"

She froze. "Oh, my God. I totally forgot to call. I saw the message, and I ran over and… I can't think."

"Okay, okay. Go call them now, and then meet me in the bedroom."

I physically turned her to the library where she could find some peace, then helped my mother get the kids dressed for outside. Luckily for me, someone from my kinky family had gifted me a bondage set underneath the tree with a note: "Don't fuck this up."

I chuckled and dimmed the lights, checking the last-minute details. Rose petals were scattered over the bedsheets, and candlelight glowed over the furniture. My heart gave a kick underneath my ribcage, and I steadied my breaths.

Laura stopped three feet inside the room and spread her fingers out in a fan against her breastbone.

"James?"

I dangled the set of fluffy handcuffs from my finger. "Are you ready to scream, baby?"

We spent the remaining days taking the kids on the toboggan, making snow angels, and sipping hot chocolate by the fireplace. On New Year's Eve, Allie married my cousin Tristan. Laura stood beside her best friend as the maid-of-honor, and our kids carried the rings. I imagined the two of us up at the altar one day soon—once Laura forgave me. She'd agreed to move in with me so we could raise Foxy together. Standing at that altar, I secretly vowed to never break my family apart, nor let them go ever again.

We took a private flight home the first week of January. Laura had questioned me about the Millers throughout the trip, but I couldn't give her the answers she sought. Her knees bounced as we drove from the airport. I parked my car in front of my house, and my mother came outside to get the kids. Laura pulled on the door handle, but I stopped her.

"Wait, we need to talk."

"That never sounds good."

"No, this is good. I have news for you—"

"You found the Millers? I don't have to wait until they get in touch with me?"

"Technically, not the Millers. Hold on, let me try this differently. I have something for you."

I reached inside a bag behind the passenger seat and removed the rectangular box from a bag. I set the bag her parents had given me on her lap.

"This is your daughter's baby box, with her first nightgown and a photograph."

Her face fell ashen and her gaze dropped to the box, her chin trembling.

"A picture? You have a picture of her?"

I held my breath through her shaky ones. "Yes, and there's more."

"More?"

I gripped her hand with mine, but she brought it immediately back to the box. "Promise me you won't panic."

"You're making me nervous, James. What is it?"

"Your daughter is inside, waiting to see you."

"What?"

"She's not aware you're her biological mother, and—"

"What?"

"I said, your daughter is inside—"

"I heard what you said. You *found* her? How?"

"I had some help. Laura, this little girl doesn't know what happened to her at birth."

"I won't say anything. I... I just want to see her. Is this really happening?"

Her teeth flashed white and broad. I nodded and let go of the square box on her lap. She lifted the lid and parted the tissue paper, removing the baby's gown. I was unsure how she could see through the tears. She wiped them away on her sleeve, set the garment aside, and brought the photograph closer to her face.

"That bracelet looks familiar."

"It was a gift from your parents at birth. It was our only connection, and it's how we found your girl."

"What? I thought—"

"Come inside, baby."

I opened the car door and walked around the front to help her out. She secured the box underneath her arm and barely held herself steady, focusing on the home's entrance. I helped her down the path and led her to the partially-open front door. Her knees wobbled with each shaky step.

I pushed the door open and met my father in the foyer. He checked his watch.

"What's wrong?" I asked.

Laura slipped out of my grasp.

"She's not here yet. She's running late."

I checked my watch. Tiffany never ran late.

"Did you call?"

"Of course, I called. Four times. She's not answering. She's probably driving."

I pulled my fingers through my hair.

"Who?" Laura asked, but I was already on my phone, calling Tiff's number.

The doorbell chimed through the house, and the ominous sound set me on alert. Then my phone screamed with an ear-pearling tone, followed by my father's phone and everyone else's. I shook my head in denial as my father opened the front door to a police officer.

"Mr. James Silver?"

"Yes, that's me." I stepped forward.

"Ms. Tiffany Miller sent me."

"Where is she? What happened?"

A chorus of phones rang with the ear-pitching sound of an Amber alert.

"Ms. Miller is at home, but your daughter, Kensi Silver, is missing."

"What?"

"No!"

I whipped my body around as the shriek echoed through the house. My mother rushed to Laura's side as her knees buckled and she collapsed to the floor. I bolted to her side on the floor, lifting her into my arms.

"It's Kensi? It's Kensi?" she screamed, her body convulsing in my arms.

"Yes, it's Kensi. Kensi's your daughter."

I expected Laura to collapse again. Instead, she swept away the tears and shot up to her feet. "We have to find her. Now." She spun in a circle.

"We will. I'm going over to Tiffany's right away."

"I'm coming with you."

"Hold on. I need my other phone. I can track—"

"Go, go, go." She pushed me toward the staircase.

The house turned into a hive within seconds. Emma came to watch Laila and Foxy while my mother helped Laura gather herself upstairs. I turned on the tracking app on Kensi's phone, but her backpack was at home, and she wasn't. Tiffany arrived as soon as I came back downstairs. Mascara streamed down her face. Her nose was red and her eyes were swollen practically shut from crying.

"What happened?" I asked her, taking her into my arms.

"She was in the family room with me one moment, and then she was gone the next."

"What about the security cameras?"

"She never came back after she was seen going in the back-yard," she cried. "Kensi knows not to leave on her own."

"She wouldn't go into the water, but we'll search the shore as well."

"Did you check the treehouse?" Laura's whisper barely carried from the room's corner.

"Yes, of course, we checked the treehouse."

"You should check again. She loves the treehouse. It's her safe space."

"We checked three times." Tiffany's voice lifted, and Laura sat up.

"We'll check it again," I said. "We'll find her. I'm leaving in two minutes to comb through the property."

"What if she's not alone? What if someone took her? I… I thought maybe you took her." She pointed at Laura.

"I wouldn't do that to you or James. I know what it feels like to have a child stolen."

Tension nipped through the room.

"What were you talking about before she left? What was she doing?" I asked.

"I… I left her in the playroom, and I went to the front. She may have overheard me on the phone with my sister." Tiffany broke into fresh tears.

"What did you say to your sister?" Laura asked.

"I told her about you. I told her you were Kensi's biological mother, and when we finished talking, the backdoor was open and Kensi was gone." She covered her face with her hands, sobbing.

"I will find her if it's the last thing I do. I promise you both."

Laura shot up to her feet. "I'm coming with you."

"No. You're staying here."

She braced her hands on her hips. "Have you forgotten I was a cop? And now, I'm more than that. I'm an investigator and a mother with an instinct. I'm looking for Kensi, and if you try to stop me—"

I lifted my hands in the air. "All right, all right. You're coming. Tiff, can you stay with Laila and Foxy?"

"I've got the kids." My mother came out of the kitchen. "They're in the basement with Emma on the pinball machine. Tiffany, come with me. I made you some tea."

"Thank you, Mom." I hugged her and took Laura's hand.

We drove to Tiffany's in silence. I pushed the car to its limit while Laura braced against the dashboard. I had planned a long speech for today, but now I couldn't find any of my words. I'd wanted to sit Laura down with Tiffany and tell them we could work things out. But now our daughter was missing. My head pulsed with pain and my vision blurred. I cleared my eyes as I turned into the driveway filled with police cars.

"Are you all right?" she asked.

"As good as can be."

"No, I mean it, James. You don't look well."

"None of us do right now," I snapped. "I'm sorry. I didn't mean that."

"It's all right. We're all stressed. Come on. Let's go look for Kensi. You know this home better than me or the police. There has to be something they missed. Show me the treehouse first."

I showed my ID to the officers, and we strode through the side yard. The stepping stones had sunken into the soil drenched from the snowmelt. My lungs filled, but not to their depth, and it was difficult to breathe. I stopped and braced my hands on my knees.

"Hold on."

Laura turned around and gripped me by the arm, trying to lift me, but I resisted.

"You're not feeling well. Sit down."

"No. Kensi." I clenched my jaw.

Laura inhaled patience into her lungs and took me under my arm, helping me up. Stress and fatigue dripped down my back.

"That way." I pointed to the mature maple. "That's the treehouse."

Halfway across the lawn, Laura let go of my arm and hurried ahead. The world spun around me and I couldn't keep up with her pace, no matter how hard I pushed forward. I stopped again about a dozen feet away from the treehouse and braced my hands on my waist for a deeper breath. My lungs couldn't fill. A low buzz pierced my ears. I lifted my head, watching Laura's fading silhouette scale the steps to the treehouse, and blacked out.

Chapter 19

Laura

I climbed up the steps to Kensi's treehouse. The handful of warmer days on the east coast had melted the snow, erasing my daughter's footprints. The air carried the smell of soaked wood and winter. Kensi's treehouse bed had a pillow but was missing a blanket. I walked around the square space, dragging my fingers along the window sill, then the desk. Colored pencils and crayons lay scattered over the surface. Underneath them were pages of drawings of her family. I lifted a sheet from amongst the drawings where fluffy marshmallow clouds drifted away in the blue sky. Hurried hand strokes marked the corner of the page. My heartbeat strengthened.

I know where she is.

"James?"

I hurried out the door and down the steps, nearly tripping over my feet. James lay unconscious on the ground.

"James? Oh, my God! James!" I ran, stumbling over my feet. I dropped to my knees beside him and checked his pale skin for a pulse and lowered my face to his mouth.

He's breathing.

"Help! Someone help! I need an ambulance."

I checked his airways and the back of the throat but found no blockage.

"James? Can you hear me? You need to wake up, James."

"Help!" I finally caught the attention of two paramedics and waved them down. "He's breathing, but he's unconscious. I don't know what happened. He followed me to the treehouse but didn't go up."

"How long has he been unconscious?"

"Maybe…three minutes?"

They turned him over on his side and checked his airways again. James stirred and opened his eyes, disoriented. "What happened?"

"You fainted."

"I don't feel well. Dizzy. Very dizzy." His eyes rolled back in their sockets.

"He looks very pale. He could be losing blood."

"We're close to the hospital, ma'am."

Two more paramedics hurried toward us with a spine board. They strapped James in, gave him oxygen, and carried him to the ambulance. I watched as the medics drove away.

This couldn't be happening. I couldn't lose him. My trip back home to find my daughter was turning into a nightmare. A stiff wind blew through the front yard, and I gripped Kensi's drawing in my hand, realizing I hadn't gone with James for a reason.

I hopped into his car, turned on the ignition, and drove to the Silver Securities building in Manhattan. I scanned into the building and took the elevator up to my office floor. It was the weekend, and no one else was there. I walked in quietly and swept through the space, slowly crossing the floor to the area with marshmallow pillows and beanbags stacked into a fortress by the window. The corner of a blanket stuck out from between the pillows. The first wave of relief hit me. The second one came when I saw the pillows move.

"Kensi? Are you here?"

Her head popped out from within the pile. "Hi," she said.

"Hi." I waved. "What are you doing here?"

"You said I could come whenever I wanted."

I stepped up to the pile and crouched down, drawing even with her face. "Yes, but I meant with your parents."

She lowered her head. "Are you my parents now?"

Her eyes were red and so sad, my heart broke.

I sat down in front of the wall of bean bags and oversized pillows. "You overheard your mom talking to your aunt about you?"

She nodded.

I lifted a pillow and set it by the window. "Come out here and sit with me. I'm going to tell you a story."

She curled back her lower lip. "Does it have a happy ending?"

"It does if you make it so."

"Okay." She climbed out, and I quickly texted Teresa that Kensi was safe. She replied that they were on their way to Manhattan General, where the paramedics had taken James. I patted the seat beside me, and Kensi plopped onto the cushion with a shy smile.

"Change can be scary, but it can also be exciting and fun."

"I'm not scared." She met my gaze.

"You're not? Well, why did you run off?"

"Because I'm confused, and clouds help me think, just like they help you think. But they haven't helped me today because it's a cloudy day."

"What are you confused about?"

She curled her lower lip inward, collecting her thoughts.

"Are you my mommy now?"

I wasn't prepared for the question and moved closer to her side.

"Tiffany is your Mommy. She will always be your mommy,

but I'd like to be your Mommy as well."

"I get it. Jessi at school has two mommies. So you won't take me away?"

"Of course, not, but I would like to get to know you better. You were in my belly before you were born."

"Then how is Mommy my mommy? Didn't you want me?"

"Oh, honey. I wanted you very much, but there were some bad people in the room who took you away from me."

I skipped the controlling grandparents part because there was no point in fuelling a dying fire. I preferred Kensi have a positive relationship with my parents.

"Did you cry?"

"I cried a lot, and I hid in a pile of fluffy pillows. But this story has a happy ending because I found my baby girl."

"Me?" she whispered, and I gave her a gentle nod.

She looked out into the distance. Darker clouds had closed in, and I was worried about James. He would be relieved to know Kensi was safe.

"You gave everyone a scare, Kensi. Tiffany… I mean, your mom said you know better than to leave on your own."

"This was an emergency."

"How did you get inside the building, anyway?"

"My dad's card. He leaves it around sometimes."

"And how did you get to Manhattan?"

"I know how to use the train and the subway. Only two percent of kids my age know how to use public transportation."

"You're smart."

"Daddy taught me."

I checked my phone and found a message that they'd transferred James to Manhattan General.

"How about we go find your daddy?" I rose off the pillows.

"You know where he is? He missed Christmas."

"Yes, I know where he is." I stuck out my hand, and she

slipped hers in mine. The touch brought peace to my heart. "And I promise your daddy won't miss another Christmas with you."

"And my mommies too?"

Her wide eyes waited for the right answer, so I smiled. "And your mommies too."

She let go of my hand, scrunched up her blanket underneath her arm, and resumed our hold.

"Laura? Does that mean Foxy is my little brother?"

"Yes, it does."

Her mouth stretched wide across her face. "Good, because I love him very much. Is Laila my sister?"

"Of course, she is. She brought you a Christmas gift from Santa all the way from Austria."

Her steps picked up with mine, along with a hop. We took the elevator downstairs and walked the three blocks to Manhattan General. A new text came in from Teresa that Tiffany and Jacob had arrived at the hospital.

"Your grandfather told me you go hunting with him. Is that true?"

"Yes, but Mommy doesn't like to go. She went once and the mosquitos bit her, but grandpa said that's because she wore underwear in the woods."

"Mommy wore underwear in the woods?"

"No, but her shorts were very, very short, to impress daddy. That's what Grandpa said."

"Aha. Hey, do you think I could go hunting with you sometime?"

"I don't know." Her nose wiggled. "Hunting can be dangerous. There are guns involved."

"I was a police officer before I came to work for your daddy, and I had a gun."

"You had a gun?" Her eyes grew wide.

"Yes, but I didn't need to use it. Smart people know when to use weapons."

"That's what Grandpa says. Maybe that's why I've never seen him shoot anything."

"What do you do instead of shooting?"

"Grandpa collects antlers in the woods, and I pick berries with Grandma. She makes jam."

"Sounds like you enjoy nature."

"I love nature. I love animals too. And birds and fish and fairies."

I listened to her chat all the way to the hospital. She told me all about the animals she'd seen in the forest on their way to Colorado in their RV. The Silvers took summer trips to their cottage home every year. She told me about how much she loved bunnies and chickens, and how sixty percent of kids her age in a big city haven't seen a farm animal.

We arrived at the hospital, and Kensi ran straight into Tiffany's arms. "Mommy!"

She lifted her daughter...*our* daughter and held her tightly against her chest, mouthing a *thank-you* my way.

"What were you thinking, sugar bug?" She brushed Kensi's hair off her face.

I stepped away and joined Jacob outside of James's room. A handful of doctors and nurses were gathered around his bed. "Did they say anything?"

"Not yet. They're discussing his scans right now."

The doctors walked out into the hall, and the nurses wheeled James's bed out behind them.

"Mr. Silver, walk with me, please. We're on our way to the operating room. James has internal bleeding, which originates in his liver. It's likely a burst cyst, but the bleeding is not stopping, likely due to the falling platelet count caused by the leukemia. We need to operate before he stops clotting."

The doctor pressed the elevator button and turned around, facing us. "Unfortunately, you cannot come to the operating floor with us, but I'll have a nurse update you. Do you have any questions for me?"

"No, thank you," I whispered, but I doubted he heard me. They were in the elevator before I realized I had never said goodbye. My chest tightened.

"Jacob, I need to sit down."

"Come on, Laura. You need to stay strong. Your family depends on you. Your whole family."

He pointed to Tiffany and Kensi. My daughter was sitting beside her mother, glued to her side. Tiffany gave Kensi her phone, which she rejected because she already had a burner and was playing the classic snake game.

Jacob squeezed my arm. "Tiffany's made her mistakes, but she loves that girl."

"I know. It will take a while to get used to this. I... I don't know how I feel about it, but you're right." I looked at him from the side. "We will make it work... If James makes it."

"He'll make it. My son's a fighter, and he has too much to live for."

"Thank you."

We walked over to Tiffany and Kensi. Jacob took his granddaughter to the vending machines, and I sat down beside Tiffany.

"How are you doing?"

"I'm broken and relieved, at the same time. Is that possible?"

"It is if that's what you're feeling."

"How are you?" she asked.

"Relieved and scared. I don't know how that's possible, either."

"Laura... I got Kensi..." She wavered and looked around the room self-consciously. "I adopted her illegally."

"I gathered as much."

"Are you going to sue me? Will you take my daughter...our daughter...away from me?"

I didn't see the point of fighting and tears when we had the same goal in mind: Kensi's well-being.

"No, of course, not. I may be her biological mother, but you're her mother as well, and she loves you."

The PA system called a code blue, and we both jumped up, staring at the elevator and praying no doctor would come with the news that James hadn't made it. After what felt like forever, I broke the silence.

"Are you okay with this, Tiffany? Me being Kensi's mother and all? Because I adore your co-parenting with James. But I can't deny I want to be a part of Kensi's life. I want to be part of your and Kensi's lives. Who says a child can't have two mothers? Don't they say it takes a village to raise a child? We're not a village, but I'm sure we can all use help, and the kids love one another—"

She lowered her hand over mine, stopping me. "Laura, you don't need to sell me on the idea of the three of us raising the girls together. It's worked for me and James for years, and you found Kensi. I can see how well she takes to you. Besides, three pairs of hands are better than two. But you're not going to sue me, are you?"

"No." I gave her a warmer smile. "I'd prefer spending the time bonding with my new family. Listen, this surgery may take a while. Do you want to get some coffee? Maybe we'll run into Jacob and Kensi. I could pass the time looking at that girl's smile."

She grinned with pride, like Kensi had gotten her bright smile from Tiffany. Well, she wouldn't be wrong.

"Coffee sounds perfect."

THE SURGERY LASTED THREE HOURS, and the doctors said it was successful. James was recovering in his room. Kensi kissed him on his forehead while he was sedated, then left for home with Tiffany, who hugged me before leaving. She held on tighter than I expected, whispering, "Thank you. We'll make this work."

I held Kensi in my arms and said goodbye. "Listen, next time you'd like to visit your mom's beautiful clouds at the office, you need to let us know. That way, I can give you a private tour."

"Really? I could visit when it's quiet, and no one is there?"

"Sure."

"Take care of my daddy."

"I will, honey. I'll see you soon."

She waved goodbye, and I returned to his bedside. I rested my head near his pillow and must have dozed off because when I awoke, it was dark outside. My stomach rumbled with hunger, and my nose caught the aroma of a veggie burger in a bag, which I opened to find a note from Emma.

Thought you may be hungry. You snore.

A fizzing Dr. Pepper was set at the side, with a healthy portion of sweet potato fries. I dug into the meal, finishing the crumbs. Another hour passed before James stirred in his bed.

"Ouch." He groaned and managed to sit up. "Kensi?"

"Hey, hey. Relax, you're freshly stitched. I found Kensi at Silver Securities, and she's safe at home with your father and Tiffany."

"Oh, my God, that's a relief." He shifted sideways and winced in pain. "Ouch. What the fuck happened to me?"

"You want the good news or the bad news first?"

"Bad."

"The chemotherapy plan to treat your leukemia has an over ninety percent success rate. That's what caused your platelet count to drop. Your markers are off, so it's time for treatment."

"All right, I think I'm ready for the good news."

I took his hand. "You have two extra people to care for you:

me and Foxy. I've already told the office you're taking time off, the house is being sterilized, and Olivier has agreed to put you on a special diet to help your immune system. We've got this, James. Your family's got this."

He relaxed back in the bed. "What would I do without you?"

"I don't know, and I don't want to know."

"Will my new scar be more impressive than yours?" He grinned, wiggling his brows.

I shrugged a shoulder. "We'll see when they remove your bandages, but I doubt it."

He shifted in the bed again, wincing in pain.

"I should let the nurse know you're awake."

"No, wait. How are you and Tiff?"

"Like sisters." I scrunched my shoulders tighter around my neck.

"Seriously?"

"No, but we're good, and I think we have an understanding."

"What kind of understanding is that?"

"That we both love Kensi."

His fingers weaved through my mine, and his eyelids lowered. I counted five breaths, and for a moment, I thought he'd fallen asleep, but he opened his eyes and turned his head my way.

"I didn't know about Kensi when we had her. I thought she was mine," he whispered. "Tiffany—"

"It doesn't matter anymore, my love. We have our girl, and you should rest now. We need you strong, so just…rest."

He closed his eyes. I waited until he fell asleep for the night before leaving for his home. Tiffany stayed over with Kensi. We removed cushions from the couches and made a gigantic bed on the family room floor. The kids slept in the middle between me and Tiffany. I tossed through the night, praying their father would win his fight.

Chapter 20

James

"Daddy, do you like it?" Kensi spun around in her peach dress Tiffany had picked out for today. I closed my laptop and pulled away from my desk. Everything was ready for the day, and I had one last task.

"It's beautiful. You look like a sunflower."

"Mommy Tiffany said I look like a rose, and my dress matches Laila's."

It was cute how Kensi had come to calling both Tiffany and Laura her mommies. I lowered myself to the ground and pinned a rose into her hair.

"You know what? I think Mommy Tiffany is right. You look perfect, but there's something missing."

I narrowed my brows and crouched in front of her.

"What is it?"

I reached behind her ear and magically pulled out a necklace. Kensi's mouth opened wide.

"How did you do that?"

"If I told you, it wouldn't be magic, would it?"

She shook her head quickly.

"Turn around, baby, so I can put this on."

I fastened the clasp and swept the six heart charms to the front.

"Why are there so many hearts, Daddy?"

"There's one for your brother, sister, both mommies, me, and you."

"It's beautiful."

"I'm glad you like it. Hey, Kens? Would you like to help with an important job today?

"A job?"

"It's actually a mission."

Her eyes brightened. "A mission?"

I stood up and checked the hallway to ensure no one else was heading our way, then whispered my plan into her ear.

"What do you say, Kens? You think you can help me?"

She gave me a quick nod and showed her row of teeth.

"Okay. I'm counting on you kid."

Hand in hand, I walked downstairs with Kensi. Foxy and Laila were waiting in the kitchen with my mother, dressed in their matching outfits. My mother straightened my shirt like I was her little boy again. She rose on her tiptoes and whispered in my ear, "Don't fuck this up."

"No pressure."

The kids' unanimous gasp forced my body to turn as Laura appeared.

"Holy shit."

"That's a bad word, Daddy."

Laura walked down the stairs in a beautiful summer dress and sandals. Her hair flowed loosely down her shoulders, her cheeks held a rosy shade, and her eyes popped like amber gems. She looked stunning.

"Look at you, all dressed and ready," she glowed. "Where's Daddy taking us?"

"Daddy said it will be a long walk."

"Let's go for a long walk, then."

We secured Foxy and Laila in their strollers and took off walking down the driveway. It had been two months since my last chemo cycle had finished. Laura had driven with me to every treatment. She'd coordinated Kensi's school drop-off with Tiffany, and taken Laila and Foxy to the new daycare at Silver Securities while working full-time. The woman was a superhero, and most importantly, she was mine. Today, I'd ensure she remained mine forever.

We left the neighborhood and strolled along the shoreline, stopping by a family of ducklings. The kids fed the birds, and we bought ice cream from one of the food trucks. We picked up fresh berries at the local market, along with a box of apple fritters. We turned the corner to the main street, and I gently squeezed Kensi's hand. She looked up, and I gave her our secret double wink.

"Oh, look, Daddy. It's a ring store." Kensi pointed, drawing Laura's attention.

I glanced over at Laura and wiggled my brows. "Should we go inside?"

Kensi tugged on my hand. "Let's go inside, Daddy."

Laura gave a shrug, and we wheeled in the strollers. The store clerk I'd met last month stood behind the counter.

"Good morning, how can we help you today?" she asked.

"I'd like to buy rings for my daughters."

"Absolutely. Let's get their fingers measured." She dangled a chain of loops, and Kensi stuck out her hand.

"Rings?" Laura stepped closer. "James, they'll lose them."

"Are you looking for something specific, sir?"

"Maybe something with their birthstones?" I lifted my gaze to Laura's.

"That would be nice, but maybe better to get Laila a bracelet similar to Kensi's, so she doesn't lose it."

"Mommy, you measure your finger too." Kensi pulled on Laura's hand, holding it for the store clerk.

"What about Foxy? Should we get him a bracelet too?"

"James, he doesn't need jewelry." She chuckled. "He's two."

"So is Laila, and Foxy will be three next weekend."

"Still not old enough to warrant a bracelet he might lose."

"Kensi hasn't lost hers since birth."

"I'm not winning this one, am I? Fine. A bracelet for Foxy as well."

"Are you upset with me?"

"No, I'm not. I just don't see why a three-year-old should wear something so expensive. Sixty-eight percent of children in this country get spoiled and can't learn how to fend for themselves when they're thirty." Her eye twitched.

"How about this one?" I slipped a diamond over her ring finger, and she covered her mouth with her free hand.

"James…"

"I like the way it fits."

I held her hand and watched as she twisted it in the light. The diamond caught streams of light, reflecting rainbow sparks on the counter's glass surface.

"Me too," she whispered.

"Mommy, look at my bracelet. Now I have two."

Laura took the ring off her finger, returning it to the clerk.

"It's beautiful, Kensi. It has your birthstone. Give your daddy a big hug."

Kensi thrust her arms up in the air, and I lifted her up, holding my girl tightly against my chest.

"You got it?" I whispered in her ear.

"I do."

I paid for the purchases, and we headed back to the house, picking up a bouquet of wildflowers on the way. We crossed behind my parents' property to mine.

"What's that?" Laura pointed to the blanket near the docks.

"I thought we could have a picnic with the kids."

"When did you get that ready?"

"When you weren't looking."

The bright summer sun shone over the bay. We parked the strollers and let the kids out. Foxy found a ball and kicked it away, giggling. Kensi ran after him, and Laila followed Kensi. I helped Laura down to the blanket and removed the champagne from the cooler.

"What are we celebrating?" she asked.

"A beautiful day."

"With champagne?"

"I could do sparkling water, but it just doesn't have the same kick. Hold these."

I passed her the flutes, popped open the bottle, and filled the glasses.

"We should drink to something." She lifted her glass higher.

"How about to health and me having better taste in rings?"

She squinted. "What do you mean?"

"You didn't like the ring at the store."

"I did. It was beautiful."

"But you were disappointed."

"Not because I didn't like the ring."

"Then what is it?"

"I… I thought you were buying the ring, and I had this idea that maybe you would propose, and you didn't—not that I expected you to propose because it should be a surprise. Forty-eight percent of partners don't plan anything, but since you're a planner, I thought—"

"You thought I would propose at the ring store?"

"Well, that wouldn't have been romantic, would it?" Her chin dipped and I gave Kensi a nod. She returned to the blanket and sat down beside Laura.

"Are you sad, Mommy?"

"No, I'm not, baby girl. I'm so happy to have you here, and Laila and Foxy and daddy. It's a beautiful day."

"Would this make you happy?" She lowered her hand inside her dress pocket and removed a diamond ring.

Laura shot up to her feet.

"Kensi, where did you get that? We were supposed to leave it at the store. James—"

She turned around and froze when she saw me kneeling in front of her. "We weren't supposed to leave it at the store." I grinned, and Kensi placed the ring in my palm. "Because I didn't think asking you to marry me at the store was special enough."

Laura covered her mouth with both of her hands as tears streamed down her face.

"Laila, Foxy, come over here," I called out, and the kids joined me in front of Laura on the blanket. "What do you say, Mommy Laura? Will you make me the happiest man in the world and marry me? Will you be my wife?"

"Say yes, Mommy. Say yes!"

Laila and Foxy joined Kensi in clapping, and Laura stuck out her hand, sobbing. "Yes, I'll marry you."

I slid the ring I'd bought last week on her finger and lifted her hand. She moved her hand in the sunlight, then threw her arms around my neck. I kissed her hard on the lips and leaned my forehead against hers.

"Are you ready to marry me today?" My lips buzzed over her mouth.

"What?" She pulled back. "Today? Don't we have to plan things? Like make a guest list, order a cake, book a venue, food. James we need time to—"

"Why waste another day?" I said. "Besides, everyone we want is already here, and we have a beautiful venue, food, music, and cake." I pointed to the deck at the back of our house. Our families waved, cheering.

"My brother Gabe flew in from Austria with his wife and newborn."

"Wait a minute… You planned a proposal *and* a wedding?"

"It's a beautiful day." I lifted a shoulder.

Her eyes skidded to the deck and back to me, growing wider.

"I don't even have a dress," she whispered.

"Fifteen gowns, all in your size, are waiting in our bedroom, and I haven't seen a single one. Allie picked them out, and my Aunt Mary already had your measurements. I'm hoping you'll like one of them."

"Allie had time to pick out dresses? She has twins."

"Laura, my love, I think you're missing the point here." I smoothed my thumb over her cheek, cupping the side of her face. I waited for the idea to settle in her heart.

Her gaze met mine, and she curled her bottom lip inward. "I guess we're getting married today."

I punched up into the air and screamed across the yard, "She's gonna do it!"

My family erupted in cheers before scattering to their assigned tasks.

We took the kids back to the house. Allie and our mothers helped Laura dress while I slipped into a suit. Laura's dad got Foxy into his outfit, and Tiffany helped Laila and Kensi with their flower girl dresses. My family set up chairs on the back deck, and I waited at the front with the minister. Our family sat in the rows of chairs they'd set out. Laura's parents and mine were in the front with the kids and Tiffany. My cousins, aunts, and uncles, along with their families, sat behind them. In less than an hour, the house was transformed into a venue with vases of white roses and clumped hydrangeas. Candles lit the rose petal path for Laura.

I fixed my bowtie and rolled back my shoulders.

Allie joined me at the front as maid-of-honor, and my brother Hunter took the job of best man. Unchained Melody played over the speakers, and I turned around. Laura stood on the backyard patio with a bouquet of roses in her hands. Her satin dress flowed to the ground, fluttering in the breeze. She was the most beautiful woman I'd ever seen. She looped her arm through her father's, and they stepped forward. I wiped the corner of my eye and locked my shoulders. The fifteen-foot walk across the patio took forever, but from that moment, I couldn't peel my gaze away from her.

I held her hands as she stood by my side, and as we exchanged our vows, it felt like a bubble closed in around us. The outside world ceased to exist, and it was just the two of us.

"You may kiss the bride," the minister said.

Finally.

I extended the smooch until someone in the back yelled to get a room. We pulled away. Confetti cannons and streamers blew through the air. Kensi, Laila, and Foxy hopped off their seats and slammed into us both.

"I can't believe we're married," Laura said.

"It was inevitable." I kissed her again.

"Okay, you two, let's get this party going because my date is a professional dancer." Tiffany tightened her grip on Christian's arm. They'd been seeing each other for a few months now, and the new relationship looked promising. She let go of his arm and gave me a tight hug. "Congratulations, Fox Silver. Thank you for being a great friend and father."

She sidled over to Laura.

"Congratulations to you both, Laura. Thank you for loving our kids, and… " She swallowed past unshed tears and went in for a long hug. "Just…thank you for being an amazing woman and friend."

"Thank you for opening your heart to me."

I took my wife's hand and lifted it high in the air. "Tiff is right. Let's get this party started."

The DJ turned on the music, and I spun Laura into our first

dance. The day passed too quickly, but our memories would last forever.

We finished the night at one in the morning, dancing until I couldn't feel my feet. Laura's parents chatted with mine, and the house was filled with love and laughter. Emma had caught Laura's bouquet, and her brothers tried ripping it out of her hands. She wouldn't have any of it. Julian and Kendra announced they were expecting, and my youngest brother made a move on Grace Wagner. Again. He pulled me aside before leaving.

"Congrats, man. I'm glad to see you happy."

"You've been awfully quiet today. Everything okay with Grace?"

"Nothing's ever been okay with me and Grace."

"Hey, don't give up so fast."

"I'm going off the grid for a while." He locked his eyes on mine. They were devoid of all emotion, except worry and fear.

"A new assignment?"

"A new assignment, and a new life. I don't know when I'll be back."

"So we're reverting to no news is good news?"

"I'll try to touch base when I can, but yeah, don't bury me before I'm dead." He winked.

"Anything I can do to help?"

"No. I'm doing this on my own."

I brought my brother in for a tight hug and patted him on his back. "Be careful."

"Thanks. Congrats, James."

I watched as he pulled out of the driveway. My brother had been in love with Grace Wagner for years. They'd dated before Grace opened her salon, and I was certain they'd make it work, eventually. Grace had left him, insisting their age gap and Hunter's immaturity were too much to overcome. They'd remained friends, but my brother never stopped hoping

The kids passed out on the couch, and once everyone left, my wonderful mother helped me clean up. I put the kids in their beds after everyone left, unbuttoned my shirt, and met my wife in the bathroom.

I took her by the hips and pressed her lips to mine. My heart whirred in tempo with the blood rushing through my veins. "Hello, Mrs. Silver."

"Mrs. Silver? I didn't know I was changing my last name."

I grazed my hand over her neck and brushed my lips over hers. "That's non-negotiable."

"Anything else non-negotiable?" She wiggled in my hold.

"Clothing on our wedding night. Why are you wearing that robe?"

A smile tweaked her lips to the side. She stepped back and released the robe's tie. "Will this do?"

She dropped the covering to the floor, and my hard-on went completely stiff at the sight of her negligée. The sheer fabric composed of straps and buckles left nothing to the imagination, yet hid everything I needed. I eyed the fastenings, calculating the quickest way to her skin. It wouldn't be an easy task.

"No, but I know something that will."

She squealed as I lifted her over my shoulder and carried her to my bed. I set her down on the sheets, shed my clothes, and climbed onto the bed, hovering above her. "If you don't tell me how to get this contraption off of you—"

"There's a latch which releases all of the fastenings at once, but Grace said only three percent of men can find it."

"Like a G-spot?"

Her face fell flat.

"What's wrong?"

"I don't know any statistic about G-spots."

I laughed, sat up, and pulled my hands over her outfit.

"Let me assure you, I'm part of the statistic of men who know how to find one."

Twelve seconds later, I pulled down on two hidden zippers underneath each arm. Her mouth dropped open while her eyes shone with pride.

"Come here." She grabbed my neck and pulled me down to her body. "It's time to consummate this marriage, Mr. Silver."

I planned on nothing less, and definitely much more.

Prologue

grace

Life was good; and tonight, my hard work building a beauty empire would be rewarded and all of my dreams would come true. Well, almost all of them, because babies didn't arrive like the award I would receive this evening, and my clock was ticking.

I pinned the last bobby pin into my hair and lowered my arms. Curled strands glittered in gold, forming a flowing fire. The hair creation matched the sparkling dress hugging my body. My mother had called in a favor to a designer from Paris, and a month later, the custom-made gold-chained gown fit me like a glove.

A loud splash drew my attention to the outside. I paced to the balcony where the setting sun bathed the backyard in orange. Below, Hunter was walking up the pool steps, carrying what looked like another toad in his hands. He crossed the lawn to the lily pond and crouched. A giant toad hopped off his hand and into the water. That made the third toad he'd saved this week.

He rinsed his hands in the pond water, shook them off, and stood, pulling his fingers through his hair. The column of his back muscles twisted. He turned around. The permanent tan from the time he'd spent landscaping the backyard glowed in the evening light. His beautiful chest, dusted with hair, was young and firm, with room to grow.

I watched him cross the lawn back to the house. He stopped and looked up to the balcony where I stood. His piercing blue eyes were drowning with sadness. His head fell forward, and my heart sank.

I'd known Hunter Silver since his diaper days. He was my uncle's nephew on my mother's side, and our families spent every holiday, birthday, and celebration together. And boy, had he grown up fast. For his eighteenth birthday, I bought Hunter a bike and asked for a few lessons on my broken Harley, which he was eager to fix that evening. Let's just say, he fixed more than my bike. He'd begun as my boy toy, and three years later, he was saving frogs from my pool.

As soon as he stepped inside, I hitched my dress to my thighs and hurried to meet him downstairs. Hunter wouldn't reject a quickie before I left, and I was ovulating.

"Hey, baby. Another toad in my pool?"

His beautiful blue eyes met mine. Jesus, he would make a gorgeous baby. He stood, dripping wet, his gaze unapologetically slithering down my body. I swallowed with an audible click, drawing my tongue over my dry lips. His shorts clung to his muscled thighs and his healthy dick, lifting my arousal and setting my blood on fire.

"Holy fuck, Grace. You look stunning. Like a queen. My Queen."

I twirled in the spot, and his gloom vanished. The half-smile and two dimples were a good start.

"You like it?" I asked, wiggling my ass.

"What are you supposed to be? An Oscar on fire?"

He stepped closer, his eyes swimming with lust, and a little bit of disappointment.

"Exactly." I cleared my throat.

"But you're not getting an Oscar."

"This award is the highest honor I'll ever get, so it's like an Oscar to me."

"You look beautiful. The dress is the perfect choice. Wish I could be there to see you accept the award." He kissed the tip of my nose.

The punch in my gut briefly knocked me off task. I stepped closer and dragged my manicured nails down his drying chest. "What can I do to make you feel better?"

"I'll ruin your makeup if I have my way with you"

The rumble from his chest vibrated along my skin. I pushed my thigh through the slit in my dress and lifted the other side, exposing my panties. I was willing to beg him to ruin me, but if I did, he would, and I'd be late. But there were other ways.

"If you stay below the belt, you won't ruin my hair or makeup."

His mouth twisted into a sly grin, and my heart kicked up a beat. He leaned into my ear and dragged his lips over the cartilage, whispering, "What if I want to ruin you, Grace?"

Yes.

His fingers skimmed up my arm, and his needy breath drew shivers down my spine.

"Touch me. There." My lips trembled over his.

He slid his hand through the slit in my dress and up my thigh. I gripped the dinette table as he dipped his palm down the front of my panties. My eyes rolled back in my head and my legs instinctively opened. His long, skilled fingers dragged through my wet flesh, and stopped.

"Aren't you ovulating, Grace?" he asked, withdrawing his hand.

Shit.

"I'm thirty-two, Hunter. It's the perfect time to have a baby."

"I'm not ready for offspring."

"But my business is booming, and we're happy and together—"

"If we're happy, my love, why aren't I escorting you tonight?"

"Hunter, we've already talked about this."

His shoulders dropped, and he strode to the kitchen where he poured himself a vodka on ice. He lifted the glass and pointed my way. "No, Gracie. *You* talked about it, and because your reputation is more important than me, you chose not to take me." He took a sip. "What are you afraid of?"

I was worried about Hunter. Last Christmas, he took a tumble down the stairs at the salon and pissed himself when he reached the bottom. Alcohol and Hunter didn't mix well.

"I never thought you'd be one to care what people think about you because you have it all. But you hide me like a dog in a shed. Is it really me you want tonight, Grace, or my sperm?"

I swung my hand, aiming for a slap, but he gripped my wrist before my palm connected with his cheek.

"Fuck you, Hunter. This is exactly why I can't take you to serious events." I yanked my wrist free.

"The least you can do is be honest. Why won't you take me? What am I to you? I fix your car and your bike. I bring groceries and cook. I take you out on dates like all boyfriends do, while most of my friends stay out and party from Monday to Sunday. I go to school, I work, and I'm in what I hope is a committed relationship. Yet you're embarrassed by me."

He took another swig.

"Hunter, you're wonderful—"

"But?"

"But you go to school, and you're twenty-one."

"Yet I'm old enough to make a baby. What's going to happen after you're pregnant, Grace? If you can't introduce me to your friends as your boyfriend, how would you introduce me as the father of your child? Would you even want me in your life?"

My child. I sighed internally.

"They would talk about you, wouldn't they? Fucking Cougar Court." He motioned south to the front of my house. My neighborhood girlfriends, all single businesswomen over thirty, liked to talk.

"We should change your address to Gossip Court."

My neighbors hadn't welcomed Hunter with open arms, but let's be honest. I did live on Cougar Court, and we all lived up to the street's name. When Hunter first moved in, Lexie came out for a jog around the court every time Hunter washed my car in the middle of a heat wave. Carly loved Hunter's help with the lawn mowing, and he'd drained Susanne's pool for the third year in a row after the company botched up the liner. But after he helped them, he was mine and all mine. Day and night, he fucked me like an animal, and I screamed past the open windows. But as amazing as he was, taking Hunter to a party would be like adding fuel to a fire, and when flames flared, so did Hunter. The bounty hunter-in-training at Silver Securities lived up to his adventurous name.

"Hunter—"

"Grace, all I'm saying is that I'd love to be seen as more. I'm not one of your aunt's manservants."

I brushed my hand over his cheek and curled his dark hair around my finger. This evening wasn't starting out the way I'd imagined, but I'd be damned if it didn't end with him between my thighs and deep in my vagina.

"Please don't insult me, Hunter. You know how I feel about you and how much I want you."

"Do I? Your friends don't know I exist, and your neighbors think I'm your boy toy."

I drew back my hand, and his curl sprang off my finger. "My family knows about you, and that should be enough."

"Yet it isn't enough to earn a permanent spot in your life."

The grandfather clock struck six times, and I let go of my

dress. If he wasn't hard in thirty seconds, we'd run out of time. I curved my hand over his dick, but he stepped aside.

"Fine. You wanna be this way, then be this way. I gotta go, but I'll see you later tonight."

I lifted to my toes in front of him and planted a long kiss on his plump lips. When I returned, I'd straddle him if I had to, and I wouldn't let him go until he came hard. His tongue sneaked between my lips, igniting my need, but he pulled away too quickly, bracing his forehead against mine. "Have a great time, Grace."

His soft voice fed my guilt.

"I won't be late—I promise."

"It's your night. Take your time. Just don't let some phantom man steal you away."

"Phantom?"

"The party's Halloween-themed." He kissed me again and whispered against my lips. "Remember, you're the queen of this party. Better get going if you want to make it."

His words buzzed against my mouth, as shame burned a trail through my heart. But I'd come back in a few hours, and everything would be normal. The hallway camera showed a limo pulling up to the front gate.

"A queen is never late." I kissed him back.

By the time Hunter had laced the gold high heels around my calf, the limousine was parked at the front and the clock was striking the half-hour mark. He helped me inside the limo and waved as I drove away.

A pang of regret sank my heart into my chest. Hunter was the kindest and smartest boyfriend; but most of my friends were pregnant or on their way to being pregnant, while Hunter made bets about how far he could ejaculate. It was far. I'd seen it. Except the sperm didn't go where it was supposed to go: inside my drying womb.

Twenty minutes later, my limo parked at the curb in front

of the venue gardens. White and gold fabric was draped over the erected Greek columns at the front, and floodlights illuminated the entrance overgrown with vines. A valet opened the back door. Camera lights flashed, and security closed ranks. I stepped out onto the rolled red carpet, and someone bumped me in the shoulder. A security guard squeezed between us, guiding me to the door. Thank God Hunter had hired his company's private team.

I stepped past the gates, and the crowd's noise settled into a hum. The sound of falling water trickled from a central fountain, and I let go of the tension in my shoulders. A warm breeze blew by, swaying the fairy lights on the trees. Beyond, a tent with tables and a stage had been erected on the main lawn, which was decorated with flowers and vines and looked like a fairytale garden.

I walked up to a tall gentleman smiling my way. He was dark and handsome, in his late thirties, and fit the description I'd given to Aunt Mary right down to the neatly trimmed growth on his face.

"Grace Wagner. You look beautiful."

"Xavier Morrison?"

He smiled and extended his hand. I hooked my arm into his.

"You're early," I said.

"I didn't want to keep you waiting. It's a pleasure to meet you. I took the liberty of getting your favorite drink; non-alcoholic, as per your preference sheet."

He motioned to the wait staff, who immediately brought an aloe-coconut water.

"Thank you. That's sweet. Have you read everything on that preference sheet?"

"My apologies. I wasn't supposed to mention the pref— Never mind. I promise not to slip up again."

My brows furrowed, and I looked at him from the side. He

was more handsome than the profile photo I'd received from Aunt Mary. His firm jaw, dreamy eyes, and confidence were toxic. One day, Hunter would mature, and I could take him to events, but now… For now, I had to make this work.

"No worries," I said. "What about your costume?" He was wearing a tuxedo with a long black cape. "Let me guess. Magician?"

"No." he reached into his jacket pocket and removed a black mask. He looped the elastic around his head and adjusted the front. "Tonight, I'm Zorro."

Cute.

We headed to the front table, where Xavier pulled back my chair. I took my seat beside my other date and my best friend, Emma Silver. Hunter's younger cousin was wearing a feathered mini skirt and a matching top embroidered with gems. The modern cowgirl outfit on her body made her look like a Victoria's Secret angel. My parents occupied the seats across from me, along with my Aunt Mary.

Emma glanced over at my date and leaned into my ear. "Where's Hunter?"

"Home."

"Why?"

"Because he's too young to be my boyfriend today, Ems."

Emma may have been even younger than Hunter, but she had the maturity of ten Hunters and knew how to behave at award nights.

"Eleven years is nothing. You two are meant to be."

"It's a lot at his age. He's not ready for things. He's not ready for a family."

My mother shushed us from across the table, and I shimmied my ass to the chair's edge. The lights dimmed and voices hushed, as everyone focused on the stage.

"I'm not ready for kids either. I've babysat enough of my nieces and nephews for three lifetimes. Besides, I have school, and Eric is my brother's best friend, so it's not like that's going to happen."

"Enjoy life before settling. Have fun while you can."

Emma rolled her eyes. "Says the woman with an escort as a date because her boyfriend's too immature."

"He has a good heart but makes bad choices."

"He chose you."

Touché.

"If I wanted a lecture, Ems, I'd sit beside my mother. I grew up with four brothers, my twin included. Trust me, you don't need your brother's permission to date. Just have fun, test out the goods, and see what he's like."

"He's a cowboy, rides horses, and reins in cattle. What else is there to know?" Emma reserved the dreamy look on her face for Eric Waters, a well-established cowboy. And since Emma Silver always got what she wanted, it was only a matter of time before she got Eric.

Someone kicked me underneath the table, and I jumped, catching my mother's deadly stare. "You'll miss it," she hissed.

The MC walked out to the front of the stage and tapped the mike. The room's focus shifted my way as soon as he introduced me as tonight's guest of honor.

I walked up to the stage, my knees wobbling and heart pounding. Bright lights heated my face, condensing my sweat into drops. My speech flew out of my head as soon as I took the mike. I barely remembered the words as I accepted the Contessa award. I thanked my team and my parents, my aunt, and the rest of my family for their support and influence. My salon's popularity couldn't have grown without them. I gripped the golden award, lifting the trophy toward my family's table, when my gaze caught a figure in the back corner by the bar. He was dressed in a black suit with a matching cape, and was leaning against a maple tree. A white mask covered half his face. The wind blew, branches swayed, and he disappeared into the tree's shade. The applause settled, and the MC walked me down the stairs and back to my table, where Xavier pulled back my chair.

"Congratulations, darling."

I set the award on the table, took a deep breath, and hugged my parents and my aunt. This was the night I'd waited so long for, yet it didn't feel complete. Celebrating without Hunter wasn't the same.

"Are you all right?" Xavier asked.

"Yes, thank you."

The commotion settled as servers brought out the first course. Soft dinner music played overhead but did nothing to settle my nerves. I scanned the room until I felt someone's stare on my back. I glanced over my shoulder, but no one was there. My heart hammered in my chest, and my hands shook.

"Can I get you anything to drink, Grace?" Xavier asked.

"A glass of rosé would be nice, thank you."

Xavier snapped his fingers, and a moment later, a chilled glass stood in front of me. I gulped half down before my bladder reminded me it had filled twenty minutes ago.

"Excuse me. I need to use the washroom." I pushed my chair back, and Xavier stood as well.

"Do you want me to come with you?" Emma asked.

"No, it's all right. Your food will get cold."

I turned on my heel, crossed the dining area, used the washroom, and broke away from the party and into the gardens. Moonlight illuminated a path with clumps of white carpet roses, and the smell of lavender filled the air. A warm evening breeze blew through my golden hair. I stood by the back fountain, watching the water splash, and then turned at the sound of approaching footsteps. A man in a cape similar to Xavier's walked toward me, except his mask was a Phantom's. I squinted. The corner of his mouth lifted, and a dimple sank into his cheek.

"Hunter? Is that you?"

"Hello, Gracie."

Oh, no.

His deep voice chilled me to the bones. Hunter only called me *Gracie* when he was drunk. He walked forward, somewhat confident on his feet, yet swaying. I looked around the empty gardens. If someone saw him like this with me, I'd be ruined.

He removed the Phantom mask from his face and pulled his fingers through his hair. On a sober night, the move was sexy. Tonight, not so much. The vodka stench finally reached me, and I recoiled.

"What are you doing here? You were supposed to stay home."

"I'm here to replace your date."

Fuck.

He stepped closer, rocking back and forth, and I stepped back.

"You're drunk. You need to go home."

"Come on, Gracie. The night is still young." He moved forward and took me by the arm, but I pulled away.

His brows drew together. "You'd rather sit beside an escort?"

"Xavier's a friend."

He burst out in laughter. Part of me hoped someone would hear him and escort him out. He stumbled forward but regained his balance as I took him by his arm. God, how he stank!

"I don't like it when you're like this."

"I'm like this when you treat me like I'm nothing."

I let go of his arm and poked my finger into his chest. "Don't you fucking blame your drinking on me." The force in my whisper surprised me.

"I drink because you're ashamed of me. Say it isn't so, Gracie."

"It isn't so. I won't be the scapegoat for your problem. We had a deal. You promised—"

"You made a promise as well, Gracie. Remember when I had my tongue in your pussy?"

He stepped closer. Suddenly, that same vodka breath I despised warmed the side of my neck, and I quivered.

"Or all the times I fucked you in your beautiful gardens, similar to these? Was that not a promise to cherish you? Did I suck you wrong?"

He didn't. The lump in my throat tightened into an unbearable knot. In bed, Hunter Silver outdid every man I'd ever been with. I'd taught him well, but he'd needed little teaching and enjoyed listening to my instruction. Then he fucking outperformed in every way.

"Do I not deserve a spot at your table, Gracie?"

I sucked in a sharp breath.

"Or did Xavier fuck you much better?"

I yanked myself away and swung my hand to slap him, but he caught my wrist in mid-air. I focused on his tight grip and my shaking hand before my gaze drifted slowly to his, and my mouth opened in shock.

He let go and stepped backward, toward the dining area, looking at me like I'd made the biggest mistake of my life. I breathed through my nose, desperate to salvage the situation and get him out of here.

"Hunter? Whatever you're thinking of doing, don't. Please."

"Are you embarrassed to introduce your boyfriend to your guests, Gracie?"

I quickened my pace, but I was already too late. He turned on his heel and headed straight for the stage, where he tapped on the microphone. The echo brought everyone's attention center-stage. The lighting technician flashed a beam Hunter's way.

"Oh, no." I covered my mouth with my hand, afraid to walk

back to my table. Instead, I stood near the stage stairs, staring at the man I loved like he was my worst enemy.

"Don't do it, Hunter. Don't ruin this," I whispered, breathing to the beat of my heart and still afraid I'd run out of air as soon as he sucked it out of the room.

"Good evening, everyone."

The two hundred people fell quiet.

Here it comes.

Hunter's mother frowned from the table occupied by his parents. Jacob and Teresa Silver had brought big business to my empire. How could I not have invited them? But now that I saw my Hunter there, slurring his words, I regretted my decision to leave him at home.

"My name is Hunter Silver, and I'd like to 'gratulate my Gracie on her beautiful Oscar. She deserves it. She deserves it all, but she's been hiding me from you all. Not my dick. She doesn't hide from my motor."

"Oh, no." My whisper fogged in the cool air.

The more his speech slurred, the quicker my heart raced in my chest. He tilted his hips forward and wiggled them like he had a trunk for a penis.

"I may be younger, Xavier"—Hunter pointed into the crowd —"but with youth comes stamina, and my Gracie likes stamina."

His hand flew to the left, directing the crowd's attention to where I stood. I covered my face with my hands, hoping the ground would open underneath me, but a beam of light shone my way. I slid my fingers open enough to see Hunter turn my way. Someone from the dining area was making his way to the stage as Hunter stated, "I'm good enough to fuck for sperm, but not good enough to have dinner with. Come on, you guys, help me give her a hand. Gracie! Gracie!"

He clapped, enticing the crowd, but the room stayed silent. Humiliation burned through my body and rage coursed through my veins. Someone dragged Hunter off the stage. I was pretty sure I peed myself that night.

And I threw Hunter out on his ass before he sobered.

Continue with Grace and Hunter on their sizzling adventure in *Silver Hunter*, Book 7 in the *Silver Brothers Securities Family Saga*.

Silver
HUNTER
USA TODAY BESTSELLING AUTHOR
LACEY SILKS

ALSO BY LACEY SILKS

Silver Brothers Securities

Silver Santa

Silver's Rebel

Silver's Pawn

Silver's Secret

Silver's Trouble

Silver Fox

Silver Hunter

Dirty Deeds Series

Dirty Cowboy

Dirty Mechanic

Dirty Con

Be the first to know!

Visit: www.laceysilks.com

ABOUT THE AUTHOR

USA Today Bestselling Author Lacey Silks crafts riveting romantic suspense filled with heat, spice, and pulse-pounding tension. Many of her endearing characters are inspired by her own life, and her loved ones often find themselves playfully woven into her tales. Her two children and her dog, Kygo, keep her days lively with homework queries and affectionate slobbery kisses (courtesy of Kygo, of course).

Outside of penning intense love stories, Lacey is an avid camper and skier. Naturally an early riser, she often finds herself reaching for coffee over water, crediting her billionaire heroes for her packed schedule.

Lacey's characters, replete with flaws and quirks, evoke laughter, sass, and emotion on every page. She cheekily measures men by their foot size, has a penchant for sultry lingerie, and harbors dreams of exploring the nation in a motorhome.

MYLIT
PUBLISHING